AF415342

Editing: Alison Greene, Nick Hasse, Ethan LJubankovic, and Tarian P.S.
Book & Page Formatting: TPS Publishing
Cover Art: TPS Publishing

Trigger Warnings

This book contains sexually explicit scenes, BDSM-D/s, a MF main storyline relationship, and Adult Language, which may be triggering to some readers. It is purely a work of fiction and is intended for sales and the entertainment to adults ONLY, as defined by the laws of the country in which you made your purchase. Please store your files wisely, where they cannot be accessed by under-aged readers.

This book does NOT contain any rape, post rape or suggestive rape. It does NOT contain any incest, bestiality, under-aged play or sexual scenes with anyone under the legal age.

Language / Explicit Sexual Content / Bondage / Full-play Dominance and Discipline / Spanking

"You can't depend on your eyes, when your desires are out of focus," ~ Maître Rashawn Matisse

TALON P.S. & TARIAN P.S.

BESTSELLING BDSM EROTIC ROMANCE

BESTSELLING EROTIC SERIES

VOTED #1 BEST BDSM EROTIC ROMANCE FOR THE GOLDEN FLOGGER AWARD

THE DOMINION OF BROTHERS SERIES

WRITTEN BY TALON P.S. & TARIAN P.S.

Five Brothers at Arms share a lust for control and bondage; now they are living the BDSM lifestyle openly, and they are the very Masters who can provide satisfaction to the world of Taboo.

Plenty of people love their kink, but when the Dominion of Brothers arrive in New York, the Lifestyle gets an empowering supporter; with not only a boost in stimulation, their fellow Lifestylers also get a guardian. As it just so happens, the Brothers will stop at nothing to protect their friends, loved ones, and those who look to them for the freedom of consensual sexual expression.

BECOMING HIS SLAVE

DOMMING THE HEIRESS

A PLACE FOR CLIFF

ROUGH ATTRACTION

TAKING OVER TROFIM

RIGHT ONE 4 DIESEL

TOUCHING VIDA~VINCE

SEDUCING HIS THIEF

UNSUSPECTING SAVING

MASTERS' GOLDEN DARK SIDE

Submit your desires within the Dominion of Brothers and submerge yourself into a world of Dominance and Bliss, but get ready~

"I'm about to make you wet"

John ps.

Domming the Heiress

Heiress Amelia Quinneth had always been known for topping from the bottom. Being Vice-President of the family fortune and firm makes letting go of control more than just complicated. Nevertheless, submission is the one thing she desires most at the end of the day and no amount of control over her life can get her to that unobtainable bliss. That is until frustrated by lack of satisfaction, she finally reaches out to the Dominus Trenton Leos to be paired up with a Dom that could take charge and satisfy her needs.

However, despite her request, she never expected she would have to meet her new Dom while remaining blindfolded for the next thirty-six hours.

Amelia's Dom turns out to be a Head-Master who quickly shows her who is in charge and strips away every layer of hers, one by one, until she finds the true euphoria that comes from understanding her surrender.

The very rules she keeps to micro-manage her fantasies have been peeled away, but in order to find out the identity of who her new Master is, there is one more rule she must let go of and she's not sure she can.

MF-Romance / BDSM / D/s / Billionaire & Heiress Romance / Erotic-Romance / Sensory Play / Power Struggle / Reverse Age Gap / Fetish Play / Spanking / Corset Training / Extreme Spicy Heat / Explicit Adult Language

THE DOMINION OF BROTHERS SERIES: BOOK 2
WRITTEN BY TALON P.S. & TARIAN P.S.

DEDICATION

To my twin, Talon

&

To our Bug and Bobcat

Special Thanks goes to:

Alison Greene, Nick Hasse, and Ethan LJubankovic

for keeping us Dyslexic-Disaster-Zone free.

TRADEMARK ACKNOWLEDGEMENT

The author acknowledges the trademarked status and trademark owners of the following wordmarks mentioned in this work of fiction:

<u>Vehicles:</u>
> ConQuest Knight Armored Luxury Trucks
> Executive Lexus

<u>Alcohol Brands:</u>
> Cointreau Orange Liqueur
> Hennessey Cognac
> Campari Liqueur
> Jenssen Arcana Grande Champagne cognac

<u>Colognes:</u>
> Clive Christianson Cologne - Imperial's Majesty

<u>Fashion Designers:</u>
> Enzo D'orsi Hand-Tailored Suit Designs
> Jorg Hysek HD3 Watch Designs
> Mont Blanc Writing Instruments
> Diesel Watches
> Greubal Forsey Luxury Watches
> Marks & Spencer Suits and Tailoring

<u>Restaurants:</u>
> New York's French restaurant La Perigord

<u>Books**Plays:</u>
> The Way of a Man with a Maid: An erotic novel penned and published anonymously – 1930
> House of Incest by Anais Nin 1936 (quoted from)
> Dracula by Bram Stoker
> Quills by Doug Wright
> Chronicles of Gor by John Norman

<u>Quotes:</u>
> *"My first vision of earth was water veiled. I am of the race of men and women who see all things through this curtain of sea and my eyes are the color of water. I looked with chameleon eyes upon the changing face of the world, looked with anonymous vision upon my uncompleted self."* ~ House of Incest (page 15) by Anais Nin, 1936

TABLE OF CONTENT

PROLOGUE

<u>TWO MONTHS AGO - July</u>

Amelia Quinneth wrung her hands together in fettered nervousness as she watched Dominus Trenton Leos sweep around her guests throughout the day, herding them like cattle, toward the kinky delights which had been planned out to entertain them. His imposingly handsome gallantry even had her entertaining some naughty bits in her mind.

All her life she pined to submit at the feet of such a man. Not specifically Trenton Leos, but someone like him; someone who could deliver her body to the impossible treasure— surrender. And it was no pipe dream that such a dominant man could control her to such findings, she knew on personal account it *could* happen.

She sat back, keeping to the shirttails of her guests, watching Dominus and recalling the moment of bliss he'd given her nearly a year ago—

~~ Drunk and frustrated, Amelia slid rather than walked down the hand rail of the stairs leading down from the private members only area at Club Pain.

She'd done every little naughty thing she could drum up to earn a spanking without succeeding in getting even a single swat. She was tired of sitting pretty while Carlton watched Dane take the violet wand to one of the house subbies. While there was never anything dull about watching the skilled Golden Head-Master at work, Amelia wanted to have a bit of shock and awe of her own. Only Carlton had grown innately lethargic in his Domming of this heiress. He didn't even notice when she helped herself to his scotch, in addition to a swallow of someone else's wine glass left unattended for too long. She then even dared request he order her something for her parched tongue, a play of words to see if he got any other ideas. *Like, perhaps, his cock.* But no such luck. Carlton hardly even took his eyes off the tight young blond suspended in a swing, hanging from the ceiling in her pink patent-leather body suit.

"A scotch on the rocks for me and whatever she'd like." Carlton told the waitress. Amelia nearly rolled her eyes before realizing the waitress was new and decided to take advantage of the offer. After all, Carlton was her Dom and if he wanted his subbie to drink then by god she would, especially if that bit about *submissives don't drink upstairs* rule slipped the waitress's mind.

Now, four Manhattans later, Amelia wanted nothing more than to just go home and abandon herself to a hot bath, a good book, and her water wick. It wouldn't do the job either but at least with *it* there were no expectations, just unfettered frustration.

But before she could make it out the door, her little naive writer friend, Katianna Dumas, caught up to her and corralled her back to her booth.

"Where's Carlton?" Amelia's petite friend fumed at her. To which Amelia just rolled her eyes in response, or so she attempted the act, accomplishing more room tilting than anything else.

"You're drunk?"

Amelia actually accomplished her stoic expression that time; her signature narrowed eyes and cocked brow. The same one she used on the men on her committee when they questioned her authority.

Katianna's attention then shifted to something outside the booth and rushed off after whatever it was while Amelia took a seat. She flipped her hair from her face, then pressed down the wrinkles in her satin corset dress. She was ruffled but she wasn't about to appear as such. What she really wanted was to just leave and she had half a mind to do just that. Katianna could either follow or find another way home. The latter wouldn't be too difficult, Dominus Trenton Leos would be more than happy to tend to that need.

She glanced out her booth, at the two clubbers standing just out her door; she envied them. They'd obviously been ordered by their Dom to stand and wait and would at some point soon be called upon. Maybe they got in trouble so he would spank them before being ordered to drop to their knees and suck his cock. Maybe he would tease them and pull his shaft from their tongues just before he might have released his prize. He would play with the hard flesh with a lazy stroke— teasing them until they begged and whimpered. The very vision had her salivating for her own experience. Why the hell did they have to stand just outside her door to flaunt and torment her? It was as if they knew how discontented she was. "Little deviant bastards," she spoke hardly an audible breath aloud.

Another minute passed and one of the regular Doms that frequented the club came to retrieve the two subs parked outside her door with a mild scolding. She knew him. He'd even offered more than once to have her as his, but she had always turned him down.

He glanced in and tipped his head causing her to blush. Just another color to add to her green-envy. She blushed just as easily with a young Dom's flirting as she would with the attention of a more mature man. But not even his ability to affect her so, could alter the course of her admonitions to turn down any of his propositions. It wasn't the *liking* that was missing. Sir Ripley was delightfully easy on the eyes with a reputation for wax, rope, and paddles. No, her taboo was strictly about age, something she could never bring herself to break; the one line she did not cross. And he was a full generation her younger. Older women did not belong in bed with younger men. It simply sent out the wrong message. However, sitting here alone and abandoned by her scheduled Dom— of mature age— she rolled her eyes reminding herself of her own road blocks, she had to wonder if perhaps it was time to shed a few restrictive habits.

Amelia grew fitful and glanced around her booth. She spotted her cape still folded over next to her on the crescent sofa and she licked over her lips as she stared at it. For how long she couldn't say, mentally drifting off, recalling an old film that touched off her dark unspoken inhibitions long ago and she had ever since, enjoyed having a cape. The only thing she was missing was a fancy mask to cover her face. The swing of her door called her back to see the Dominus stepping in. *Another handsome face to taunt her.* And there was no Dom or Master more thorough and Alpha male than Trenton Leos.

She let out a deep sigh, figuring this wasn't a chatty friendship visit. "Dom-minus-s," the small, inebriated slip got away from her.

"Heiress." Trenton greeted her tightly with the title she refused to accept that her title at least inside the club robbed her of her desires to fully turn over all control.

Amelia was as readable as any woman a man could ask for, but she had yet to learn, despite such yearnings, to actually let go. Of course, for a woman of her stature and position, it was understandable why. Heiress Amelia Quinneth: Head Chairwoman and Vice-President of the Quinneth fortune of global businesses. As Heiress, she controlled such a large empire it was hard to stop being in control of herself.

It was through the Lifestyle of bondage and dominance she had a chance to find a haven that would ultimately care for her deepest needs; to let go and submit herself to a Master for delivery of those precious moments of distinct non-control she needed the most. But as it were, for the many years he'd known her, both as friend and as a client of his security services, Amelia Quinneth topped from the bottom, down to the last detail, whereby always overriding her Dom, she got in the way of her own needs.

Just like tonight, Carlton had grown fed up with her backseat driving that it didn't take much for his attention and own desires to shift to Club Pain's newest in-house subbie. Nevertheless, Carlton had broken more than a few rules that should have been addressed immediately. Trenton was just on his way up when had heard Katianna's fussing coming from the top of the stairs and decided to let the chips fall.

He couldn't help himself. Katianna was notorious for her fears of nearly everything, but she'd also been coming down for the self-defense classes at Diesel's shop at the insistence of Diesel and himself. What better chance than now to see if she'd actually learned anything?

He had quickly ducked out of the stairwell before he could be spotted and came to wait it out here alongside Amelia. He scooped up her cape then brought it over to where she sat with a rather sullen look. With a kiss to the top of her head, he draped it over her shoulders, clipped it closed, and then sat down and waited for the show to begin.

Per club rules, Katianna never made it past the stairs, but did manage to convince the bouncer, Jon, to bring Carlton to the door. The second the Dom was in reach, Katianna caught him by the leather straps of his harness that crisscrossed over his chest, pulling him off balance. She leaped out of the way and down the stairs, the man went with a thud at the bottom.

She dashed down to catch him before he could gain a position to fend her off with a reminder to herself that at five foot nothing she was not so big to overpower anyone. However, she'd been taught she didn't need to be if she acted quickly.

Katianna quickly snatched the Dom's finger and twisted it until it threatened to break. A trick Diesel Gentry had taught her one night when he stopped in at the VIP booth to amuse himself with a quick game of *Name That Skirt* with her. Those nights were always fun.

Carlton was now in a position to do only as Kat demanded if he wanted the pain to stop and she began pushing for him to head to the booth, catching the attention of a number of club guests along the way. Even with Carlton on his knees and his fingers bent over backwards, it was a physical struggle on her part to get him to do anything.

When she finally made it to the booth, only to find the two clubbers she had placed to watch over Amelia were gone. But discovering in the next instant as they came around the front, Trenton Leos was now sitting with her, and Kat let out a sigh of relief as well as felt a bit of empowerment from his presence.

Despite the bit of confidence, Katianna stepped in cautiously with Carlton still trying to keep up, while crawling on his knees. She was apprehensive that she might end up in trouble herself, but she had a damn good defense: Carlton broke the rules.

"Where the hell did the other two go?" She shot a gaze at Trenton with little effect as he rested leisurely in the booth with one arm up over its back, while the other was dropped onto the leg he had settled on the edge of the table.

"Never use a sub for security. They will always obey their Dom and abandon their places when called."

Kat's eyes shifted to the cape that was wrapped around Amelia, "You?" She asked him to indicate to the restored modesty her friend, landlord, and publisher lacked while tipsy. Trenton merely closed his eyes in a slow blink, silently answering in the affirmative, but Katianna was grateful for it. While she couldn't argue that Trenton was better suited for watching over Amelia anyway, at the moment of need, she had simply grabbed the first two people she came across.

"So, what are you going to do with him?" Trenton's eyes held some amusement as if anticipating a show.

"He broke the rules. Now he has to apologize while on his knees," she puffed, ready to make her argument of defense to Trenton if need be.

Trenton's gaze jerked ever-so-slightly., "That's all?"

She blinked at him, having not expected that response. "Well, what else would be expected of him?" She didn't know what went on upstairs. She'd never gone up there and she never asked Amelia what she did privately.

"A good Dom always leaves his sub well pleased by the end of the night. Ask Amelia if her Dom made her feel like a beautiful woman."

Katianna grinned. *Dom class 101.* She gave it some thought then looked back at Amelia, "Amelia? Did Carlton sate you, tonight?"

Amelia's drunken attention wavered, but managed to make contact with her friend and she shook her head.

"First thing's first—" Kat twisted Carlton's arms tighter, another valuable lesson, courtesy of Diesel Gentry, until Carlton was cursing under his breath. "Apologize."

"Let go of me, you stupid bitch."

Unsatisfied by his response and lack of understanding of the overthrow of power in the room, Katianna stepped into him, keeping his arm in the tight twist, and it forced him face down into the floor.

"I said apologize, not call me names." She took hold of one of his fingers and bent it back again and Carlton cried out, part pain, part anguish.

"Fucking Bitch."

Katianna lifted his arm, taking a step back, and pulled his face from the floor, then with a stomp of her boot, slammed him back to the floor. *That one* she learned from watching Desiderio Olla Chaves, a big boned, champion body builder with a whole lot of Spanish attitude and a whole lot of curves and muscle power to force her subbies to comply. When she told her submissives to do something, they obeyed, or they ended up being ridden like a pony on the stage; all while Desiderio Olla flogged their bare asses in front of the dance floor until she was certain they had learned their lesson.

"Apologize, damn you!" Kat turned to look over at Trenton who was still watching, thoroughly entertained. "Can't you make him? You're the Dominus." She would plead with him if she thought it'd do her any good. After all, it would not take Carlton much strength to throw her from him if she let his fingers slip from her grip.

"Sorry, I don't Dom men. But perhaps if you weren't trying to break his bones or beat his head into the floor, you might get a better response from him. Try letting his arm go and see if he'll cooperate." Dominus passed the gavel back to her with a flat sardonic tone.

"Let him go?" she stammered, "If I do that, he'll hit me." And with her response she revealed her lacking vote of confidence on her hold on the older man.

Trenton's face darkened. "Not in front of me he won't. He even thinks to raise a hand at you, Katianna, and he won't be seeing the light of day for at least a week," his tone growing serious, losing all the amusement he'd just had moments ago.

"Hear that, Carlton? The Dominus will stuff you in a dumpster if you don't do what I tell you," she warned the man still folded over on the floor, just a little too over-empowered and smug by the security Trenton had revealed to her. "I even bet if this doesn't get resolved you might be banned from Club Pain." And that bit of information seemed to get Carlton's attention. After all, death threats weren't exactly the Dominus's modus operandi— getting banned from the club was. No one who was in the Lifestyle wanted to be on the blacklist, as it tended to stretch well beyond just Club Pain with a domino effect.

"I apologize, Amelia," Carlton quickly spat.

"Heiress Amelia." Katianna corrected him with a snap.

"I apologize, Heiress Amelia."

"Good. Now stay there until I decide what else you should do." Kat let go of his fingers, but even with the proclamation Trenton had made, she jumped back putting safe distance between her and the older man, just in case. She stepped over to Trenton looking to him for suggestions, but he offered her none, only looked up at her. That amusement was back in his eyes, watching her try to *suss* out the particulars of being a Domme and what to do with the one who had broken protocol.

Katianna dropped down in the seat next to him and gave him a pouty look. "You *could* help."

Trenton forced himself to look away, biting at his lips to fight his own defeat if he so much as gave in to her pouting.

He had assessed a long time ago he would fold to it.

"Some help you are." The little woman nearly stamped her foot in protest.

Don't look. Don't— look.

Damn, he looked.

And he was instantly leaning in, heading straight for her lips when lucky, or unlucky, for him, her expression brightened as though the flickering of a light switch as an idea came to mind.

"I know— he should perform oral sex on her, right here."

She said it so clinically. It surprised Trenton, considering what she wrote in her books. But the disruption broke him from his tumbling spell to devour those soft lips that puffed out in frustration. "Katianna, we don't allow that kind of display downstairs in the main club area. It's only allowed upstairs in the private section."

❦

Katianna let out a hard huff; she just got through dragging Carlton's heavy ass *down* the stairs. *Now she has to get him back up just so Amelia can get hers?* Kat's mind was thinking and she shot a glance at Trenton reclining back again his arms stretched out across the back of the booth seat, watching with acute interest, finding it all very entertaining.

"We could take them to your booth. The glass to your booth tints on command." She suggested with a touch hopefulness.

"You're not taking him into my room, Kat." He was quick to block even the mildest suggestion of it. "I'll take you any night, but not him."

Katianna's shoulders slumped and she rolled her eyes, "I wonder if maybe the glass on this room does the same, only your brother hasn't made us privy to it yet?"

Trenton grinned. Like a Cheshire cat. Or the Proud Lion King— *King*— *Dom*— she'd never forgotten that.

He was nearly laughing at her; he was enjoying this so much she could tell. But he didn't offer any trade secrets as to whether the glass on any of the other VIP booths contained the same holographic tinting ability in their glass partitions or not. Probably not. After four years since the club first opened, Amelia and the other private members would have surely figured that one out by now.

Katianna gave Trenton a leering look then stood, stepping back over to Carlton, and parked her fists on her hips.

"Dominus, get your pet off of me," Carlton huffed from the floor.

"Shut up," Katianna barked. She relaxed her fists and tapped her nails at the front of her hips, contemplating for any alternative, "Oh fuck it. The worst they can do is throw me and Carlton out. Right?" she proclaimed to no one in particular.

"*You* and Carlton?"

"Yes. Carlton— because he's the Dom in the contract. He takes the responsibility therefore the blame for Amelia, and me—" she shrugged "because of what I'm about to make her do." Kat gave the empty explanation, with some silent wager that perhaps Trenton's odd fondness of her really did have some merit and she wouldn't get banned after all.

She caught Amelia by the arm and lured her up and steered her over to Carlton. Katianna gave the man a kick of her boot, knocking him off his knees, and she quickly maneuvered Amelia over him, guiding her friend down over Carlton's face.

"Get to work, Carlton, until she is well satisfied."

⚘

At first nothing happened other than Carlton's breath against her not so moist lips. Amelia had yet to feel even the smallest bit of excitement this night. But then Katianna was moving behind her and she felt the pressure of Katianna's knee on her back, pressing her down harder on Carlton's face and a moment after that a wet tongue darted out, and licked over the entrance of her pussy with urgent direction.

It was hardly the tentative act Amelia had grown spoiled with from reading both in Katianna's books and the many other erotic library Amelia published. But it was more attention than her cunt had had for some time.

She caught the movement out of the corner of her eye, Trenton had snared Katianna around the waist and pulled the petite woman into his lap. His gaze intensely on herself and Carlton, but his heated whispers were for Katianna only.

Amelia envied the attention her small friend got while still naive of such treasure being offered to her.

She let her head drop back and she closed her eyes, talking to herself to get into it. She let out a soft crooning sound which seemed to encourage Carlton further. He grew more active in his licking and sucking. Then lifted his arms up, looping around Amelia's thighs and pulled her down over his tongue so he could probe her deeper.

There was a blur across the glass front and Dane was suddenly standing at the door, pushing in, "What the hell, Trenton?"

Amelia didn't respond, grinding her hips into the face, planted between her legs. She wanted to cum, the need becoming painful as it remained out of reach.

"Hmmm, guess I should do something or the whole club will start fucking downstairs and then we'll really start to get in trouble with code enforcement," Trenton good-humored, then planted a pillowy kiss on Katianna's lips, not too soft, not too hard, just right, and always with the hint of moisture from a tongue that promised euphoria.

He pushed her from his lap, setting her down on the bench next to him then tore his lips from hers, licking at the kiss he had just stolen from her, and then got to his feet.

He stepped over to Amelia and took over the scene. This way he, and Dane as well, could say he'd been in a special mood to give a show for all the little kiddies that never get to go upstairs. It was, after all, taking place in a private booth, separated from the general public. It was a far stretch of allow-ability of law and club rules, but workablc if cvcr questioned.

Trenton stood straddled over Carlton just behind Amelia, taking her arms, and raising them over her head. He clamped her wrists together in his grip and lifted her slightly to add tension to his hold, "Fuck him, Amelia," he commanded firmly. "Fuck his face."

Amelia pouted, exhilarated by the moment of restraint Trenton created on her arms as he held her tightly. But she was in pain. She wanted to cum, but Carlton just wasn't delivering. It wasn't enough for her.

"I'm going to let go of you and you're going to take his hair and force him deeper into your pussy, you hear me?" More of the deep resonating voice Trenton was so well known for. The kind women couldn't ignore.

"Yes—" Amelia gasped.

Trenton released her and she bent over grabbing Carlton's hair and pulled him tighter against her body as she undulated her honey sodden mound into him. She gasped, her thighs clenching, and her head dropped back. But still only a whimper of need came from her lips.

◈

Trenton shot a look over his shoulder to his brother and grinned, "Got a paddle handy?"

"You better finish her quickly before somebody I don't want to see this walks in."

"Then find me a paddle. You know she'll cum with a good spanking."

Dane was quickly yanking one from the hip of a random patron as they came up to watch as did many of the others in the club, and he passed it over.

Trenton knelt down beside the couple, turning the paddle over in his hand for a careful inspection and gently eased Amelia to bend over, his hand gently stroking her back. He at least knew Amelia— he had watched her take the paddle and even the cane a number of times. He knew she didn't require a warm up to be prepped for a full masochistic spanking. She loved a good paddling and was always willing to receive. He'd have her cumming in under twenty smacks.

"Too much clothing—" he was talking to her as he pulled up her tight skirt, raising it up to her bound waist, revealing her powder white ass. He smoothed the paddle over her flesh, teasing her with the implement. It had only taken the suggestion of it and she was humming with anticipation. She was so ready; he was considering lowering the accomplished bar down to the price of only ten.

—PHWACK—

Trenton brought the paddle across both cheeks with a firm smack and instantly her skin was blushing a perfect shade of pink in the shape of the paddle.

Amelia crooned with delight and her hips rocked into the mouth that was still trying to work her to her goal.

Trenton gave her a set of teasing, stinging smacks. Two per side, then one right after another until five had landed firmly on her ass, turning white flesh a radiant red.

Amelia's head shot back with a cry, "Oh yes!" And she was instantly shuddering. "Oh, yes, yes." she cried out again.

Trenton dolled out another half dozen when Amelia's body curled then snapped in a hard, arched back.

She bolted upright, grinding her hips into the man below her, "Eat it all up and don't you dare waist one drop of my champagne," she was suddenly fierce in delivering the command, intent on savoring every tingle through her body.

Trenton waited until the tremors subsided in Amelia's body and her shoulders drooped with the released tension. "Are you pleased, subbie?" his question soft and reassuring.

Amelia's eyes rolled up to him and she smiled with a sultry gleam, one of her sexiest looks. "Yes, Dominus, I am. Thank you, Sir." And she lowered her eyes out of respect for him. ~~

The bitter sweet memory faded, leaving Amelia still unsatisfied. She had never gone out with Carlton again after that. They both agreed they were not a good match. But then it seemed that no such thing existed for her.

Dominus Trenton Leos.

He was a mastermind of matching Masters and Doms with their perfect submissives. And the other way around. Yet she had never gone to him.

It was time for all that to change.

It was a bit of a surprise when Dominus found her first just when she was chatting with a guest near the grand stairs of the main hall in her home.

Amelia immediately diverted her eyes to the floor. As hostess to her own party, in her own home, she was not subject to the rules as sub, but Trenton wasn't just any Dom, and even in her house, she did so out of respect for him. Not to mention, when she wanted something, she knew it was the best way to approach him.

Trenton strolled up, reaching for her graceful hand, bringing it to his lips, and kissed her like the true lady that she was. He caught the light fragrance of her perfume, a sensuous floral with honeysuckle, Sicilian lemon, chocolate, and musk. Somehow it all smelled quite luxurious. The perfect scent for a woman of such power, who just happened to be one hell of a tasty treat if a Dom were so lucky to overthrow her micro-dictated contracts for her submission.

The other woman next Amelia kept her face bowed as well, but he could glimpse enough of her seeking gaze to see the expression of envy as she licked her lips greedily. "You're dismissed," he ordered the girl away.

"She does not please you tonight, Dominus?"

"These young subs watch you— watch how you sway from sub to heiress, and they get to thinking they can get away with doing the same."

"Lucky them, if their Dom chooses to punish them for it." She smiled, her mind already scheming to find what would whet her appetite. "So, is my girl tucked away busy with her writing?" Amelia's sheepish smile deepening with the knowledge he had been playing with Katianna earlier.

"Mmmm, she is— sad to say." He stepped in to hover over Amelia, letting his threatening stance affect her— asserting his overruling dominance. "However, I'm pretty certain she's *my* girl."

"Remember, you parked her in my garage. Where you've left her, going on what? Four years now. I'd say that makes her mine by law of possession. Besides—" Amelia went on, "I like having my favorite erotic-romance writer right here." Amelia could see his frustration. He didn't care about the subs around him anymore. He hardly acknowledged they were even there, not to mention he was fighting a serious hard-on for her star writer, and she knew it.

"Well, just so you understand, those days are numbered. Katianna is mine, and I will be claiming her soon."

Amelia heard the certainty in his voice. It sent a chill down her spine and fired off the nerves in her clit, not that Trenton was the man of her desires; only that she wished that one day a man would say the same for her. Her greatest desire was she would meet a Dom that could take control of her and as the Dominus termed it— *claim her.*

Amelia fidgeted, something she never did, and right away she knew that Trenton saw it in her, and his gaze was turning suspicious as he watched her more intently.

"Out with it," was all he said with a stern command.

Amelia shifted her weight; her hands clasped in front of her, but finally after a deep breath, she relinquished her question of need. She had always searched for her own Doms, but for the past two years they had been unfulfilling and short lived. She was tired of always having to look for the next one, only to come home unsatisfied because they hadn't mastered her needs yet. "Dominus, I need your services."

"What are you wishing?"

"I need the perfect Dom—" her eyes dropped as did her voice, like a whispering song bird, "I need a Master to know me and keep me."

Trenton let out a chuff, "You micro manage too much, and in doing so you would cancel out the perfect match."

"Dominus, please," the request came out nearly a whimper.

❦

"I'm curious—" he leaned one shoulder against the wall, crossing his arms over his chest, still close, still breathing down on her. "How is it after all these years, you've never approached me about any one of my brothers to Dom you?"

Amelia instantly blushed.

He'd never seen the woman blush quite so deeply before and it was a new surprise.

"Dominus, you and your brothers are still so young. Why I'd feel foolishly out of place next to your tight bodies." She grinned shyly with a deep sigh, her fingers moving to clasp in front of her, absently twirling a large fanciful gemmed ring on a slender finger. "I prefer a man closer to my age; they tend to make me look as youthful as I feel." The corner of her lips quirked to one side in a wicked smile, "Not to mention I'm a client of TL Securities. Like you, I never mix business with pleasure." She dared to look up at him but did so at a side glance.

Trenton seemed to study her collectively for a long moment. Always more thoughts in his head then he ever spoke aloud. His eyes narrowed with some unspoken thought, followed with a deep drawing breath that made his nostrils flare as he calculated his response. "And what if the perfect man for you was truly on the other side of the scale? Would you be able to let go of these self-placed limits so that you could be happy?"

"Oh Trenton, really. Why play with me in such ways. What possible happiness could a woman find in a man half her age?" Amelia grew more astute now as the subject grew more detailed. "Is it not bad enough having to suffer through such tabloids as the paparazzi chases after an actress and what boy toy model she has seduced to play on her arm for golden coins and free vacations. All so she can fool herself into thinking she isn't growing old."

"And you, Amelia, are not a Hollywood face, but the heiress of a wealthy family fortress. Do older men not do the same as you claim the younger do? Men, you yourself have contracted with for unfulfilling dates. So wealth and paparazzi aside, as a submissive woman with particular needs with a man who has no need for your money, just need for your submission; will you still cling to your taboos?"

The alarm on her face was genuine though he could tell she was likely grasping at far more than what he was suggesting, but he allowed them to storm her thoughts none the less. He wanted her to face her fears. He was deliberately turning her about to face the things she refused to let go of the very things that had gotten in the way of her happiness. And would do so again if she wasn't willing to step beyond her comfort zone.

Trenton dropped his gaze down on her, studying her for a long moment.

Amelia Quinneth was the Bettie Page and Marilyn Monroe pinup, all wrapped into one body. Any man would be considered lucky to have her. But that she was head of a powerful family didn't help her situation to find the perfect Master who could handle her. She had to be let off her leash almost daily. Trying to reel her back in during the after-hours could be tiresome for a Dom. It would definitely take a Master to handle her; he just wasn't so sure she was really ready to relinquish that much control. She topped from the bottom on a regular basis which was also why she was unsatisfied. A submissive can't enjoy the bliss of surrender if they haven't actually surrendered. But he knew she had run out of *wanna-be*'s and *weekender* Doms to play her game with, and he could see she was in burning desperation for the real experience that perhaps she was finally ready to let go.

At the end of the day, Amelia needed the control to be taken away from her entirely. That was where her deeper sense of femininity lie.

He knew the perfect Master for her, he'd be just the right match to train her away from her bad habits and the reward would give him exactly what he'd been searching for in a submissive of his own choice. Trenton was certain the man he had in mind would accept the offer to explore the match up. He'd hate to see the arrangement suffer over something as petty as age differences.

He pushed off the wall and leaned in closer. He knew the answer to this problem. "If I do this, then you will meet him blindfolded." He pushed in on her, backing her against the wall, displaying his own control.

"But—"

"No buts. I choose who your Master will be. I alone make all the arrangements and take you to him blindfolded, which you will remain so for the entire time you are with him unless he himself removes it."

  Amelia swallowed hard, and she felt her body heat rise.

"Is this clear?"

Another hard swallow and she found she had to lick her lips just to get them to work. "Yes, Dominus. It is clear."

"Then say it."

She chewed— stalling—

He turned as though to walk away.

"Green." She closed her eyes and sucked in a deep breath. "My safeword is Green."

CLUB PAIN

Trenton Leos, the man everyone revered as the *Dominus*, stood before her, the blindfold of merlot colored silk held resolutely in both hands as he brought it up to her eyes.

"Wait." She wiped her hands down her thighs, taking another deep breath. She was growing increasingly anxious with each passing minute. Two months ago, she went to Dominus pleading for a Dom. Then just three weeks ago, he brought her a contract written on parchment paper, sent by an approved Master agreeing to claim her as His sole property and to be used at His leisure and pleasure for the ascribed time frame. Thirty-six hours, that's how long she was to submit to Him. The missive had even been written with a fountain pen.

The very elegance of the letter swooned her so deeply, she nearly signed it before reading it. But the contract was more involved. It contained a complete checklist of things one might do in a scene together. And she was required to answer: *yes— no— I'm not sure if I will be ready.* There had also been a health section. He requested her personal comforts, even her favorite foods, and it included her first order to be tested by her doctor of choice. While it wasn't the fifty some pages of questions Dominus's forms had contained, her Master-to-be had not left many items unsecured.

The contract also detailed what to expect. That at no time would she be called by her name. Referred only as *His pet.* They would use the universal safewords: *Red— Yellow— Green.* But she would also have a two other safewords. The first, *Magenta,* for' when she needed personal pauses, such as breaks for the restroom or being hungry outside of meals. The other, *I am the Heiress,* was the all-stop *Red.* Reference to herself meant it all ended. Their thirty-six hours coming to a full stop and she would be returned to Dominus the same as she came, blindfolded and without a Master.

Lastly, there was a personal note from her Master, to let her know he was looking forward to their exploratory time together and that he would send one final letter to her after reading over her answers on the contract. She answered them all and within five days another letter came. Same as before, elegant Calligraphy, handwritten on parchment paper.

When His correspondence arrived, it came with the details of his plans for the weekend, including a list of personal items she was to wear and bring. Now, with her suitcase waiting at the door of Club Pain, standing here at the threshold of her greatest desires— she hesitated.

Trenton paused, allowing her the moment and lowered the blindfold slightly, but kept it close to remind her the moment had come for her to stop being in control. "It's time, Amelia. Unless you want to use your safeword."

"Yellow. I need to use my yellow."

Trenton shook his head, "There is no yellow here for this. Either you do it or you don't. So say red or green."

"What? Why?" Her hand went up to catch the silk cloth— anything to stall this a little longer. Get a better grip on the night's plans.

"Because you've been riding with your foot on the break for years. Your body desires submission like no other, yet you continue to micromanage it away like a fleeting orgasm, which leaves you unsatisfied. You cannot have it both ways," He let it sink in a moment. His expression controlled blocking any hint that he might pity her. His eyes looked deep into her, and his head titled ever so slightly as the remains of his conviction were given over. "In order to enjoy the pleasure of ultimate submission you must surrender completely. You came to me asking for a Master, now I've found one. One who is willing to take on the challenge of your submission and it is time, Amelia." He gave her a gentle smile, one that touched deep inside her with a promise to deliver succulent pleasure, and he waited.

She took a deep breath, feeling his promise all the way to her core, but it wasn't enough to relinquish her last thread of control. "Why must you blind submit me?" Her lips rolled in to be caught by her teeth. Her attention flickered to the mingling crowd just outside the glass walls of her VIP booth, then back to the Dominus.

"Amelia. I said it would be done this way. This is how you will surrender. To keep you from attempting to micro manage. Your new Master will not tolerate it and he agrees with my decision."

Just another Friday night at Club Pain, Amelia's eyes scanned the crowd of people outside her booth once more. Some went on without so much as a glance their way, others had definitely taken notice. Her new Dom was out there somewhere— but no discerning face leaped out at her.

She swallowed nervously. Dominus didn't play around, the moment she went to him asking for a Dom who could handle her, he took over and gave her no reins whatsoever and brought her a Master. Now she was about to be truly stripped of her control and it frightened her beyond comprehension, but she could not disregard the excitement that pooled inside her either. Total submission to a Master seemed, for so long, like a mythological desire— inescapably unobtainable. Now, here it was, and the heat flux it created was beyond measure. It had her breath catching in her chest and a myriad of anxiety, need, nervousness and anticipation fluttering about her insides that it had her heart pounding, despite the restrictions of her corset.

Once more, she rolled her lips in, biting back the yearn— she was very wet and for the first time she wished the glass around her VIP booth was able to tint digitally as Trenton's private room did, so no one could see.

"What do you need to say to me, Amelia?" Trenton asked, not an ounce lost in his patience or stern guidance.

Amelia took in a deep breath, willing herself to relax, and let go of the silk scarf, "Green." A nervous cool escape poured from her lips like a favorite dark wine. "My safeword is *green*."

"Good girl." And the blindfold came up over her eyes as he spoke to her. "Your new Master will join us in a moment."

Domineering, yet warm. Reassuring her in the darkness, talking her through her new experience into submission.

"If at any time you have reached your limits use your safewords. If you call *yellow* he will pause and work you past it or switch into something else, depending on what he thinks you need. If you call *red,* he will stop the scene. If you use *magenta,* he will pause or stop the scene for your needs then resumed at an appropriate time. Should you refer to yourself as *the Heiress*, your weekend with the Master will come to an end. However, the blindfold does not come off until he has returned you to me. Understood?"

A new wave of tantalizing fear rippled through her, sending her new lust escalating. Her eyes tried to see past the cloth, but she was as blind as a new slave should be. "May I ask why, Dominus?"

"Because calling a full-stop forfeits any privilege of discovering who your Master is. That must be earned." His fingers tested the tension on the blindfold making sure it wasn't too snug, "How does that feel? Not too tight? It would be on for a long time so I want to be sure it is on comfortably so as not to trigger a headache during your stay."

Amelia sucked in a deep breath, letting it out with a soft sigh that accented the surrendered word she was ready. "Green."

"Good girl."

She felt the soft kiss to her now partially covered forehead. Comforting her. She heard him circle her then took a few steps back, no doubt enjoying the display from her body language. "Now stand there and don't say a word unless you need to use your safe words. Understood?"

"Yes, Dominus." Her heart strummed in a merengue beat in her chest and her belly began twisting and flipping as though it were a dance floor filled with salsa dancers that took up the beat in her chest.

The time was coming.

The surrender she had always desired.

Such sweet fear. She prayed for a brief moment, perhaps not the ideal prayers one should send up, but she did so anyways, because she truly did hope to make her Master happy with her, for what he was already giving her. *Exhilaration.* Succulent heat radiated out from the epicenter of her cunt, stretching out, and licked her ear all in a single heated whispered word.

Master.

Rashawn Matisse waited in Trenton's booth, watching from across the way. His skin tingling with electricity as the Dominus took her sight from her. *Bon sang*, he wished he could have been right there to see the rippling of her control being stripped away. That very first step was always exquisite, the most dramatic. But with a woman as powerful as Amelia, he was certain there would be plenty more to come over the course of the next thirty-six hours.

He watched from afar. With the blindfold now in place on his pet, Trenton stepped back, and waved him in. That was his cue. He held still a moment to enjoy the rush of excitement he felt. He was about to have Amelia Quinneth in his world.

"You will follow me." His attention moved to Katianna who sat quietly on the sofa, "Your Dominus wishes you to be in his arms as he watches this. You're to keep silent. Never at any time are you to allow Amelia to become aware of your presence. *C'est bien compris?*" He paused reminding himself that she may not speak French, so he translated to be sure she understood the command, "Clear?"

His revered friend's slave looked up at him with a tender, playful glance of anticipation for her friend and publisher.

"Yes, I understand," she responded obediently, "I promise not to ruin it for her."

"Merci." Rashawn held his hand out to her. He would expect her to walk in extreme close proximity to him for Trenton's sake. Or perhaps for his own. He'd known Trenton for some time and never before had he seen the Dominus be so taken by any one woman. Even for the short walk across the club, Rashawn felt the pressure of having the man's Unicorn in his charge. He had to admit though, the little woman everyone playfully called *mouse,* flourished under her Master's intense control very well. Any other slave would perhaps have found it too much. Not even the best of slaves could handle the amount of smothering Trenton placed on his— *except Katianna of course.* Though, Rashawn had put considerable contemplation on how healthy this would be for her. Would it only seem that such sheltering would encourage her to become timid and fearful? Those thoughts quickly found misplaced when after arriving to New York to work directly with Amelia's firm and what he'd learned of Katianna Dumas, the author was already those things before Trenton claimed her as his property. So, Rashawn couldn't foretell how their future would turn out— for the best he hoped. Until then, he would escort her across the club as if she was the blue Hope diamond wrapped around the neck of Mona Lisa herself.

Rashawn walked along the line of booths toward Amelia's on the end. Katianna walking just a step ahead of him, his hand lightly over her shoulder to ward off anyone's thoughts of approaching. Which was unlikely, everyone that was a regular at Club Pain knew the small exclusively owned slave belonged to the Dominus and everyone knew to keep a clear distance unless Trenton was with her.

Alas, the moment had arrived. Rashawn took a deep breath to steady his excitement. The mouse turned to watch. An all-knowing twinkle in her ghostly eyes drawing out a triumphant warm smile of his own, then he pushed the glass door open, waving Katianna into the Dominus's arms and he stepped inside.

He inhaled deeply, taking in the scent of his new woman. Sweet, aroused, and very beautiful. His cock was already throbbing to attention. He bit at his lip reminding himself he could not rush through this. This weekend was for her. To deliver the ultimate experience as a surrendered sub.

❧

Amelia stood at attention. Her body shivering with anticipation as the door to her booth opened, letting the swarming sounds of the club spill in before it closed once more. She waited, her shoulder tingling for her Master's fingers, but no touch came. No words or commands to introduce her Master's presence. Outside the booth, techno music strummed out a hypnotic beat, but inside it was deathly silent.

"Domin-"

"Silence." Trenton's voice snapped her back to attention. "Just stand there. Not a word."

Amelia bowed her head and waited as the Dominus commanded. Her ears straining to hear what her eyes could not tell her. Again nothing. No talking, no touch—not even the shuffle of footsteps. *Was he contemplating? Was he having second thoughts about domming her? Was he even in the room? Oh lord, not Trenton!* Her mind panicked. *He wasn't going to be her Dom— was he?*

"Strip." The potently whispered, male tone broke the silence. Her head snapped a fraction to one side, toward the new voice that'd just spoken. Panic sprung up. *In front of the club?* "But—"

"Unless you need to use your safeword, you are not to speak. Not even a sound from you," the new voice spoke to her again. Stern, but not overbearing. And finally, she felt him, felt a presence— more like— dominance circling around her as his body brushed up against hers in several feathery touches— just enough to let her feel the heat from the backs of his fingers.

"Another refute from you and you'll earn a punishment," a deeply majestic, manly voice. An accent strained and held back that she couldn't place it but definitely European.

He spoke clearly and decisively, as if to mask the European accent. Or perhaps, added a gentle, mocking of one to disguise any familiarities she might have detected. Wait, *did* she know him?

Her new Master paused, standing just behind her. She could feel his breath cascade over her shoulders, his strength— his presumed power over her. Her insides clenched. Just the hope that such a thing was true made her grow wet.

"Do you need to use your safeword?" The man behind her asked, giving her permission to bow out now.

Amelia shivered. "No, Sir."

Then she felt his breath on her ear. "Head-Master," he whipped her skin with his warmth.

Amelia licked her lips slowly. "Yes, Head-Master," she responded back with the corrected title.

Wait!

Head-Master?! It couldn't be, did Trenton set her up with Dane Masters? Was this why she had to be blindfolded?

No! She couldn't do it. She would be utterly embarrassed. No— humiliated. She would never be able to look Dane in the eyes again, being the arrogant Golden Master that he was. Never again could she blush at his playful flirting and not feel utterly naked, knowing he'd secretly dommed her.

❧

Rashawn saw the panic rising in her, he knew it was coming, and enjoyed it as if having his first sample of a fine wine. For a fine wine she was.

"Dane?" Amelia sputtered.

"*Pshh!*" Rashawn snapped into her, "Do not attempt to call me by an identity you've assumed. I am no one you think I am. I, from this moment until 9:00am Sunday morning, am known only as your Head-Master." It was almost upsetting that his name did not come before any other, but Rashawn reminded himself he had done well keeping his personal life secret from his professional one. Even around her. She didn't even know he played, but that would be remedied soon enough. Just not this weekend.

He took a deep breath, inhaling her perfume. Such an exquisite delight that he leaned in for another, more deeper, more intimate smell of her. Her body's arousal mixing magically with the scent of the *Clive Christianson design: Imperial Majesty*. The very same one he bought her for the Christmas exchange. She smelled tantalizingly rich in it. He'd never met a woman who could wear such lavish scents, as if it had been designed specifically for the Heiress.

He circled back to stand before her. "Is this understood?" He watched the quiver in her lip. Fighting back questions sitting at the tip of her tongue. Bon sang, if he didn't want at that very moment to just dive in and plunder her mouth. Taste her tongue. Chew on her raspberry red lips. He sucked in another deep breath— *soon.* "Pet?"

❦

Amelia fought to still her emotions, "Yes, Head-Master."

"What do I need to hear from you?"

Amelia rolled her lips, her fingers curling at her side grasping for strength, "Green."

"Good, my pet. Now strip as you were told, but leave your high heels on, and we will begin your first punishment."

Amelia gasped, preparing to protest.

"*Ahhh*— do you want that to be two punishments?"

She could almost see the single digit finger wagging at her to behave. The image perfectly formed in her mind, the way his tone nearly *tsked* at her. "No, Head-Master."

"Good, not a sound then," his voice softened into a near caress and the room fell silent as she began to remove her clothes. "Remember, you wanted this. You went to Dominus and asked for a Master. I am here because you want me to be here. Now give in to all those desires. For you no longer had control over what is done to you, Because that is what you asked for."

Trenton was nestled back into one of the easy chairs. His mouse curled up in his lap so he could play with her freely. His fingers having worked her dress up to toy with her clit while his other hand cupped her mouth to prevent any sounds from escaping her lips.

Watching Amelia struggling with herself was amazing. He'd really expected more outward resistance from her than this, but her body truly desired total submission and Rashawn managed her superbly. He gave no quarter and it was working exceptionally well on the heiress.

If only she didn't cling to such hang ups as age differences. The sight of the dark haired Mediterranean Frenchman had to be an eye candy for even her. Perhaps even more so. Rashawn was near the same age as he and having grown up with two separately wealthy parents and his father being in the Lifestyle, he was groomed to be the perfection of a Master of sexual kink. She was truly missing out. How she ever missed his attentiveness toward her was another matter of denial. He'd spotted it right away, during their trip to Paris for the summit meeting. It was how he knew Rashawn was the only choice for Amelia's request to be matched with someone.

Trenton had no doubts Rashawn would be able to deliver her to the ultimate quest. The true challenge would be in whether or not she would let down her guard to let him in when his face was revealed.

Rashawn took the blouse from Amelia once she had it free, but when her skirt slipped down her legs to the floor— he let the hiss slip through clenched teeth.

Who would ever have been able to envision Amelia Quinneth, the heiress of the Quinneth Estates, standing here in front of him, cinched and gift wrapped in a satin blindfold and a gorgeous chocolate brown burlesque style corset with crème colored ruffles across the top? A mix of red and crème colored satin bows danced about the bones to tease his eye. *Voila! Behold such succulent candy dipped in exotic spices.*

A deep low groan threatened to rumble in his chest as he took in the sight of her. *Bon sang, couché!*— he had to tell his own cock to settle down with an amount of cursing. But the whistled expression escaped him. "Very nice. Now stop there. We'll get to the panties in a minute."

Rashawn circled around her, taking in every detail of her body. His hand went to his throbbing cock in his pants and stroked at it through the fabric of his tailored slacks. It was going to be torture getting through tonight, but it would be damned worth it once he got there. He circled around, stopping just in front of her.

One of the nice things about Burlesque corsets was, while the waist and hips were cinched up beautifully in the stiffened whale bone structure, the brasserie was usually soft fabric. Which meant— as he pulled at the ruffled fabric at the top— he could easily access her breasts.

"Now those are some of the prettiest little, pink jewels I've seen in a long time," he coo'ed.

Amelia was enjoying the praise, but when she felt the warm wet mouth come down over her nipple, sucking it in deep and hard— *ohhhh,* she loved that even more. No stalling or holding back. He swept right in and delivered a tantalizing contact. And a hot breathy O floated past her lips. Her pleasure made known when her head fell back with an expressed gasp. Her Head-Master's lips tightened around the tip then opened up to suck more of the full plump roundness of her breast into a swirl of his caressing tongue. She could feel the quickening he caused all the way down to her sexual core and it was getting wetter by the minute. Her thighs tightened, pleading to have a man's hips between them.

Her Master's lips were replaced with his palm and he pressed it against her, rolling the taut button under the friction of his palm, like a rough massage, while his lips arrived at her other nipple. Giving it an equal amount of attention.

Amelia arched into him. She loved receiving affection on her breasts and yet it seemed she never got quite enough. It was always over too soon or just not the right touch. But this? This was making her head swoon, his mouth so perfectly pampering her needs that must have caused her to sway as she felt the firm press of his free hand on her back to steady her.

She stifled the whimper when it stopped. Her Master's lips and hands gone. But the absence was short and his fingertips hovered around each hard nipple, drawing circles around them teasing her. Amelia arched her back, opening herself for the return of his lavishing attention. She wanted to feel his tongue lick over them again, as if savoring a favorite delicacy—

The image shattered quite suddenly, feeling something very much different than the anticipated mouth. First, just a tight pressure to both nipples, but the pressure quickly bit down mirroring little teeth.

Amelia tried not to cry out. She wasn't prepared to get clamped. She'd never allowed a Dom to put them on her before, but she knew it could be nothing else. Her breasts ignited with the first experience of fire, warm then hot, and they shot out a powerful pulse as if little supernovas.

She felt herself drifting away from him as if doing so would make the clamps disappear, but a strong arm slipped around her waist to prevent the retreat, and she couldn't hold back the tearful moan any longer.

"*Shhh*— easy— the first minute or two is the hardest. Remember, you earned the punishment," his voice formidable and strict, yet soothing and then she felt his tongue tease over her throbbing abused nipple. One, then the other, moving back and forth between the two as if the very touch of his tongue could put out the fire caused by the clamps.

"Oh god, take them off please."

"*Shhh*— you want this— you can't see them, but your nipples look magnificent in clamps. Small succulent buttons of red candy begging to be plucked by me."

Again, he dropped his mouth over one then the other, sucked and licked over them, voraciously devouring her nipples. She could feel them swell even more as pleasure and pain stung through her senses, and she found herself arching into him farther.

"See? Your body responds so wonderfully," he praised her further, making her feel just how much the sight of her appealed to him. She could only play it in her mind that his pause was him taking a moment to enjoy her body visually as he watched her injured nipples bordering on red and purple. His fingers fanned over the hot buds like he had his tongue. And he let out a coarse sigh before withdrawing. "Yes, we will definitely come back to these later. So beautiful, so incredible."

She heard his deepening breath, adding to the physical elixir. He had enjoyed it as much as she had. *Oh, good god, did she just admit she had enjoyed this? The clamps?* Her thighs shifted; she felt the wetness building in her theca, to borrow a tantalizing word from her star author. Yes, she definitely had enjoyed it.

"Nice, was it?" he crooned close to her ear.

"Yes, Head-Master, thank you," she barely managed to squeak out the response he waited on. She felt the faint kiss to her forehead through the satin blindfold and heard his footsteps circle around her without removing the clamps. "Will you take the clamps off now?"

"No, they'll stay for a while and when they do come off, it will be incredible." He paused behind her and pressed his lips to the back of her head. "I promise, my pet." He sounded so seductive, so sultry she believed him. A reverence most Doms practiced, the kissing of the forehead as a reward or reassurance, but never before had it touched her as it did now. Before it was just something her Dom of the week did, about as mechanical and fulfilling as putting the keys in the ignition to start a car. But when her Head-Master did so, she felt her emotions swoon like a little girl, beaming with pride that she'd pleased him.

"Tell me, my pet, where does your waist measure now in your corsets?"

"I believe I am at twenty-two or twenty-three. I had no one to measure this evening."

"Very good. I appreciate your honesty. I would like to do some training on you tonight. Let's see if we can get you down to twenty by the end of the night, shall we? We'll do this one inch at a time, yes?"

"Yes, Head-Master."

"Good, my pet."

She listened to his movements and she felt the laces on her corset come undone.

Her Master's hands freed the braided cords then instantly began tightening the lower set, starting at her hips, and one lace set after another, working them tighter with a firm pull until he reached her waist.

There was an art to corsets. A man's hands either fumbled clumsily, or his fingers worked the cords like magic. There was no doubt, this unnamed Master knew his way around a corset. Precisioned, even draws of the cords as though he'd been lacing girls up all his life.

He crisscrossed the cords then pushed them around front. "Hold the laces, pet, and don't let them slip."

Amelia did as told. His voice so smooth and deep like a lover's kiss with words. Any word and they bid her to obey him. Her fingers held the laces while her Master repeated the lacing procedure with the upper part of her corset making his way down toward her midsection this time. Again, he crisscrossed the cords, reached around, retrieving the first set of cords from her hands and pulled the combined laces back behind her, and then gave them a final firm tug.

Amelia's breath clutched from the hard pull and she felt every bit of that one inch sucked out of her. She felt the cords secured behind her once again then felt something different wrap around her waist. *Had he actually carried a measuring tape with him? Had she ever met a Dom that did?* He had requested that she wore a true boned corset tonight and had been very specific that it had to be a lace up ribbed corset, not a *for-show* lingerie or fashion styled corset.

"Twenty-two and a quarter inches, mmm. We're off to a good start." His fingers glided over her narrowed waist and across her abdomen. The light sensation through the heavy material tickled and she jittered under the touch. She heard the faint hum of approval as he enjoyed the nuance of her body's responses. He truly *was* a Master— none of the Doms she had gone out with before had taken any notice. It touched her deeply that this man did.

"Now I want you to take off your panties, but I want you to bend over at the hip, keeping your back straight as you do. Nice and slow so I can enjoy it," his rich, deep voice commanded softly against her ear.

Amelia lost all will to hesitate. She reached down, snaring the sides of her lace panties with a manicured thumb at each hip and then tugged them down. Slowly sliding them down her thighs, bending straight over to accommodate her reach as well as the wishes of her

Head-Master. The commanding man remained snugly pressed against her ass, his hands stroking her skin.

Yet when she reached her ankles, she noticed one of her Master's hands vanish. Though, just as she wondered where its destination was, his left hand's grip tightened on her hip and then she felt the sudden —*SMACK*— of his right— directly across an ass cheek. The sting came down so hard she yelped. And she would have toppled over had he not kept her secured.

"What was that for?" She snapped her head in his direction behind her, despite her blindness.

"For not responding to me properly." Her Master told her as his hand smoothed over the warm sting on her cheek then switched hands, "Don't move. Now I have to even out your color." And just then his left hand came down, just like the first. Hard across the opposite cheek with a loud smack and right away Amelia felt the gorgeous blush develop over her skin.

"Now I think you should be thanking me, since I took the extra effort to see to it you're even on both sides."

Amelia bit back what she really thought to say, *balance me out*— he got plenty of pleasure from that. No need to be thanking him. And suddenly his right hand came down on her ass again. Her breath hitched.

"You know, my pet, there is a reason why there is a difference between being just a Dom and being a Master."

"What is that, Head-Master?"

Rashawn couldn't pass up a chance to light the fires inside her with some exultantly naughty, albeit also egotistical, anticipations. "Some Doms are just barely grasping the power they have. Like little boys masturbating for the first time. They have just barely scratched the surface to explore and have any real understanding of the human psyche. However, a Master is going to give you the greatest pleasures you've ever desired, his dominance isn't displayed with shouting and demands, but with the slightest touch of his hand to your back and whispered words that make your head spin. He will also punish you *every* time you desire it." And his left hand came down—

—*SMACK*—

"Now, what do you say?"

Amelia caught her breath. Feeling the electricity travel from the sharp sting on her derriere to the front of her clit. It was all she could do not to groan just then. It was delicious. "Thank you, Head-Master." That groan purred out with the sultry gratitude. Not even an ounce of the sassiness she had thought up on the first delivery. Not even a tiddly bit. Her Head-Master knew her all too well.

"Very nice." His hand smoothed over her skin, easing away the burn, "Such a good pet." His hands guided her to straighten and he rewarded her with a gentle brush of his lips on her shoulder. Then a brush of his nose against the side of her head, inhaling her scent as if she was the most succulent flower he had ever smelled. The little girl hiding inside Amelia swooned once more. Then he was the one kneeling, his hands caressing her legs, gliding down her thighs and she discovered the smooth polished skin of his palms. Not a single telltale scratch of a callous. His hands were not rough by any working man's means. A manicured man. Gears began to move once more to decipher who her Master could be.

"Lift your foot." The gentle command came and she felt his hand at her right for support as she lifted it and was surprised when he removed her pump, then returned her foot to the floor. "Now the other." And he did the same with it. "Spread your legs apart, my pet, I'm going to inspect you now."

Amelia shifted her feet until they were nearly shoulder width apart.

"Mmmm, that's very nice, but I want you to spread them a little farther."

Amelia hesitated, the pose making her feel utterly lacking in grace.

—*SMACK!* —

Amelia gasped when his hand came down on her ass without warning.

"I really hate waiting and I won't repeat myself."

Amelia stepped her feet out farther.

"There. See how beautiful you are now? And to think you hesitated on such a small thing. What will you do when I command you to your knees and tell you to lean back so that sweet pussy is looking up at me?"

"I- I will do as you command me, Head-Master."

"We shall see, I suppose." Not convinced she would be so complacent and that alone hit like a welt on her desires. *She had already displeased him.*

He reached around the front of her between her legs, his fingers grazing her wet folds, finding something he hadn't expected.

"What's this?"

She felt her hood piercing move from his touch. "My slave chain, Head-Master."

"Slave chain?" He looked over her front, down at the small gold chain now draped over his fingertips. About four inches in length with a ring on its end, lent perfect for tugging on the captive-bead ring pierced through her clitoral hood. "Why you naughty little pet." And taking it in his fingers, he did what it was meant for and pulled on it. A firm gentle tug, then lifted it up as he stood.

Amelia moaned, instantly rolling to her toes; her weight shifting slightly using his body to keep her balance.

"Mmmm," he crooned in her ear.

Amelia felt the warmth of his breath cascading down her neck as he spoke more praises.

"I am going to thoroughly enjoy you as my submissive this weekend, my pet." He released the chain and pulled away.

Amelia felt the sudden relief. Her anxiety leaving her that she had passed his scrutiny.

"I accept her as mine for the next thirty-six hours."

Her thrill quickly shifted to surprise, realizing he had not directed the announcement to her. "What?" Her head snapping around toward the other movement when she realized they hadn't been alone all this time. Trenton had been so quiet she'd forgotten he was still there. It wasn't as though he'd never seen her with a Dom before; he had plenty of times. But this man? He was different he— *he* was in charge. And Amelia felt quite embarrassed suddenly.

"Silence. Not a word from you," her Master corrected her racing thoughts before moving away. "What are the rules upstairs?" Again, his question directed away from her to no less the Dominus.

"The lobby allows pretty much whatever you want to do. There's a considerable amount of equipment, but most fetish items are light and the acts themselves are expected to be light as well. There are private rooms to the side. Club subs are available for play and they have the same safewords: Red, yellow, green." Dominus filled in a few details.

"Can I feed her say a glass of wine?"

"Subs and slaves are not allowed to drink upstairs. It's necessary to prevent gratuitous advantages of their submission."

"I understand."

Amelia felt his fingers in her hair. An attentive gesture that said many things all at once, to remain still, he was still admiring her. *Yes, I am talking with someone else, but my eyes are still on you.* And perhaps he was fantasizing over what her hair would look like spilled over his lap and she couldn't wait until they reached that part of their time together when he would use her log locks to mop his lap with.

She sucked in a deep breath, her lips rolling in with the tantalizing thought, and it was mirrored with a chuckle from her Head-Master. "I think she's ready," he cheered and oh she wished he could see the purring delight in her eyes just then.

"Do you wish to take her up now?" Trenton asked from his spot in her booth.

"Yes. Yes, I do."

Rashawn carefully restored the cream-colored fabric of Amelia's brassier to its suitable place over her still clamped nipples. He grinned deeply with anticipation of watching them come off. Next, he stooped down and guided her feet into a pair of luscious lace panties he'd brought for her. Basked in dainty ruffles and an accessible slit along the crotch for his fingers to find and play as he pleased.

He glanced at Trenton as he pulled them up over her hips and caressed her mound with his cheek. His eyes closed a moment as he breathed her in, letting out a mild groan. "But I don't think I want to stay long. I have other plans for her and I'm eager to get started."

Rashawn took Amelia's hand and draped it over his arm as he turned his back to her. "Keep just a step behind me and you will feel where I am guiding you, keep your senses trained on me and you won't stumble," he instructed her and waited for her response before taking her out of the room.

Upstairs, only this time with a Dom who knew what to do and would deliver. "Yes, Head-Master," she whispered with divine anticipation. And out into the crowd they went.

Once upstairs, Rashawn wasted no time taking advantage of a couple of the club subs to torment his new pet for a little while. Placing Amelia on her knees and bent over backwards on one of the ottomans in the center of the upstairs lounge, he'd directed the two subs to lather her body with their tongues. Watching, he held a riding crop in his hand with a relaxed grip, drawing the leather tongue across Amelia's skin so she could anticipate the coming strikes. Her body quivered like a nervous virgin as he did so. *How exquisite.*

The first flick came. Right across her left nipple taking the clamp off. Amelia coiled to the side instantly and cried out as blood rushed in to fill her abused nipple. A nod from Rashawn and instantly the female sub dropped over Amelia's breast and sucked the red nipple into her eager lips.

"Ahhhh!" Amelia gasped, coiling and recoiling. A snap of the crop against the inside of her thigh called her to still her movements.

"You may move some, pet, but do not attempt to escape what is inevitable for your body." Rashawn circled around her, watching as the club-sub sucked and licked over the tender nipple, taking in every writhing shiver of his pet. He dragged the tip of the crop over Amelia's body up and down several times, adding to those tantalizing ripples until finally he saw fit to remove the second nipple clamp and did so by smacking it off with the crop.

Amelia's head shot up and her cry filled the room. Her teeth found her lips.

She dropped back down and right away, Rashawn gave the second sub a nod to move in.

❦

Amelia's whole body shuddered with pain that shot out from her freed yet tortured nipples and then instantly being licked over by not one, but two mouths. Each so very different from each other. One small and soft as a dainty tongue circled around her engorged tip. The other, larger and more demanding mouth, devoured her with rough suckling and teeth. She tried to remain still, but it was impossible and then she felt the first set of switches to the inside of her thighs. Small stinging snaps across her skin, licking them to open farther. She struggled to spread her thighs wider, then wider again when the second set came, one thigh then the next. Back and forth, tiny snaps of leather flicked against her skin with a pink sting. Then they stopped and the leather wrapped rod was used to strum over her labia, sliding between the accessible slit in the panties her Master dressed her in and slid against her wet folds before delivering a whipped strike on her clit. It throbbed awake as if it had never been woken from a lifelong slumber.

"Please, Head-Master," she pleaded.

"Why, dear pet, you are pleasing me."

She chewed on her lips and groaned when the next set came and when it ended, she felt two hands one large and rough, the other soft and dainty slide down her belly, snaking through her pubic hairs then together they dove into her cunt, twirling and pumping together inside her. She felt it instantly, her walls clamping down on the two intruders. "Oh god, Master, I can't—"

"Stop now," the command came quickly and the fingers which pumped inside her honey slicked walls stopped instantly and retreated. "You are not to cum until I tell you to, my pet. You weren't going to cum, were you?"

"No, of course not." Amelia gulped. Her own pleas stopped when the fingers had retreated. But it wasn't an orgasm she couldn't hold back, rather it was one that clutched at her painfully and frightened her. A ball of energy floating just over the cuspate of release and yet so far away she could never reach it. It hovered painfully behind her clit and she clamped down every muscle inside her, wishing she could do just that, but knew it had been just the opposite for her. The very reward always denied her, and it had come so close. She would lie and cheat if to only snatch it and run. Even if it meant to disobey her Master's pleasure. Though she knew it would never happen.

"Good, because I want to be sure to feel every inch of you shiver when you do."

She felt the knee press into the ottoman next to her hips, felt it sinking her own as the weight of her Master eased down over her. Like lightning, two fingers thrust deep inside her until his knuckles bottomed out against her hooded jewel. "Now, my pet. Cum for me, now." He whispered just above her.

His fingers scooped and danced inside her, and she pleaded with her body to obey his command. The small white ball of ecstasy just out of reach of his fingertips. The needy pain ripped through her. Oh god she wanted to, but could not. Her body convulsed, straining to catch it, lifting her hips off the cushion, forcing her body over his fingers farther.

"That's it, let me feel you come right to the very edge," his voice grew husky as she rocked her cunt over his fingers, pumping to trigger every last ounce and quiver from her before sliding out.

The squeal of torment broke free from her as his hand slipped away. The stalled tactic made her feel as though she was free falling from high above. Yet her body still owned every bit of the tension that had been there at the start.

Moist fingers traced her mouth and she tasted the hint of her own pooled moisture as he pushed his fingers past her lips, urging her to open, and receive the gift. The scent of her own silk filled her nostrils, painted over her tongue with the brush strokes of his fingers. The pain ebbing but never vanishing as her body failed him.

She moved all her thoughts to her tongue, to the fingers offered her, and she sucked on them in a display of her eager tongue's talents. It pleased him, she knew it, as he moaned with delight and quite suddenly his fingers were replaced with his mouth, licking to steal the taste of her juices he'd just brushed over her lips. She loved every bit of it. If only it could have been more, but she wasn't about to disappoint him with her failure.

"That was very nice, my pet." He leaned in to whisper in her ear, "however, next time I expect you to actually cum when I tell you."

He knew.

CHAPTER TWO

Taking Amelia from the club still blindfolded could have raised some issues. For one, they were breaking one of the club's rules, it also had a tendency to draw unwelcomed attention to the club's entrance. However, their evening had been planned down to the last detail. So when Trenton came up and drew a cloak around Amelia's shoulders and pulled the billowing hood over her head to cloak her face in shadow, Rashawn knew that the Dominus had gone to great lengths to honor his requests, and to ensure the start of their night went as planned. Once outside the club, all would be reliant on him alone.

Quite extraordinary actually, how the rich velvet cape swept around her body, its hem barely skirting above the ground as Rashawn led her toward the chauffeured car that waited for them at the curb. Trenton and Diesel, both escorted them to guard their departure which was neither interrupted nor tainted with any calling out of names and titles. Rashawn had to hand it to the man,

Trenton Leos truly was a Master of design as well as control when it came to seeing one's fantasies fulfilled.

During the short drive from the club to the marina, Rashawn kept silently toying with her shoulders, drawing soft lines down her arm with the light brush of his fingertips. Simply enjoying the nervous breath coming from the woman he'd desired above all others for some time. Just the thought of his success to finally have her had him ready to cum if he even so much as adjusted the erection trapped in his slacks.

When Trenton came to him asking if he would be interested in spending an evening with a hard to control woman who was in great need of a discipline Master, Rashawn had almost turned it down. He had no desire to waste a moment of his time to be hindered by just any woman; not when his time could be better spent plotting the pursuit of the heiress of his desires until she surrendered to his arms.

Perhaps it was some insight he'd had that the Dominus didn't take Rashawn's first answer. The cosmic moment when Trenton spoke those magical words now echoing in Rashawn's mind as the car drove them down the wharf toward the large, three-mast sailing yacht awaiting them.

—Amelia Quinneth can be quite the handful. Though, I assure you, she would be well worth the effort and the rewards—

Rashawn had lost his composure to stammer out his answer to take her. Even he could not have accidentally seduced such a perfect arrangement to happen between him and the woman he desired above all others.

Getting Amelia on his yacht without giving too many hints away of their location was another challenge. The blindfold and an iPod were used to help buffer and disorientate many of the details of their surroundings.

While his own clipper's rigging were almost entirely internal, functioning from inside the three dyna-rig masts. Nearby sailing vessels were not so quiet, and the slapping rigs would send out a distinguished sound if a strong enough breeze swept through. But even Mother Nature seemed to be on his side. The water in the harbor was fairly calm at the moment, so the 289 foot sailing vessel sat quietly at her moors. The only thing that might give him away was the gangplank. The ribbed ramp meant to move with the ship was an unavoidable detail so he decided to add one of his own, first delivering a nice swat to the round rump that hid under her cloak, then swept her off her feet, and carried her onboard.

Once inside, Rashawn had little concern for such details, his focus was purely on her and he planned to have her too busy and too aroused to know the difference between the soft rolls of the boat and her senses being pitched off her axis.

"Are you ready to serve your new Head-Master?" he asked after returning his pet to her feet.

Now arriving inside the mystery location where she would spend the next two days, Amelia took a deep breath to steady herself, her heart fluttering excitedly in her chest, and the exulting warmth that trickled over her was too sweet to deny. "Yes, Head-Master."

She stepped cautiously, but not too slow that it might upset her new Master. Nevertheless, being blindfolded was not a common playground for her, and it certainly presented a challenge when walking in a place where she had no sense of navigation. Her self-control completely benevilized as she relied on the steady hands of her Master to guide her, as too, did his words. Suddenly her mind fell from his florid spell and she nearly let slip the embarrassing laugh at her thoughts.

"What is it that makes you laugh so?" Her Master's gcntlc voice quizzed her.

"My apologies. Just something I thought of and then realized—" she paused then corrected her babbling, "It was nothing. I didn't mean to laugh."

"Nonsense, laughter is good. Please, tell me what it was."

Amelia tried to lick the smile from her lips but it was useless, even as a turn here and there, then a step had her so perplexed of what direction she was going. "I have an author who likes to make up her own words, no matter how many times I tell her not to. And well. I just had a mental slip and actually used one of her words."

"And that is what made you laugh?"

"Yes, Head-Master."

"It is a humor word, like to make jokes with?"

"No, just funny because her definition, it fit so perfectly just now."

He paused her, using nothing more than his own body as he stood before her, his hands still guiding her but now they guided her to step close, against him. She heard the purr of his breath in his chest, felt it brush the side of her head as he bent down to whisper in her ear. "And what does the fictitious word mean?"

"It was a hybrid word between *Benevolent* and *Obliterized*, which meant: to be gently or kindly done away with."

"I don't believe I have ever heard of the second word."

"I know. I lost that argument with her two books ago. Writers can be such stubborn creatures," she purred with another laugh. "Sometimes more so than their editors."

"And who is this wily crafter?"

"Dominus's Life-slave, Katianna Dumas."

This time the laugh came from Rashawn, so it would seem the timid and petite woman had even more hidden strengths than ever given credit for, if she managed to win a contest of wills against Amelia.

Amelia could still feel his face next to hers, hovering close, breathing her in, "What is it, have I done away with?"

Amelia swallowed nervously and once more licked her lips. Only this time it was nervousness she battled. "My control," she whispered.

"Mmmm— I like the sound of this word. Whisper it to me."

"Benevilized."

He remained silent, only his hands responded with faint touches that brushed down her body one side then the next, letting her know he circled her. Then led her to continue their journey within this place he'd brought her for the weekend.

It was arousing how the rest of her senses came alive and she was vaguely aware that her surroundings seemed to have a strange fixture about it. As if her environment moved, even if only the slightest bit, but enough that the floor beneath her feet didn't seem as solid as it should. And she loved how it added to all the other nuances of her experience. This is what it felt like to be completely dependent on another.

Her Master's hands moved to her shoulders, pulling her to aa stop, then slipped to the front of her breasts, undid the fastener of her cape, and then slow and tantalizingly, pulled it from her shoulders. His fingertips grazing over her skin as he did.

Where the cloak went was not any wonder to her, but rather that continuing caress on the skin of her arms while it moved up over her shoulders, tracing lines along the tenure of her neck and combed through her hair. She felt a handful of it being lifted and she swore she heard the hiss of his deep inhale.

"Lovely," his deep voice praised her, "My pet, there is a bed post directly in front of you. I want you to reach out and take hold of it."

Amelia did as instructed, her arms nearly colliding with the post, when she discovered she was much closer than she had anticipated. Her fingers felt along the carved texture of wood, while she felt his hands once more set to the task at the ties of her corset. When the first set of lacings were pulled, she made sure her arms where in proper place, hugging the post to steady her body as her Master yet again drew her waist in to reach their goal was suggested earlier that night. His hands didn't fumble, not missing a corded loop or leaving uneven draws in his wake just as he had throughout the night. Like a man who knew precisely what he was doing by experience and not wishful thinking.

"Take a deep breath."

She sucked in a deep breath, filling her lungs that stretched her body upwards as there was no expanding in the bone-ribbed constraint.

"That's it— now let it out."

Amelia huffed the breath out properly. A final hard tug on the cords and she felt her waist cinch in to what felt like more than that last inch he was hoping for, and a pleasant sigh escaped her lips that she would please him so.

The measuring tape threaded around her and a proud *mmmm* resonated at the back of her head and rewarded her neck with a kiss.

"Very beautiful. You have trained well."

Even his choice of words bespoke he knew the culture of corsets and she felt a small swelling of love for her Master— *but not too much*— she giggled to herself, she didn't want to spoil the progress she had made.

Oh, but perhaps just a little more— she admitted silently when his hand brushed her hair aside and she felt his face press against the back of her neck again— heard the tight inhale then felt his warm breath in her hair. Even blindfolded, closing her eyes made an exquisite difference and she teetered off her balance deliciously.

Every cell in her body followed those lips now kissing a trail down her neck, along the concave line that led out across her shoulder. It all ended with a soft lingering press of his lips returning to the base of her neck. That erogenous spot where neck and spine met. That singular connection did more to her body than all the others combined. The encapsulating result was that cascade of tingles like a waterfall of stardust that trickled down every nerve ending and gathered in her pudendum and then waited for permission to be released. It was the sweetest agony she had ever felt.

A firm hand on her neck replaced the kiss and silently guided her down on her knees, her hands still holding the bed post, and he left her there.

She waited silently, ears pining for a sound— a clue— all adjusting her anticipation up another notch until her Master revealed what would be next. When she heard the clink of ice in a glass and the stopper of a glass bottle, she couldn't help the warm appeasing smile come over her.

While her new Master's voice didn't have the tone of an aged man, the moment of play that included him sitting back to admire her while sipping on a toddy was definitely *old school.* And to be sure she was the perfectly painted picture of art for his viewing pleasure, she tightened her pose.

She pulled her shoulders up, tucked her chin just enough, and kept her hands on the bed post delicately. She even added a little pout to her lips to make them desirably kissable. The effect she hoped for delivered, when she heard the tumbling of his upturned glass pause a moment before turning up the remaining tilt. Ice cubes jammed against his lips, followed by the clunk of a heavy glass bottom returning to the bar for a refill.

Rashawn leaned back on the bar as he sipped his Hennessy, granting his thoughts, and his dick, just a moment to rein in some. Never before had he wanted to just jump for the finish line and be inside a woman as he did with Amelia. Her submissive equanimity simply did him in when he was in her presence and he desired nothing more than to just ravage her for hours. But why stop there— he did after all have her for the next thirty-six. So, some pacing was in need, but that was nearly *bon sang* to hell when he saw the small correction to her posture as he watched. The results had his cock balking against the zipper of his slacks instantaneously and all else froze a moment to stare at her elegant form.

Putain, he thought, drawing in a tight breath then forced himself to glance away and top off his glass. Though the movement had the effect she wanted, it also showed the problem. She was still calling the shots on her submission. Something he would have to train out of her. His mind going into planning mode of just how, while he poured another double shot. Handling her was much the same as his drink. One would not often think to create a dirty mixer with an expensive cognac— he perceived as the spirits splashed over the melted ice cubes in the crystal tumbler. He could drink it dry but instead, he added a spritz of fresh lemon, and a heavy drop of Cointreau orange liqueur so that what was considered the perfect drink beforehand was transformed into a delightful un-neat cocktail after some proper ingredients. Like Amelia, she just needed some distingue training to undo all that perfectly misplaced controls.

"We're going to start off by going over the rules of our contract. I know you have answered the questionnaire I sent to you prior, but it's always good to review before starting. You may start by stating yours for this weekend, my pet." He took a tentative sip for taste testing, then a longer for pleasure, drawing his thoughts back to the business aspect of their arrangement. They had played lightly so far at the club, but it was time to get past the innuendos and get down to some serious fetish work.

"I don't believe I have any to be concerned over, Head-Master. I belong to you and you may do whatever you wish to enjoy me."

"That sounds very nice, my pet. And I assure you I intend to do so." He strolled up behind her. He bent and cupped her elbow and gently pulled her up to her feet. Her fingers gracefully following the bed post to steady herself. "But there are always rules and we need to go over the foundries of them before we are free to begin. For example, I have many. In time, you will be taught them all, but we'll just go over a few of the essentials for now."

"As you wish, Head-Master," she answered back with a sultry purr.

When he was confident, she had her footing, he guided his blind pet out of the room and into the large study. Wall to wall and ceiling to floor bookshelves enclosed in glass cabinets covered two of the walls fronted by an impressive American Eagle Presidential Executive desk. Hand carved exotic woods of black and burl walnut made it a masterpiece meant to impress.

Two leather sofas added to the rich masculine décor. A cream colored suede ottoman was situated just slightly off center in the room. At first-hand, the elliptic shaped piece of furniture looked completely out of place, unless one had had the pleasure of being a guest on a night Rashawn chose to entertain, then the misplaced colored ottoman made ideal sense— and the perfect stage. The bondage restraints were color matched to hide in plain sight, however, viewable upon closer inspection.

The centerpiece never ceased to arouse both men and women guests.

Rashawn led Amelia over to the plush stage and settled her to sit on it. "Pose for me and wait for further instructions while we continue going over the rules," he spoke gently then left her on the ottoman and took a seat behind his desk. From where he sat, he could see every part and act he commanded of her, and he tilted his chair back eyeing the alluring beauty that now belonged to him. His hand dropped to his lap, using the heel of his palm to adjust the aching hard-on and took another long sip of the Sidecar mixer.

"Let's go over the house rules, shall we?" It was more a pronouncement than a question, but when she spoke up, he allowed it.

"How many are there?"

He watched the rise and fall of her breasts, accentuated by the waves of dark burgundy hair. He grinned, though he knew she could not see it. "Many— but we'll just start with the first six, which are the most vital to our arrangement." He watched as she adjusted her pose perfectly for him. She sat straight as an Egyptian chair, breasts thrust out, chin tucked, and her hands folded perfectly in her lap. Very dowdy and proper— ready for naughty spoiling. "House rule number one: you will wear no items of clothing other than high heel shoes and whichever articles of fabric candy I have selected for that day. If, when you wake or after a bath, no garments have been laid out for you, you're to remain naked with only your heels until told otherwise." He paused letting it sink in and then he gave her the second rule. "House rule number two: The correct response to most things is *Yes, Head-Master.*"

Ruby red lips curled up in the corners and she spoke fluidly, "Yes, Head-Master."

At that response, the heel of his palm was no longer suitable enough, and he unzipped his pants and slid his hand inside. A gruff moan gasped from his lips when his fingers coiled around the ache he was sporting— *soon—* very soon, it would be wrapped inside the warm, wet bliss of her pussy and he was likely going to die once there.

"On occasion, I will allow a less formal response where *Yes, Sir* will be just as acceptable. I will tell you when this is allowed and when it is not. House rule number three: when spanked for being naughty— *Count.* When spanked for pleasure, you will always say— *Thank you, Sir.*" He paused taking another sip of the un-neat cognac; letting the bold mix of candied fruit, wild rose flavor of the *Hennessy Eclipse* paired with the citrus and candied liqueur burn longer over his tongue a moment, while its earthy aroma seeped into his olfactory senses. It all seemed to infuse with the sight before him, how her body so tantalizingly burned into his mind and furthered his desires.

"House rule number four: Worshiping my cock is always a good start for anything." And he very much liked the sultry curl to her lips then. In fact, it was time for her to start some show and tell for him. "Now I want you to spread your legs out. Lean back on only one arm, set your feet as far apart as you can, and show me that beautiful rose." His instant gratification came out in a groan as she did as told. The manicured patch of burgundy curls dappled just over the glistening mauve petals— looking as beautiful and as tasty as he ever imagined. Perhaps even more tantalizing with the gold accessary. Now he had no choice but to free his cock all the way out of his slacks and he began to stroke over the hard length slowly; his gaze locked onto the sight in front of him, and he downed the last of his drink. "Touch yourself. I want to watch your fingers drawing out the silky honey hidden away inside you."

Amelia took a deep breath, listening to her Master give her first commands for the night. His tone strong willed and precise. Her emotions reeling with the excitement after she had placed her valued, intimate possessions on display for him and she brought her fingers around to fulfill the next command.

There was a loud inward hiss from his direction, then carried on with more of the rules.

"When sucking my cock, you will always be a good girl and swallow every drop."

As he told her the extensions of his fourth rule, she traced over the entrance of the moist lips between her legs. She eased her fingertips through the silky wetness that seeped out and made her so ready for not just her fingers, but she wanted her Master's cock up inside her. She felt the rush of blood in her chest and neck at the lascivious thought. It'd been a long span of time since she had actually lusted after a Dom so readily, to want to be in his bed on the first night.

"I want you to bring yourself to the very edge of your orgasm and then stop there." The firm addition to his order for her came across the air like a hot kiss in her ear.

"Yes, Head-Master."

She parted the entrance right down the center, slowly to give the teasing visual he allowed while noting every nuance of the contact on her body. Relishing the shiver it sent up her spine and then slowly slipped two fingers all the way in, imagining they were her Master's.

Warm soaked walls hugged around her fingers and she crooked them inside as she withdrew and slathered the wetness around her clit. Her legs jumped at first glance of the sensitized nub then she pushed back in.

"House rule number five: Your orgasms belong to me. They are my gift to you. I will give or withhold them for my pleasure. So, you will cum when I command or not until I have given you permission to do so."

He did so seem to enjoy giving that one, she could almost hear the proud smile on his lips. The very tone of his ownership rang out more in this one, and it had her breath kicking up as she continued her masturbation show for her Master, and her body ached as it waited for him. However, there was one problem that was already casting a shadow on her pleasure.

Even as her hand did as it was commanded, the orgasm he promised as a gift, was as foreign an idea as an investment prompted to a man with not even two cents to rub together. And she feared she would not be able to satisfy her Master if he demanded a show.

Rashawn watched through a half-lidded gaze, his hand still stroking over his shaft lazily as he watched her do the same to her own body. He studied her, looking for the small tell-tale signs that said she was enjoying this, not just going through the motions, and the blush and deepening breath told him she was definitely into this. Yet, there was something amiss— something he couldn't quite put his finger to— or perhaps that was exactly what he needed to do, put *his* finger on it. "The last one for this visit is house rule number six: Remember who you belong to." And the slight whimper that threatened to come from her lips just then was exquisite. "Now, my pet, tell me what your rules are, so we can get on with the things we both want. Mind you, your fingers are not to stop until I tell you."

Amelia spoke softly, and too smoothly for a woman who was supposed to be working herself to the edge of orgasm, but not so feeble to suggest they could be ignored.

Dammit— Amelia's thoughts argued as her body also seemed to refuse to comply with the command from her Master to go to the edge. She just needed a little more time to get there, she told herself. Though his commands did do something to her, she feared her own voice would break the spell of hope she was on the edge of being delivered to.

Her fingers chasing and searching for what was not there. Having to answer a question only sent the unobtainable edge she was supposed to be standing at, all the farther into the distance. But when she failed to answer promptly, he repeated rule number six, along with the command, reminding her he was awaiting her answer. She sucked in a breath, mentally sending a plea to her clit to stay happy while her mind did the thinking.

"No blood-play, water-works, or degradation-play. No needles or suction cups— please, Sir. I love a good bit of pain, but my skin bruises easily sometimes and I would prefer not to go home with too many of the darker trophies from our first weekend."

"Thank you, pet. That is good to know. I will be careful of your skin this weekend then. Please do not stop your hand, keep working yourself to the edge."

She fell silent, her mind going back to her body and what her fingers were doing, and the goal she was failing at. The stress of chasing the ungettable orgasm robbed her of all the other pleasures she'd been swooning in.

Rashawn watched and listened to her hard rules. None of any a surprise to him. A woman of her stature was never likely to be willing to be subjected to any of the harder degradations nor did he plan to demean her in anyway. Nevertheless, rules had to be stated, not assumed. She was a goddess to possess, and he intended to be sure her submission was so thoroughly seduced at the end of their thirty-six hours together that she would not want to ever be released from him.

He brought the glass, he'd still been holding, up to his lips, the cognac-tainted melt of ice hit his tongue while he watched her fingers with a fierce hunger. *Time to play.* He sucked one of the cubes into his mouth and nearly slammed his glass down as he stood up from his chair and marched for her. Without warning he snatched her wrist from between her legs, enjoying the startled gasp but it didn't slow him down one second. Bringing her hand up, he sucked her fingers into his mouth, nursing the honey that coated them with exquisite delight. His tongue dancing about, pushing the ice cube over her slender digits.

Having taken the treat from them, he pulled her hand slowly from his mouth and let her hand drop to her lap. His eyes falling to her breasts that rose up and down with a hard breath. One of the fascinating things about corsets, it made it challenging for ladies to breathe, bringing the full amount of her efforts to her breasts. The details of this gave a nice rise and fall to the upper toys men loved so much.

He traced the hemmed edge of the ruffled brassiere that covered them, just like before when they'd still been at the club, he pulled the fabric down to reveal tight raspberries ready for the picking. He fished the ice cube from his mouth and teased her, "Try not to flinch." Then used the ice to trace rings around one of her perfect nipples. Her breath caught with the surprise chilled contact, but she held to his wishes and managed to keep still. Too bad really, he was scouting for an excuse to spank that snowy white bottom of hers. Then again, he was the Head-Master, he could spank simply because it would please him to do so. "Good girl, you've earned a treat."

He pulled his slacks open fully, letting his cock, still thick with need bounce out before the blindfolded face. There was something about the luscious lips shimmering with her evening gloss waiting almost innocently, barely a few centimeters from the broad tip of his aching organ. "Open your mouth, pet, and stick your tongue out—" he nearly hissed, already allowing himself to be captivated with the sight of her mouth and at the way she followed his instructions perfectly. He slid the hard bulbous tip of his cock over the flat of her tongue. Enjoying the self-serving male chauvinistic act for a moment. Little micro movements, pushing into the cavern of her mouth then back out, then abandoned her mouth. "Now tell me, my pet, are you close to cumming for me?"

Even behind the blindfold that complimented the color of her hair so well he saw how her face went white. "Looks like you are in for your first hard lessons, my pet."

She was so beautiful, even the nervous swallow was a work of art, displayed by her body. "Do not move, pet," he commanded gently then stepped away. He touched a key pad on the wall and a panel slid to the side, revealing a hidden closet space recessed in the wall. He reached in, pulling something from a hook on the wall and carried it back to his prize toy still waiting like a good girl on his ottoman. The item in his hand was little more than a right angled triangular shaped wedge in matching upholstery, which once he placed on the ottoman behind Amelia, became a back rest for her. Rashawn took her shoulder with a light touch and guided her to recline back on it. "To start, I will ask the question again. Did you bring yourself to the edge of orgasm as I ordered?"

❧

Amelia was instantly alarmed that she had failed such a simple task and to be tested so quickly on her obedience, she was at a loss for words, save the one she knew she had to utter. "No, my Head-Master, I did not." She already felt so ashamed.

"Hmmm—" his voice drew closer. She could feel him hovering over her, so close— so disappointed in her. "That is very bad. Do you not wish to please your Head-Master?"

"No!" Amelia quickly began to stammer, "I mean, yes, I do." Oh she was going to make a mess of this so quickly if she didn't get a hold of herself. But if she thought that was going to be her tactic, she was quite wrong when the hovering body added fingers right over her wet slit, taking thoughts of self-control from her, and tossing them to the wind.

"Did you forget or not hear my command for you to bring yourself to the edge of orgasm when I gave it?" His questions so precise like a doctor determined to find the cause of the illness, while his hands followed through with a physical examination of her body.

He curled his fingers and raked them through the playground of curled pubic hair. "I love this. It is just as I fantasized it would be," his voiced growled to her while his hand fisted into it, locking the short curls between his fingers, and pulled tight. "My cock is going to look so damn good in all that burgundy hair." His thumb found her clit and went to work. Circular movements, delivering just enough pressure to tug her clit into a gentle twist. Even using her piercing as a door knocker to add to the already avaricious contact.

She felt his hand grab hold of the backrest she was propped against, his breath spilling over her throat as he spoke— fingers— heart beat— *Oh yes question— breathe.* "Oh—" she gasped instead of words coming out when two fingers abruptly entered her. No delay, no timidness. They commanded her awareness just as his words did. She felt them sliding in a crooked bend, scooping up the silk, then drew it out, and the swiped over the outer entrance to be sure she was wet with it.

"When I ask you a question, I expect an answer, my pet."

Amelia swallowed hard, retracing her intended response, "I did hear you, Head-Master."

"That is good to know. Did you not want to please your Head-Master then?"

"Yes, I do want to please you, my Head-Master," Amelia answered formally, hoping her manners would make up for it— she hoped.

"Do you need to use a safeword then?"

Amelia bolted up only to smack right into the body that truly was just inches away from her. "Please no! I—" a kiss to her forehead pressed her back down.

"Shhh— just answer the question, pet."

Again, she swallowed, fearing this was going so awry, yet the fingers— oh the fingers still working her over— making it hard to remain on her fears or— or anything— thoughts— answers both lost in the swelling haze that warmed her flesh. "No, I do not wish to use a safeword." She gasped.

"Then I am quite vexed as to why you did not do as you were told. I thought you were a good little girl who enjoyed serving her Dominant."

She felt the rush of heat that filled her cheeks then, bringing with it some small amount of shame. She did want to please him. How he swayed her so easily with just a few— fingers— *and oh words too*. She chewed at her bottom lip. Her body aching and wanting. She was nearly screaming to meet him at that edge. Her breath hitching in small increments as he set into a rhythm of fucking her with a full slide of his fingers into her soaked cunt and all the way back out. The edge of his palm scrubbing over her clit, setting it on fire like matchsticks scraped over the grain strip.

"So, you *do* wish to please me?"

"Y-yes, I do, Head-Master," her voiced strained as the tension built up in her body. Her back arching, her legs curling in, and she rocked her hips on his hand. Still her release was nowhere to be found.

She felt him lean in, felt the whisper of his breath in her ear, "Then cum for me, pet." And he thrust his fingers deep into her theca, laying the demand before her as physically as he had spoken it.

Only the orgasm didn't come as commanded. She was still painfully chasing an unreachable condition. And it *was* painful. Both physically and emotionally.

Sudden movement and she felt her body flying— no, she was being flipped— and just as quickly as the movement of her body started, she came to an abrupt stop, her breasts crashing down over a firm thigh. Another caught her belly and without delay, a firm hand came down over her ass.

There wasn't even a pause when the next came down in a loud smack, stinging over bare skin and then the next. Only the slight shift in where each landed, the epicenter of each never finding the same spot on her buttocks, delivering a rapid sting that made sure every inch of her fanny was kissed by it until it was over.

After ten spankings of his hand were delivered, she was turned back over— returned to sitting with his hand grasping the back of her neck, guiding her to lie against the cushion, and his fingers found their mark inside her cunt, once more.

"What do you say, my pet?"

"Ten! No, I mean, thank you, Sir!" Amelia cried out. The sting and shock rocked her right out of her pit.

Heat swelling over her thighs and she let out a moan as two fingers firmly caressed her inner walls then teased her slit and back again.

"Cum for me, pet," he demanded.

Oh god not yet, her mind screamed, she still wasn't there. But why wasn't she? And wasn't this too soon? The other Doms had always deprived her. Now for the second time tonight this one was demanding her orgasm at the very start of the play and her body just didn't know how to comply— salacious fingers— *oh god his fingers.* Her hips moved on their own volition, pressing down onto his hand. Fighting against her needs, she feared her lips were likely to be chewed off before the night was over. "Please— I can't."

Alarm! *Oh god she did not just say that!* But before she could correct it, her body was being flipped over once again, her poles of gravity lost within the darkness. Without a single word, nor did he miss a step, she was over his lap just as before, and ten more stinging slaps of his palm came down over her ass, one after another— oh such wondrous heat blanketed her flesh. She felt every red hand print as it soaked into her skin— and gathered in her juices inside her cunt. Ten more— *oh ten sweet deliveries* and then back to her seated position. His fingers going back to their task, teasing her labia apart, tracing the inner entrance then thrusting all the way in.

"Thank you, Sir," she whimpered.

Amelia's head kicked back, sliding off the backrest. A loud gasp escaping her throat and mutated into continuous moans as he finger fucked her. Oh, the alluring firm caress of his hand, fucking her hard then soft. To one side then another— *oh so wondrous— toes curling— soooo something else she could not define. Wait. Was she truly getting close?* Her stomach twisted while some invisible part of her body clamored out to find the command, seize it, and claim it. Then, as if her Head-Master heard her mental thoughts, heard her mind dare make mention of the words *claim* or *control,* her dark world was toppling over and she was once more over his lap.

"We will keep doing this until you have learned that when I tell you to cum for me, you will do so as commanded. You will find I am not like others you have met before, pet. As I find no thrill in depriving you of my gifts unnecessarily. I prefer to spoil you with them. This way when you misbehave, depravity has some grounds of punishment. So, you *will* cum for me and you will do so several times tonight." And with his claim of the land, her Head-Master delivered ten more of his spankings to her already fiery cheeks.

The hot burning on her skin growing and spreading, rattling her senses to let go. Oh god! That was what he was doing, she had held her orgasm back for every Dom she played with. And then when they ceased to even put forth the effort to bring her to such bliss, she had forgotten how. It wasn't that she was holding back now, she simply did not know how to give it. And because of it, she was not giving her body to him as she was supposed to.

Tears poured from her eyes, because she found herself in the worst, most bitter conundrum, because she didn't know how to let go. She didn't know where the lock and key to her containment walls were. But she felt them crumbling with each strike landing over her burning bottom— *so close now.*

Three rounds of reprimanding to her ass and once more her body was to the backrest and her Head-Master's fingers working her over— sliding in, sliding out, a grinding pass over her engorged button, and back in again, harder and faster—

"What would you like to do for your Head-Master, pet?"

Oh god, fingers— fucking— anything— something— oh fingers— a collective thought would have been nice, but she knew what he wanted to hear and she was so there now. "I- I w-want— to do as— my Head-Master commands and cum for him," she pleaded, grateful to have even managed to get the whole sentence out, even if it wasn't delivered as fluidly poised as she would have preferred. But there lie her flaw. *Now* wasn't about what she wanted but what her *Head-Master* wanted, and he had commanded her to cum and been graciously patient with her failure.

Tears spilled from the sides of her eyes only to be sopped up by her blindfold.

The coil winding ever tighter around her clit, building pressure threatening to explode with bodily juices that it frightened her.

A honey soaked hand pressed both her thighs to open wide and just then a hard slap came down between them, striking over both mound and swollen clit. One— two— "Oh god, Master!" she squealed out. Three— and then his fingers plummeted deep inside her and everything went black in her mind.

The muscles in her belly knotted then expelled out in an explosion. A squealing sound pitched in her ears as she curled up off the backrest, coming in contact with her Head-Master's body. A solid arm wrapped behind her, steadying her, holding her as her world came apart. And she felt the release rush from her body and over her thighs. The gush of fluids that flowed seemed too humiliating, but she was unable to do anything but ride out the violent spasm that gripped her entire body.

An age of time went by before it seemed the ground beneath them finally began to settle. The possessive arm around her back still held her, guarding her, and lips— his lips pressed to daub over her tear-soaked cheeks through her blindfold, welcomed her back.

"So much better when you do as you are told, is it not, my pet?" he spoke to her with warm admiration and not a single reflection of shame for her. Just blissful comfort. "Taste what you gave me, pet."

Amelia felt his wet fingers on her lips and she opened her mouth to receive the gift from him, then stolen back when he removed his fingers and kissed her. His kiss as deep and commanding as any word he had spoken so far. It said one thing to her. *She was his and he was pleased with her surrender.*

"I want you to touch me now. Use your hands to become familiar with your Head-Master," he gave her new commands, his arm pulling her to sit upright and she felt every inch of her burning derriere rebelling that she should be made to sit on it.

The moment of pampering adoration was brief but relished, just as much as his charge made her giddily happy. Reinforcing she had done well to earn more commands and their night was not over yet. She nearly purred under it. She had been bad disobeying her Head-Master and he had seen to it she did as told after all. This time, she would follow his orders with pleasure. Her confidence returning with a requisition she knew she could follow.

She leaned in, discovering his body first with her fingertips then she took a deep inhale— turmeric, dried tobacco, and sandalwood. The blend of colognes hinted over something else, an after-thought that insisted he was remembered not only as being dark, but edible as well. She took another deep inhale and caught the note of toasted coconut and dark chocolate. It was a soft hinted undertone, but there. The flavorful mixture only called her to eat him up all the more. And just to show him how much she appreciated the smell of his body laced with the delicate cologne, she buried her face into the soft nest of hair at the base of his cock. Her bold move rewarded her with more of his fragrance. *Had she ever met a man who doused his body and private parts with scent?* She rubbed her face into the hard flesh of his cock, relishing the thick throbbing shaft, pressed against her cheek. She ducked down between his legs to give his scrotum a confident swipe of her tongue from the underside.

All the way up the hard shaft, she trailed her tongue along the journey, until she found the broad mushroom cap, and she made the deliberate adjustment so the licking caress of her tongue ended with a suckling kiss to the sensitive glans. Stealing the droplet of essence that was weeping out.

"Mmmm—" Rashawn groaned, "That felt very good. Too bad I didn't give you permission for it. So, it seems you've just earned more punishment of the night, my pet." And damned if he didn't spot the hint of her smug little smile.

"Yes, Head-Master," she answered back too proudly.

He didn't miss the proud curl of her lips or the red flush to her cheeks set off in contrast by the dark blind fold,

"Well, aren't you the *femme fatale*? Guess I'll have to give you two." Because he wanted to, anyways.

"If it pleases you, my Head-Master," Amelia cooed for him, still showing a hint of her showy smug pride.

A femme fatale indeed, he thought as he stepped out of reach with a light chuckle. She was all too aware of her fault. One he was going to allow, because for tonight it meant she was enjoying him and it's just not that much fun if they are always good. He walked behind her, placing his hand firmly on the center of her back and with the same sternness of his words, warm yet unyielding, he pushed her over until her forehead touched the edge of the ottoman. "Place your arms down flat around your head, elbow to palm." He waited as she did so, then fastened her wrists into the shackles lined with soft sheep's wool. Next were her ankles, leaving her softly rouged ass up in the air. Only it wasn't going to be pinkish for much longer. He ran his hand over the curvy globe. Mmmm, it was going to be extraordinary once he was done with it.

Rashawn pulled the leather belt from the belt loops of his slacks and folded it in half, keeping the buckle-end at his grip. He gave the belt a snap to announce the implement to his pet. He watched the exquisite shiver roll down her spine and the twitch of muscle in her fine ass. "We'll start with ten, then do another set after we've played a bit."

He reached around, caressing her cheek with the leather strap for further soft teasing nuances— and more shivers on her part.

"Head-Master?" Amelia's head turned to look blindly over her shoulder toward him, but it wasn't shock expressed on her face, her lips were clearly drawn up in a purring content of a smile.

"What is it? Do you need to use our safeword?"

"N-no, Head-Master. I-I just thought maybe that a belt spanking was a bit much— for such a small infraction."

Rashawn smiled fondly to himself. *It was a bit much.* "Perhaps. But you wanted it so badly, I have decided to make it all the more pleasurable for you. Since I am in a *giving* mood tonight. Shall we proceed?"

☙ω❧

"Yes, Head-Master. Thank you," she purred and right away the first sweet sting of leather strap came across both cheeks. Not high and not low but perfectly placed on the plump flesh of each.

Amelia sucked in a breath and expressed a small moan that hissed out her nose, then she remembered to count, "One, Head-Master." And so came the next four. Each one slightly higher or slightly lower from the first, spreading the heat evenly over the left globe of her derriere and she counted each one delightfully.

When he paused, she made certain to thank him. "Thank you, Head-Master." And she was rewarded with a smooth caress of his hand. Purely for his own pleasure to admire his handy work, but the balmy caress of his palm as soft as buttered tanned leather was— *wwwonderffffullll.* So smooth— again her observations noting not a single callous. A business man— but before her executive mind could go to work, the next five straps came, one across the full of her ass then the remaining four to just the right side. *Oh how she salivated with each one.*

A belt.

She couldn't recall a time a Dom took his own belt to her. Always a paddle or their hand. Even a few flogger varieties and once a crop, which had left exquisite thin purple lines on her skin that lasted for a week. Nevertheless, to be spanked by the very belt that came from her Master's waist— oh the intimacy that it spoke to her prevailed in her mind and the juices flowed.

The tenth count landed. She was grateful she remembered to count them and once more she thanked him. She licked her lips and willed herself to speak up so he could hear her. "Thank you, Head-Master, they were wonderful." Perhaps not quite as clearly as she had the first time as her head swooned with crimson delight.

The chuckle behind her made her suddenly aware that she had said a little too much, and she feared she may have just lost any chance of getting the other half of her punishment. "Forgive me, Head-Master. I did not mea—"

"Relax, pet. Lessons can be difficult, even painful at times, yet it's good you are enjoying your punishments tonight." His hand came over her fiery rump and once more, he caressed her as though making love to a smooth porcelain vase. "Of course, there will be some punishments not meant for such pleasure. But I trust you won't be that bad." The deep tenor of his words told her his thoughts were more on her ass than the warning. Or maybe he was looking forward to those punishments too, someday. Her tongue slipped out with the thought that she would be brought back to stay with him, over and over again, and she just might get the chance to be— *that bad.*

However, not this time. She intended to be his very best naughty girl. And to prove it she pressed back, rocking her ass into his palm and shifted, hoping to get a little connection toward her wetter regions. A loud smack rang out along with the sharp contact of his bare hand on her right cheek. And she gave out a delightful moan.

"Mmmm, you are wet aren't you, my pet?" he spoke and just then she felt his fingers glide over her clit and tracing a path right up between the folds of her still pulsating cunt. "Mmmm, delightful," he hummed.

She heard the ruffle of his steps then felt his fingers on her lips.

"Open, pet."

Amelia did as she was told as two of his fingers coated in her own juices pushed into her mouth and she sucked them willingly.

"I'm going to fuck that tight cunt of yours in a moment. Would you like that, pet? To have your Head-Master fuck you?" His fingers left her mouth so she could answer him properly.

A gasp escaped her lips; just the words alone had a ripple of warm arousal moving through her at his suggestion. "Yes, Head-Master. I would very much enjoy that," she sighed, hoping he wasn't going to make her wait too long.

His fingers caught her under her chin and raised her up on straightened arms and then she felt something else press against her lips, the distinct blunt engorged head of his cock and the slippery sensation of his precum as it wept from the slit. The blunt shaft swung from side to side, brushing over her lips to add its own gloss to hers.

She rolled her lips in, taking a deep breath. It was the only way she was going to keep from opening up and licking over the prize that teased her. But her Head-Master had not told her she could, and she nearly had to bite her tongue to prevent her disobedience. Two punishments was plenty for tonight, she wanted him to do as he wished to. Suddenly, thirty-six hours seemed too short of a time, when several of those hours had already come to pass.

"Open, pet," the tenor command came.

Amelia eagerly opened her mouth and her Master's cock slid past her lips.

"Now suck me like a good little girl."

There was no hesitation on her part and just as readily his hips moved forward and his turgid flesh filled her mouth.

Creamy soft skin drawn tight, slid past her tongue. She closed around it, sucked, and was rewarded with the sweet nutty flavor of his precum. Mmmmmm, a woman had to love a Dom who understood his rewards were quintessence of dessert when he tempered his diet properly.

"Ou- yes-ssss, that's it, my pet. Suck my cock." He nearly let his French slip when he praised her. It was good he'd done so now when he still had a mind left to catch himself. It was a warning to be more mindful once he started to fuck her. The bliss of her body was likely to doom him if he wasn't.

He rocked his cock in and out of the cavern of her mouth, enjoying the caress of her tongue as she suckled and washed him eagerly with every stroke. He could spill within minutes of this if he allowed it, but he didn't want this night to end without feeling the liquid caress of her orgasming pussy. He had to live tonight as if it was the last night on earth. Just in case it truly was.

"That will be enough for now, pet." And he withdrew from her mouth. The air rushed in to tap at the vacancy, and he nearly disregarded his own plans just to have that tongue back, wrapped around his cock. But there was still more to come, *and cum,* so he willed himself to pace, if for only a little bit longer.

He stepped over to his desk, fetching something from the top center drawer then returned to his sub. Wordlessly, he tapped an inner thigh and she repositioned her knee to widen her legs. The sight of her glistening flesh peeking through the groomed burgundy curls, beckoning him, had him chomping down on his lip, then pressing his tongue against the backs of his teeth. "So beautiful," he hissed, then reached in, his ring finger seeking out and zeroing in on her clit while his forefinger and thumb delivered the clamp to it.

Amelia let out a small gasping yelp. Not a *thank you* in sight. He chuckled silently— *they never did for the clamps.*

Ten more strokes of his belt landed across her ass, leaving bright red stripes that spread, turning her ruddy skin a delightful dark rose. He palmed over the heat, caressing down the sting.

It was time.

Leaving his slacks on, he snatched Amelia by her hips and yanked her back until her knees were at the very edge of the ottoman and few inches between them so his jutting cock slapped against the hot flesh of her fiery hot cheeks. He had a reason for not disrobing fully. It was an act of separation between Dom and a weekend lover. Pure overpowering. Because Amelia needed to feel used tonight, as well as cherished.

He stood directly behind her, holding his cock in line of the world he had desired for so long. He pulled a condom packet from his pocket, tore it open with his teeth then rolled it on. He dropped a hand down at the small of her spine and eased her to rock back until her wet cunt pressed against the head of his cock.

The hiss got away with from him with the wet contact and without any grace he slipped past those moist lips.

Silky walls encapsulated his cock and welcomed him with the essence of heaven. He could have spilled that very moment, had he wanted to give her his reward so quickly. A tingling ripple shot up his legs and traveled along his spine that forced him to shoulder the shiver.

He arched his back and curled his hips, bobbing his shaft inside Amelia's perfect body. Making no rush to throttle, though his pandering stillness would last only so long before baser needs drove him into movement.

He felt her inner muscles flex and hug him. The very heat of the sensation had him dropping his head back, letting a slew of French escape his lips. "*Ayyy, Ta chatte est un tel délice. Un homme pourrait se damner pour connaître une telle beatitude,"* he heard his words as his discretion fell away briefly, voicing his belief that such succulence could be the end of a man. If only he hadn't said them in French, but there was no taking them back either. He could only defuse the slip with a new directive. He shoved himself deep inside, bottoming out in a single stroke, then brought his hand down one side of her ass, and then the other to disrupt any coherence cognizance Amelia may still have had. But he hoped she was just as mentally dislodged as he was and his slip had gone unnoticed.

And he planned to find out. Unlike his own undoing, he expected her to be so completely derail there would be no second guessing her tumultuous condition.

Another smack to her ass then he began to kick up a rhythm. In and out, her walls clenching to keep him inside, made the wet friction exquisitely euphoric. *Putain,* how he had desired this woman for so long, and now she was his. The soft mewling sounds that came from her lips, begged him to let loose and ride her. She needed to be fucked. He knew this. He had drilled Dominus for every detail he could when he was approached for interest. He wanted to be sure he was as versed in her needs as a professor of elements would be. But those details of knowledge did not compare to the intimate connection he was spiraling in now.

His pelvis and slacks slapped against her ass, greeted with hot skin on each contact. It was time to deliver what they both needed. Time for abandonment, to shed away eloquence. He grasped her hips and with every forward push of his hips, he slammed her back to counter him. Not allowing any soft buffering between them. He pounded into her cunt, until her mewlings became unequivocal moans pushed out with each throttled entry. He felt the beads of sweat break across his shoulders and back. His own breath kicking up in a husky sound that echoed around her feminine ones. His cologne and her perfume heated up and filled the air carrying with it the heavy saturation of sex in the room. The thick aroma only drove him further— harder— faster—

He could feel his scrotum drawing up. It wouldn't be long before his pleasure would be shadowed by the effort to not release so soon. He slowed inside her and folded over her. Holding his weight up on an outstretched arm planted on the ottoman while he unhooked her wrists. Then wrapping around her waist, he lifted, bring her body up to press against his chest as he did.

Amelia's senses were in a whirlwind, now a firm arm held her around the waist while the other roamed her body. His hand taking delight wherever it desired. His lips found her neck and traced it with kisses down along her shoulder. His breath spoke whispered desires with each deep, slow sinking of his cock inside her theca.

"I want to feel you cum around my cock, pet," he commanded with a husky breath and his hand dropped down and flicked the clamp free from her clit.

The rush of blood and pain startled her, a shocking reminder it had even been there and she let out a howl of no volition of her own. It just happened. His hand became rough and demanding, circling her engorged bud. His fingertips drawing her juices from her moist lips when he withdrew his shaft then used the silk to dance around her clit some more until her body obeyed. The wave drew the muscles in her legs tight, lifting them off the ottoman and she curled as her orgasm came in an almost painful explosion followed by a warm flood of juices and emotions. Throughout the dark storm— her master's body, his arms, his hands, and his whispered approvals remained consistent.

"That's it, my pet. Such art to watch you cum. And so, I shall again."

Her world dropped, landing her back to hands and knees on the soft brushed suede and her Master's cock drove in with fresh deep, hard thrusts. His movements became wild and untamed. Slamming her to the edge of the universe. He gave no respite to gain her gravity. Her head swimming in the pool of sensation, she could hardly contract a deliberate response or action to meet his thrusts. His hands gripping at her hips did that for her.

She felt the small bite of a zipper against her fiery flesh. But the sweetest of all was the heated growling behind her. The deep tenor of his breath had to be the sexiest sound she had ever heard. The very note of his growls made her spine melt and her cunt clamp ever tighter. Riding his cock as he throttled her at will.

Gasps and moans were forced from her until she was nearly ready to beg him to stop. She was so high. It was as though she was flying over the Earth on the very edge, waiting to be dropped from the highest thrill ride.

Time left her.

Not even the rhythmic slaps of his body against hers could count out the time, only the shift of such motions mapped out their durations, but never did it end. Her Master slowed, now rocking from side to side. She felt him leaning away from her and she wondered if he was watching the turgid flesh slide in the glistening wetness. And she envied such a vision. Wishing she could be freed of her blindfold and look upon her handsome Master's face and watch his thick cock slide in and out of her, claiming her as his. Fucking her into tumbling rapture.

Before she could adjust to the slower pace, her Master's arms ensnared her waist once more and her back found his body. Hands roamed freely and she felt his heavy breath against the shell of her ear. He didn't need to say a word, she felt what he wanted her to. Somatic lust and love-making intertwined. It was that last bit of revelation that startled her. She'd never felt the likes of it. Lust and cheap dates. She'd known love but lacked the lust. This was completely different.

His cock dove into her between pile driving and slow claims, his hands possessed and molested her. His breath kissed and growled. And she slipped a little further for her Master.

When his fingertips found her clit and demanded another release, she didn't think it possible but one touch and she realized she was nearly there. All she needed now was his command.

"Let me feel you cum one more time, pet, before I do."

Her body obeyed.

Her release exploding behind her eyes in white flashes that matched the exploding coil of electricity deep in her womb as he sent shards of inexplicable pleasuring pain across every nerve ending. She cried out. Or so she thought, it was odd her own voice seemed muffled. She couldn't catch a deep enough breath. The world spun like a top with her on it. She heard his growl shift to a grunt and felt the final plundering of his cock sink deep inside her theca. Then everything seemed to turn heavy and far darker than even the silk wrap over her eyes actually was.

Rashawn tightened his hold around her waist when he felt her go limp, still consumed to ride out his own violent release. An unexpected surprise.

He eased his pet's unconscious body to the ottoman, letting his cock slip from the heaven between her legs. Had he planned properly, he would have moved her to the bed sooner. A minor mistake, one that in the future once he had her collared, he would enjoy the nights drifting to sleep with his cock buried inside her.

He discarded the spent condom in a waste basket behind his desk, then collected his pet and moved them both to the guest room he'd had prepared for her.

Every inch of her glowed. It was magnificent.

He fetched a warm wash cloth from the attached head, washed her body down then loosened the laces on her corset until he could unclip the steel fasteners in the front, releasing her body from its confines to allow her to sleep comfortably. He hesitated a moment, staring down at her listless form, still radiating from his handiwork. Which had taken a considerable amount to accomplish the end results. He'd presented her with an unexpected challenge then rewarded him with a breath taking surrender of consciousness. He would treasure this moment for the rest of his life, but he most certainly planned to see to it he had all his life to repeat this with her many times over.

He took a few minutes to refresh himself; removed his slacks in replacement of a pair of comfortable boxer-briefs, then climbed in behind her, pulling her body to nestle against his, and he drifted off to sleep with his treasured Amelia.

CHAPTER THREE

DAY TWO

Amelia sucked in a deep breath as the morning light began to drift passed the silk barrier that covered her sleepy eyes. But she kept them closed, not wanting to move just yet. She'd awakened briefly in the middle of the night. And it took several minutes to reorient herself. The possessive arms wrapped around her that tightened even more when she stirred had been the bonus clue to her whereabouts. In the hands of her wonderful Head-Master and she soon drifted back to sleep. But now, morning had arrived and she didn't want to lose any more of her time with him just sleeping. She sighed again and was suddenly greeted with a kiss to the back of her neck. Followed with the sliding of her Master's cock between her legs from behind.

"Good, you're awake," he murmured succulently.

"How did you know?" She beamed, feeling every inch of the warm glow that had to have shown in a blushing smile on her face. She had to be smiling, she could feel the ache already setting in on her cheeks.

"Your body told me the way it pushed back and offered itself to me." He breathed heavily against her ear and kissed it lightly. It sent a chill down her spine and culminated in her nethers, already growing damp. A tight clench of muscles snapping the shiver back up to her shoulders.

❦

"Hmmm, that was nice," he praised the reaction, chasing after it with the palm of his hand, sliding farther down her body. A momentarily pause in his traveling caress, reaching around her front to scoop up a breast. He loved her pert nipples, such succulent morsels of candy always ready for sucking. He tweaked one between thumb and finger until it was firm. So many things he had planned for them, but for now he abandoned it to sweep down her belly.

He combed his fingertips into the small patch of hair, then continued to move farther south.

He teased her with a flick to her clit piercing then slipped past her folds. Her still sensitized flesh shot more shivers through her and escaped in a soft gasp from her lips.

"So wet and ready for me this morning. I believe I will reward you later for your morning willingness to my taking," he hissed at the back of her head, kissing her several times, until need took over and he nipped the soft skin. The motion of his cock sawing back and forth, teasing her entrance. "Mmmm, raise up a bit," he gave a soft command.

Amelia lifted then felt his right arm slip under, relieving his left hand around her clit, teasing and playing, while the rest of his body fell away.

She heard the tear of a fresh foil packet. *Oh yes-ss, Head-Master, take what you want from me this morning.* Amelia sucked in a deep breath and pushed back with anticipation. And was soon greeted with his cock and a slap to her ass.

Her Master's thick cock slipped past her awaiting walls still sensitive from last night— in and out— slow and mind boggling right from the start. His entire body pressed against her with every rocking motion.

He draped a leg over hers, pinching her thighs closed which added to the sawing friction. He pulled his cock all the way out, leaving a glaze of honey on her thighs then pushed back in, so that every return tapped the slave ring in her clit.

So slow. Too slow. It took everything she had not to press back against him. But she truly wished he would slam inside her just as he had last night. Maybe after a day or two of this, she could still her desires enough to handle a slow embrace, but she hadn't been placed on the edge of uninhibited lust in so long she wanted to be set on fire and kept burning bright until completely singed with the heat.

And as if he heard her thoughts, his arm tightened and they were rolling. But not to put her to hand and knees as she expected. Her Master was going to his back and with her laying backward on his chest. His knees came up between her thighs and spread her legs out wide as he set his heels into the bed. Firm hands took to the sides of her rump and she was instantly lifted and his cock chased after her— slamming in until he bottomed out in her. A quick retreated and then ramming upward again.

The pace instantly hard and pounding, she felt the quivering in his arms as he held her up off his body. She let her head lull back over his shoulder and great moans escaped her lungs. Tender flesh wrapped around his pounding cock, taking every thick inch over and over.

She felt his lips against her ear, he kissed her then gave his orders between husky breaths.

"Play with the jewelry on your clit and let me feel your fingers teasing my cock as it slides in and out of you. Show your Head-Master how you have learned your lesson on how to cum for him."

Amelia scrambled to gather the motor control of her hand and quickly sought out the hooded bundle of nerves. Her hips and legs quaked with imminent Earth shattering convulsions at the first contact of her sensitized flesh. Between their prior play and the direct aim of his cock now, she was well engorged and it was not going to take long at all to fulfill his orders.

She pushed her fingers to reach farther, finding the honey soaked rod of flesh sliding in and out of her cunt. She V'd her fingers to capture the sides of his cock and used the back heel of her thumb to work her clit until she was at that very edge, awaiting his command.

Shivers raced up and down her body and tore her legs from his; kicking up as if she was in a fit.

"Keep it there," he growled, pounding harder and faster inside her. His husky breath grinding at the side of her head, she felt every dire nuance of his words carried out further in each exhale. Pure alpha male sounds that growled his pleasure.

But the edge he had her at was growing painful. She drew her hand up her belly, unable to handle any further contact or she was certain she would cum without his approval.

"I didn't say to stop. To the edge, my pet. Don't step away. Stand up on the highest mountain far above the universe and look down. Let it exhilarate you, not frighten you. I'll let you know when it is time to jump."

Her breath came out in staccato huffs in the rhythm of his unrelenting, pounding ride. His cock sliding— shifting— drawing in and out, making her mad with the succulent friction and heat that singed her insides. It stoked her walls as she clamped down to hang on. She fought to keep her fingers in position yet, at the same time, she tried to minimize the stimulation her clit received. She wasn't sure she could hang on any longer.

"*Pleeeeeeaaaase!*" Amelia shrieked.

"Now, my pet. Let your juices flow and cum over my cock." He dropped her down on his cock, slamming as deep as her body allowed him. His hand moved to her, forcing both their fingers past saturated lips, his thumb crashing down over her engorged pearl and together they both exploded. Despite the thin film that protected them both she felt the hot jets hit against her back wall. And then all strength slipped from her and she felt blissfully limp over his chest, but aware this time.

They both lay listless and lazy, spooned together. His deep breath brushing the side of her neck had finally normalized while their bodies cooled. "Hungry?" he finally asked with a lazy investment.

"*Mmmm—*" was as close to a response as she could come up with.

"*Mmmm*, me too." He leaned over her and planted a firm kiss to her covered temple. "I'm going to slip out. The restroom is to your right. You may take the blindfold off while you freshen up but save your shower until I join you. In which time, I will have your breakfast brought up and I will have your day's plans ready for you by then." He kissed her once more, then she felt him slip from the bed, and a moment following, she heard the soft click of a door when he left.

Amelia dropped to her back and let out a deep dreamy sigh. She really didn't want to move just yet, and still, she couldn't wait for him to return. She pulled the blindfold from her eyes and glancing up seeing her reflection looking down at herself, tangled in the frumpy pile of downy covers and crisp blue linens. She broke out in a warm giggle. She had wanted this for as long as she could remember and yet she had never known it would feel this gloriously welcoming and soft. Who would ever think that such kink would create such a warm convectional bliss inside her? She blushed and giggled some more then finally hopped up and skipped off into the restroom.

Once inside the privy, she paused to take in the sight. It wasn't the marble stone tiles or the dark stained wood or the polished steel trim that had her brain ticking away like a time piece to count down the last remaining seconds before you can give your answer on a closing deal. It was the odd familiarity. Not per se that she'd been here before but yet it still managed to trip a switch that in a way maybe she had. She stepped along countertop of marbled greys, polished to a matte finish where she lightly touched one of two bamboo-shaped, brushed steel fixtures. Money— and much as her own family, a lot of it.

She glanced into the mirrors, her eyes falling upon the unit of drawers behind her. She pivoted around to admire their smooth polished wood, curvy edges— and how they were embedded into the walls—

"Ahh ah ahh—" a stern voice broke her attention just as she intended to open a drawer to peek. She snapped her hand to herself and glanced around. Something on the far side flickered, just inside the shower stalls. *No, it couldn't be.*

She stepped closer and realized the flicker came from a monitor and there on it was a man. Well, part of him at least, the top part of his head cut out and only a glimpse of his chin and on down from his chin down, his chest, and a hand that rested on a leg was viewable as he stroked his fingers in a rolling impatient gesture.

"I do believe I told you to take care of your morning needs before your shower." His hand waved in an offer, *"As you can see, I have already set out the items you will be needing. So, no snooping. I can tolerate some disobedience, but there are other actions that would have our weekend together brought to an instant halt."*

"Sir?" Amelia wasn't completely understanding. She understood the scold, it was the rest she didn't understand.

"The sub is not the only one who can call a safeword, my pet. A Master or Dom can as well. Though, it is rare a particular designed word is used, the Master or Dom can stop a session at any given time. Given only the understanding that any particular aftercare needed, dependent of the activities, is still carried out. The playtime is ultimately over. This is a contracted blind weekend between you and I. If you choose to break that rule, our weekend will end. Understood, my pet?"

There were no two ways about what he meant, and she quickly dropped her gaze to the floor and gathered her hands before her. "Yes, Sir."

"Ah, good. Now, I will give you a few moments of privacy and will return so I may watch you shower."

The screen went dark. There was no spoken reminder or warning of the rule he'd presented. He expected she'd understood when she said she did, a reminder would look poorly on her submission. And she was beginning to feel a whole new understanding of herself and the needs she'd never been able to fulfill.

As told, she went about her morning ritual, she relieved herself then washed her face and brushed her teeth, always mindful to keep her eyes down. She didn't dare, she did not want her weekend to be cut short and she had been reminded it could be. The very threat had served its own purpose. She felt like the school girl at the convent, when she'd just been reprimanded and threatened to have her fieldtrip privileges taken away. That was one threat Amelia always heard and obeyed. She never dared it, because when else would she be able to be naughty but during those fieldtrips? While her days in private school were not a memory she missed, the control that led to naughty delights was. And it'd just been touched.

Wearing nothing but a warm smile, she turned on the shower, and stepped in. Bringing the basket of goodies with her and started with a quick wash and condition of her hair.

Just when she was lathering up the handmade soap that gave off only the faintest fragrance of jasmine, the approving sound of her Head-Master popped in.

She turned and there he was on the monitor again, just from the neck down, tan skin with the barest dust of dark hair peeked through his robe.

How decadently naughty. She'd never thought to be watched while taking her shower. Obviously, he had. One does not just order a surveillance system installed into their shower overnight.

"Mmmm, very lovely, my pet. Please continue while I watch."

"As you wish, Head-Master," she invited with delight, slowing her hands down as she spread the foamy suds all over her body.

"You can call me Sir, for now," he offered the more relaxed title.

"Yes, Sir, thank you. I do enjoy calling you Head-Master, if it's okay?"

"Most certainly, if that makes you comfortable."

She cheated a glance at the monitor while he palmed over the well-established bulge still clad in nothing more than a fresh pair of boxer briefs, viewing the entire time and she washed precisely where he told her to and when. It was an entirely new experience for her. In the past, she had bathed her Doms, even been bathed by her Doms. But never before had she bathed *for* her Dom.

Why had she not gone to Dominus sooner? She thought with some internal admonishing.

As she continued to wash putting in a little extra to extend the show for her watcher, she began to note a developing heightening sensation between her legs, and she paused to analyze the feeling.

"Is there something wrong, my pet?"

The minute warming sensation was still subtle, it could easily just be a tenderness from last night, stirred by the soaps. "No, Sir. I think I am still sensitive from this morning."

"Mmmm, I do relish such post tender bliss, but perhaps it is something from the shower products you are using."

Amelia's eyes popped up with a touch of alarm but quickly lowered her gaze before he needed to scold her for it. "Products, Sir?"

"Yes. While I don't particularly care for the fragrance because it will interfere with the ones I have selected for you, the products and their effect came highly recommended."

Amelia returned her focus to her body. The building sensitive sensation was most definitely there, growing warm with a hint of tingling now. She closed her eyes and sent out a silent curse, recalling Katianna's tale of agonizing woe. *Why that little brat.*

"Are you feeling its effects yet?"

"Yes, Sir. Thank you, Head-Master."

"Quite lovely, my pet. Now I want you to rinse off then take the towel that is laid out for you and wrap yourself and then sit on the stool. Do not dry yourself. Merely draw it around you, sit facing the mirror and wait for me." The monitor screen went black.

Amelia did as told, sitting on the stool where the towel had been placed for her. And it was there, she started to feel the full strength of the strange tingling warmth between her legs. She chewed at her lip as she realized the sensation was building and she feared it was only going to continue to build until she went mad. *Ooo, I am going to get her back for this.*

She glanced at her reflection in the mirror and then it dawned on her she didn't have the blindfold on yet. *Had her Master let that slip his mind? Or was he going to let her see his face so soon?* She glanced around, thinking the answer to neither of her questions could be yes. As it had been reminded to her, this was a *Blind Contract* and to break it was to forfeit the remainder of her weekend with him. *But how could she if it wasn't here?* Panic began to coil in her belly. Then unexpectedly, the lights dim; suggesting they were remotely controlled from somewhere else. And then the door opened.

Out of habit, Amelia's head snapped around, to looked.

CHAPTER FOUR

Amelia looked right at him as her Head-Master stepping in as if every detail was masterly laid out by him. Nothing was left for fault. But if she thought she was about to see his face, she'd underestimated her Master's degree of planning.

Rashawn had anticipated the reaction, despite the disapproval he felt from it. These were things he would have to train her against. But he gave her some credit when she no sooner looked, in her alarm she dropped her gaze to the floor. Amelia was far from being turned over to him as yet and such a slip would have been detrimental. So, he'd not given her the leeway of seeing his face. Using the aid of a mask of his own along with the dim lighting diluted any recognition. Yet the polished silver gladiator style mask gave the same romantic appeal that a masquerade ball mask would.

"Close your eyes and lift your head, my pet," he spoke with a soft command as he stepped behind her and pulled free the sash of lace cloth that hung from around his neck then drew it over her eyes and tied it behind her head. "Now you may open them."

He glanced in the mirror, watching her reflection together with his. He loved what he saw. The two of them, her burgundy hair set a flaming contrast against his skin. He loved watching his tanned fingers moving smoothly down the milky white skin of her arm, then pulled the towel from her body, letting if cascade down around the stool she sat upon. He caressed her belly and pulled her to lean back against him. Her head relaxed, her damp hair kissing his shoulder. Full red lips awaited his kiss.

He reached up, taking her chin and turned those lips to where they were more accessible so he could do just what they were meant for. He took his time, not being taken over by the frenzy to touch and do everything just yet. He'd entertain that need later. Right now, he just wanted to touch and taste her just as she touched his mind. Deeply and passionately.

He released her chin, then using the press of his lips, he rolled her head to the side and brushed his lips down the ligature of her neck. He felt the shiver in her sigh and it reflected how she affected him. No longer watching their reflection, because what made them so perfect for each other wasn't something that was reflected in the mirror. He knew she was older than him, but he didn't see it. He only saw how sophisticatedly refined she was. She wasn't a copy of some Vogue magazine cover model or a body stripped of her sexual identity to be more masculine for the competition that only furthered people's delusions that the world belonged to men.

She was radiantly sexy in the way her strength and demeanor glowed on her skin. He was quite certain if she had set her mind to it, she could own the Vogue cover with Wall Street dangling from a charm bracelet around her wrist. Amelia was the epitome he'd never found in any other woman closer to his age. She had not given up one thing of her womanly beauty or sold herself out to them. Younger women were often still searching, seeking a lofty goal and ever changing to reach it or change their minds for something else. Both often perilous consequences for a relationship.

An added bonus was Amelia's family's wealth, which meant she didn't need his. Nor did he of hers. He had a full life; he was right where he wanted to be. The only thing missing was sitting right before him. After so many years of desiring her, she was finally delivered into his expertise. Now he need only to convince her to stay.

He moved his fingers over her trained waistline. So perfect.

He picked up the towel waiting on the counter and used it to blot her skin dry. Then traded it for a swatch of felt from a tray set out with a number of perfume bottles. He selected a fragrance, soaked the felt with some, and without a word spoken, began to rub it into all the warm places of her body. A gentle stroke across the skin like a paint brush, only here his media was fragrance, not paint. Behind her knees and against her elbows, then just under her breasts along her rib cage. He lifted her arm and swabbed it into the pit of her arm and she wriggled under his touch and he made out the quiet chime of laughing under her breath.

"Head-Master, you place cologne in the arm pits as well?" she asked him softly.

"Absolutely, wherever the body sweats is the best places to put perfume; this way it comes to life when the body warms up." He brushed her hair aside with the backs of his fingers, laid a kiss on her clean, dewy skin then touched it off with a brush of the perfumed felt and then tracing it farther down her spine, just a few inches to create a small shiver in her. Feeling satisfied he'd hit all the perfect spots, he tossed the swath square to the counter then wrapped himself around her, taking in a deep breath, and letting her scent along with the perfume fill his senses.

"*Mmmm*— god you smell good in this," he murmured his approval of the fragrance on her body. It was far better than the scent of the shower gel Trenton had given him with a playful suggestion to use it on Amelia. It hadn't been bad, Jasmines and something else, but he never was one for simple smells. He preferred them more sophisticated and complex redolent. He savored a scent which aroused him, not put him at ease.

He lifted her arm again and buried his face in the crux of her shoulder, inhaling the wash of cologne he just placed there and licked it for a delivered tickle.

His pet recoiled from the touch with a giggle, but his hand tightened around her, not allowing her more than an inch of escape. "You're going to set my lust on fire when you start to heat up." He took another long strong inhale and nearly devoured the side of her face with a lustful kiss.

❦

Amelia could hardly see a thing despite her blindfold was now black lace instead of the solid silk sash. Yet, the view gave only silhouette lines of his body, and enough of her surroundings to gift her equilibrium back with little more than glimpsing teases of her Master's body. But what she could make out only furthered what her hands and body had been saying all along. She was happy to submit to the handsomely built hedonist. He'd obviously taken good care of his body. Refusing to grow ungracefully aged.

She had been both surprised and startled when he stepped in before her blindfold had been restored to proper place. She hadn't meant to look either but couldn't help herself at the same time. She saw a thousand details before quickly dropping her eyes. Upon his face he'd donned a mask and dark cowl neck scarf that further shaded his features from her. Even now as she watched the movement through the shield of black lace, only the pewter gray mask was clear in her mind. It was certainly unusual. Not a typical fetish mask one thinks of when chatting about Bdsm. His mirrored some old Greek gladiator mask, which covered only two-thirds of his face. Yet, she couldn't even pull up the vision of his lips. Because not only had the mask covered his forehead down over his nose, but part of it also extended down either side of his mouth and down to his chin. It was odd, but effective how it distracted. Even in her brief lapse of behavior, she had failed to look past them to see his lips that had kissed her so many times since her arrival into his possession.

The arousing warmth, she concluded must have been caused by the bath product, continuing to take its effect on her. Feeling aroused, moisture pool between her legs and further delivered to unscrupulous wanton from the sensual touch of his hands as he overindulged her body with the new perfume fragrance. Her mind within the swirl of pampering touches, attempted to identify the fragrances in the mix, the barest hint of spicy incense, some tart citrusy note that made her nose tingle and a mellow woody scent of flowers— alyssum perhaps and maybe a touch of hyacinths and tuberose. It was quite wonderful, the balmy mix was clever in that it was not too sweet but didn't turn masculine either.

But it was alarming that this man who was making her body dance on his fingertips was so into the perfume. She'd known few men that took notice of a woman's perfume and even fewer still that looked at it as an art— oh god. Definitely refined European breeding. Her mind was reeling suddenly, her eyes darting up to look at the reflection of the man hidden under the hood. There wasn't enough lighting from the overhead sconces to allow her even a glimpse of his face, furthered obscured by the deep shadows from his mask that obscured his identity.

"Rash—"

"*Ahh ahh,*" his voice grew strict and prepared to scold her. "Don't dare think to speak a name that is not mine. I will be very offended that you might utter the wrong man's name while you are mine. And you will find yourself hard pressed to earn your way back to my favor." He reached for a garment of slinky see through silk from the serving tray on the counter and gathered it up in his hands, "Lift your arms straight up over your head." His command returning to his gentle tone. She raised her arms and he draped the garment over them letting the narrow lace straps fall to the inside. His hands then gliding the rest down until his touch came to her shoulders and he let the rest fall. The sheer blushing mauve chemise cascaded over her body perfectly. A simple garment with only a touch of lace trim made up the straps with no other embellishments or stones. Meant to be worn under the corset with nothing to pinch or chafe against her skin.

"Your time here isn't a word puzzle for you to solve, my pet. It is a time to be explored and to be delivered to a state of satisfaction you have sought but never arrived to. Now close your eyes and let your body tell you what it wants and hush your mind."

Amelia couldn't bring herself to close her eyes, she was far too mesmerized with the movement of his hands reflected in the mirror as he dressed her to suit his own desires. But she let the scene hush her thoughts, refusing them to come forward again. For she did want this.

Next, her Master wrapped a navy, satin under-bust, jacquard corset around her body.

He spoke not a word as he laced her up. Enjoying the pleasure of cinching her tight all to himself.

She watched his reflection moving in the mirror, obscured by the lace, but she was certain she could make out the glimmer in his dark eyes from behind his mask. The hint of a soft smile revealed his deeper pleasure as if she were a piece of art work and he controlled the brush strokes.

When he was done with her laces, he brought his measuring tape out, and took a reading. An unstoppable smile broke over his lips. "You're already at twenty-one and I have yet to pull you in tight. I figured I would wait until after you've had some breakfast, but I believe you will reach the goal I have set for you. Perhaps in the first adjustment."

She couldn't contain herself, "Is my Head-Master pleased?"

⚗

Rashawn paused, observing her. It was minor. Perhaps she'd gotten away with it with lesser experienced Doms, or they let it slip as being a lessor warranted offense in the myriad of so many Topping antics she posed. But it was very prevalent to him. And when her question went unanswered, she seemed perplexed as to how to take his silence. She had been seeking his approval. Her very question perpetrated to fetch a response for her own satisfaction. A submissive *no-no.*

His eyes shifted to her from behind the mask, then to the last few items placed purposely on the tray for her eyes. Taking each one by one, they finally arrived on her body.

A collar and matching cuffs of creamy tan leather were buckled in place. The collar with its three D rings, while her wrists had two each, plus a clip for easy, on the spot restraining. He looked at her reflection. How perfect the ensemble went together. As if fate had him preparing for her arrival all along. And when he stepped in against her, rewarding her waiting body with the warmth of his, she surrendered to him, letting her head drop back to his shoulder completely given over to him. Even her hips rolled forward in offering to his delight. The gold jewelry between her thighs capturing just enough light to draw his eyes to it. But his pet's movements were not the movements of a true submissive, but one of a seducer. Someone who had been calling the shots for far too long. And he realized a change of itinerary was in need.

CHAPTER FIVE

As much as she would have loved for some more frisky play in the bathroom, Amelia found herself led away, back to the bedroom and to a small table already set with breakfast. *Odd, she didn't recall hearing anyone come in.* It was almost unnerving, though she couldn't say why. She employed plenty of servants and stewards of her own. Many who had borne witness to her privileged guests of the private parties she held, so why would it bother her to know that her Head-Master also had a staff and one had prepared and brought a meal for her while she was occupied elsewhere? Their time had still been private, yet as her Master sat her down, she could not help but feel as though they had had an audience.

She found her hands in his as he placed them on the table where her fingers found the cool, metallic touch of high quality silver that upon further exploration with her fingertips was finely crafted into the delicate curves and edges of cutlery. She felt the soft pressure of his lips on the crown of her head and felt the sought-after, but alien warmth flutter inside her. Much the same as he'd stirred in her last night with his loving forehead kiss. He reached around her and pulled the cover from her plate and the aroma of a well prepared meal wafted up to her nose stealing her thoughts away. She sat still, listening for him, then heard the door behind her click.

She kept her head down but strained to see through the mottled view from behind the lace blindfold. Just beyond her plate sat a flat screen monitor and within a few moments it flickered on, and there sat her overseer. Her Head-Master.

"Now we can eat together," his voice came over the built in speaker.

She felt the blush in her cheeks as she made out the faint details of his arm moving up along the screen. Then drop down and the clink of his fork on his plate explained it all.

"Pet, eat. Our day is already planned, but you must be nourished first."

"Yes, Head-Master." Amelia found herself blushing further and dropped her gaze, to some extent. She could still see his hands and his exposed chest as she began to eat as told.

She could make out the chinaware through the black lace over her eyes. The simple design offered no insight to its owner, but the meal did.

Crispy Mollet Eggs served with creamed asparagus. It wasn't the commonest of recipes, but a certain favorite for the pallet and anyone who loved egg dishes. As she certainly did. She hadn't realized how famished she was until she took her first bite. She almost forgot her manners. She just couldn't help herself when she bit into the first deep fried egg. Golden light on the outside and it exploded perfectly with the soft creamy yolk. "*Mmmm—*" She closed her eyes and just simply vanished into the rich flavor. She was accustomed to fine dining in her life, but for some reason she had not quite expected it to be included in her blind-weekend arrangement. Then again, she hadn't really developed any sort of prospects as the Dominus had given her absolutely nothing, no hints for her expectations to toy with in preparation.

Finishing off her breakfast, Amelia had been offered a selection of freshly baked crumpets and popovers, both still warm from the oven. Having not missed her Master's comment about a full day ahead, she figured she needed her strength and ate one of each; using the popover to sop up the extra egg yolk from her plate; the crumpet she piled up with a warm compote mix of kiwi, raspberries, and strawberries and topped it with clotted cream.

It was an extraordinary bonus that in finding a Dom that was beyond any hopes for herself, she would also find herself not having to give up any of the comforts she was accustomed to. That's when Amelia started to let her eyes wander a bit. Not enough to get scolded for it, but the small peeks one could gain while still keeping her chin lowered.

Unlike the chinaware, the furnishings spoke volumes about the enigmatic man whom she was spending her time with. Her chair, for starters, was crafted from dark mahogany wood, with the seat and back upholstered in soft tan suede; not overly lavish in design but she understood understated quality when she encountered it. The table was out of place, perhaps better meant for a breakfast nook, but again the quality of wood leant that it came with more than just a hefty price tag. Even the carpet under her feet, soft piling with extra padding, was a light, creamy off-white.

She paused in her meal contemplating that one. White or near white carpet wasn't found in just any house. It was notable only in homes that afforded endless opulence and far more than just one or two staff members employed for the upkeep of its color purity.

⁂

Rashawn watched her though the monitor screen, catching the slight tilt to her head, as she risked fragmented glances of her surroundings. He had anticipated this part of their time together. He knew meals would be difficult while blindfolded, and returning some sight provided a variation to her experience, allowing some sight, but still only some teasing glimpses of himself while giving her eyes some time to rest. A parameter many overlooked how stressful blindfolding could be both for the eyes and the cranium.

So much careful planning had gone into it. Calculating care, both along the way and prevention of what could go wrong. The guestroom playing a large part in the plan, so he could control what was visible and make sure there was nothing even remotely recognizable to him and his family. But it was still very much the interior of a yacht; that much he could not change. Unlike land bound homes, the furnishings, such as dressers, wall units, cabinets, and light fixtures, were mostly built into the walls. Even the walls themselves were unique for even a lavish home. Burmese mahogany, varnished and polished until it simulated marbled glass rather than wood, encased her environment. He'd granted her some room to make eating easier and shift the experience around some. But now, looking at the view from a new perspective, he realized perhaps it was a mistake. He feared if she realized it was him too soon, she would very likely throw up her shields before he could win her over and accepted they made a perfect match.

Before she could make the fatal mistake of actually looking around, Rashawn called Amelia's attention back to him on the monitor. "Eyes proper, my pet. That is enough wandering gaze for this visit. Now finish your meal while I prepare the study for some training.

After they'd finished eating, she was taken into his study, the lighting kept dimmed to a golden glow, which made seeing through her lace blindfold as effective as trying to see through the fog at night. She could make out little more than his movements, the slow ambiance was reminiscent of peeking through a keyhole at her very own desires being played out in one of those erotic video tapes made to be paired up with even sexier music.

A click from something in his hand and that too was added to the walking dream of fantasies. She didn't know the music but it was soft and hauntingly mellifluous— a coalesce of provocative modern tunes, made to sway and enhance the building mood of intimacy.

In the center of the room was a large round ottoman upon which she was made to sit. She was instantly struck with a chord of familiarity culminating in the realization that this was the same spot she had occupied last night.

"Sit and wait for your instructions," he spoke smoothly to her then moved about the room without a care in the world. As if he'd just gotten in from work, his movements having little tell of purpose or urgency. She could imagine him coming in and dropping his keys and wallet down on the table in the foyer, then fingering through the mail before going to his study to have his evening toddy and finding her waiting for him at the foot of his desk with nothing more than a collar and high heels on.

While in her vision he wore a hand-tailored suit by *Enzo D'orsi* as he made his way to a cabinet against the wall across from his desk and opened it to put its contents on display. Presently, he was more at home and relaxed in nothing more than a pair of dark, silky lounge pants and complimentary robe with its belt hanging lazily from its loops.

"I'm going to do some training with you today to cover obedience. The rule is simple: other than breathing, you will not move unless told otherwise. The theme of this lesson is depravity of movement. If you cannot do this on your own submission then it will be taken away from you."

"Yes, Head-Master." Her gaze following him, but her mind wandered, wondering to what form of training he meant. *Look at me, I'm sitting like a pretty lark on a bough for your pleasure and dutifully waiting your commands,* she thought in protest that he should suggest she needed any training. She knew how to be a good subbie.

He stopped behind her and she felt his hands take charge of her corset lacings. His fingers never fumbled, he knew precisely what he was doing and in a matter of a few minutes he was cinching her waist, despite the rebellion of her breakfast, but not enough that she would lose it. Then, rather than use a measuring tape, he used his fingers, spreading them around her and hissed his approval. In the adjustment, one of the straps to her chemise fell from her shoulder, and she reached up to return it to its proper place when she felt the sudden sting on the back of her hand from a horse hair flogger.

"*Ahh ahh,* leave it."

Amelia's hand sprang back, the reaction causing the other shoulder strap to fall from her shoulder. She couldn't leave the straps dangling and disorderly as they were, so she slowly started to slide her arm out of one with every intention of mirroring the adjustment with the other. But the first of such movements rewarded her with yet another swat from the horse tail; one to each shoulder.

"What did I do wrong?"

"If I wanted the garment returned to your shoulder, I would put it there. If I wanted you to undress, I would have ordered you to do so. I have done neither. Now reach back and take your ankles and then bow your back toward me."

Amelia did so and as soon as she did, the flogger came down in a spiraling landing of three or four swats across her breasts one then the other. Delivering the sting of tiny pliable hairs.

"Now relax back as you were."

He stepped around her, his fingers at his lips moving in a habit formation that said he was deep in thought, enjoying her same as one might enjoy a piece of art. When he came to a stop behind her, darkness shaded over her eyes, and she saw the burgundy silk blindfold from last night returned to its place.

"Head-Master? Have I done something wrong?"

"Indeed, you have. And for each wandering about, you risk, I will take away." And the sash was pulled tight behind her head. Closing off what little gift of sight he had previously given her. "Now, sit quietly."

He'd almost forgotten he had set out a surprise to share with her. He'd placed it outside on the deck so that the sun could turn it to just the right consistency for what he had in mind. Everyone had their particular sweet tooth, his was dark chocolate. Dessert wasn't complete without it and neither was his kink. Leaving his pet to suffer out some more of the waiting, he stepped out and down the corridor to the great room, then out the sliding glass doors that led out to the primary deck. He paused to suck in a deep breath of the salty air, not as fresh as he'd have preferred with the drift of New York making its way out into the harbor, but enough to remind him this was home. And one day, hopefully soon, he would have Amelia out here basking in the sun while he applied sunscreen to protect her vibrant pale skin. He remembered the time he swore to her he'd move both their desks from the office onto his yacht and whisk her away for a year, having her all to himself. How many times he had entertained such a vision that she would say yes and not playfully ask for a rain check?

His gaze fell upon the box wrapped in gold and brown foil, sitting on one of the built in tables just out of reach of the shade from the upper deck. He grabbed the box and carried it back inside to where his pet was waiting.

He flipped the box lid off letting if fall to the floor with disregard and inhaled the rich aroma of dark decadence. Inside, perfectly sun-melted chocolates barely maintaining their original confection design sat in waiting in ruffled cups of silver foil, ready to play and be eaten— in any manner he chose. He plucked one out, the chocolate coating instantly oozing around his fingertips as he delivered it to her lips. He traced each one, consciously causing one dark dribble to fall to her chin, then wordlessly pressed the remainder past her lips and into her waiting, watering mouth, his fingers lingered there for her to lick them clean. The next piece made its way down her neck, followed over the curve lushness of one breast and around the pert, dusky nipple then mirrored the path along her other side with a third; when he fed his fingers to her this time, he pressed her head back forcibly and dove down to kiss the melted confection from her lips, then followed the trail of chocolate over her body. Chocolate was always a decadent gift to the tongue but it was far more fun when melted. His pet moaned with the rich flavors on her tongue and no doubt what his tongue was doing as well.

He licked and sucked each nipple until they stood into hard, pink thimbles, then sank his teeth into the soft globes of her breasts, as he pressed them in and ran his tongue between their crevice, back up her neck and into her mouth. His tongue danced with hers, pressing her back on her heels until he heard the combined moan and whimper. All while his fingers dappled more of the melted sweets to other areas of her body. A shoulder, a wrist, the palm of her hand. Wherever he wanted to nibble from, he did so. He took a piece and smeared it on his chest then pulled her mouth to him. "Find it all and lick me clean, pet." He dropped to a knee on the ottoman and let his head fall back as she did as told. Her tongue licking out as the wicked greedy thing it was, searching and mopping up the chocolate mess. He pressed her head farther down even though he'd not put any of the confections there, but he wanted to feel her tongue lower, to tease his own baser needs for a moment before moving on to other, more deviant things.

Thirty-six hours had seemed a decent amount of time, yet now it revealed it was not enough for all the exploring he had in store for her.

He sucked in a deep breath to regain his will and eased his pet back on her heels. Dessert given and taken; he was ready for some serious play. "Sit, hands on your thighs and wait quietly."

He left her there to grab a few things from the open cabinet on the far wall. He glanced over the variety of toys he might choose from as the day progressed. While he had some outline of the things he wanted to try on her, none of them were fixed. So he took a mental preview once more of his choices to see if anything called out to him right away. He picked up a pair of cuffs letting them jingle in his grip then tossed them back to the velvet shelf. He loved playing with cuffs. They gave a different vibe than leather shackles did, but he already had her outfitted in such for easement. Mostly he wanted her to hear them and pick up on the distance he had placed between them.

He glanced over his shoulder at her, watching her deep breaths causing a shallow rise to her shoulders and breasts. Her head angled perfectly. Her hands resting on her thighs. She was exactly as he had placed her. The test was to see how well she understood the waiting.

He pulled out a magic wand. He'd never used this style before but had picked one out for their weekend together. This particular model had a few bonuses, having a heat element, but also had a chill plate. Anything that offered all-in-one variable stimulants was always a must have for the toy box. And today seemed a good day to test its abilities.

He picked out a pair of nipple clamps and set them aside for easy reach later if needed, then took the rest over to the ottoman, before returning to the closet.

He had a variety of paddles, a short broad leather strop, and even a few leather tawse thongs. He appreciated variety— never having a preference of a single implement. It often depended on his mood. Whether he was in the mood for lines, broad stripes or solid blushing skin.

"Is there a service Sir would have me do?" the question called out to his position in the room.

"You have already been given your instructions, pet. I will let you know when I am ready for you to do something else." He kept his tone cool, then pulled out a pair of leg restraints to which the wrists restraints already on her arms. He took his selection back to the ottoman and stood there, letting the leather shackles drop from his hand next to where she sat. He sucked in a deep breath, inhaling all that was her. Kneeling before him, waiting his command. It was heady. Making her wait like this. The power surged, sending his blood into a race through his body. He could see all the visions of such pleasure and pain he would take her to. Visions that had his cock eager. Even if he made her wait all day and well into the evening before he gave her the fucking she craved, he would want it long before. But he would see her to the edge until she was begging. Only then might he take his pleasure with her. He was contemplating what he would do first when her hand floated up, her fingertips lightly fluttering over the tops of her breasts. A slight crook to each in a false appearance to scratch an itch then drifted— teasingly slow to move down over the mound of one. The twitch in her lips was the true give away. The seemingly innocent movement was anything but a ploy to draw his eyes to her assets.

He sucked in a deep breath then walked behind her, scooping up her hair in one hand. He twisted the locks around his fist until it tightened and certain to sting her scalp, then with a hard yank, pulled her head back. His other hand snapping around to her throat clamping it in his fingers. "The only command you were given was to not move and wait," he growled against her cheek with a heavy, sharp tone. "Put your hands back where I told you to keep them." He released her neck, pulling his fingers down her chest and over her breasts with only enough contact for her to feel where his hand was moving. "If I want to look at your breasts, I will do so. But it will not be your hand that guides me." He made sure his fingertips brushed her thighs as he dropped his hand down to the ottoman and picked up the Wartenburg pinwheel to be their first torture toy. The contact of his soft fingertips were transformed into a wheel of needlelike points against her skin. Drawing the wand handle over the tender roll of her inner thigh. His pet instantly flinching from the prickly experience. "*Ah ah,* do not move until I tell you to," he reprimanded her when her leg hopped away in the attempt to escape the contact. He enjoyed the minuscule twitches of each muscle as he slowly used the wheel wand to trace up one leg then down the next.

"*Now,* spread your thighs." But she could only move so far and he saw to it the pin wheel pressed into the soft inner skin of her legs until he had her spread out to her limit. The breasts, she had attempted to lure him to look at, were next to be tortured, rolling the seven prickly wheels over them leaving a faint trailing footprint of red points across her skin. "I can spoil you with intoxication, my pet. But you will also come to find my commands precise. I will have my orders followed to the letter without any translated variation. Is that understood, my pet?"

"Yes, Head-Master," Amelia whispered, but he could hear in her voice she did not fully grasp what her offense was.

Time to teach her what it meant. No more words. She would learn by means of action. He tightened his fist in her hair and shoved her over until her cheek pressed hard into the edge of the ottoman. "Stay," he growled and took one right ankle in his grip and lifted her leg back. He leaned in, licking a broad line from the back of her knee up the back of her thigh and over the rolling globe of her ass and then sank his teeth into the succulent flesh. Baser lust smoldered inside him, wanting nothing more to pin her down and ravish her like a wild animal. To temper the need, he bit into her again, letting out a low resonating growl to vocalize his claim on her. This time his teeth exacting a sharp whimper from her.

He returned her knee to the ottoman and moved his hand to her wet folds, drawing her moist lips apart with the tip of a finger and pushed in to collecting the pooling honey.

He moved farther over her, letting her feel the slow possessive approach of his body over hers. Then, reaching around to her mouth, he placed his soaked fingers over her lips with the honey from her body. Her mouth opened and he pressed his fingers in to land on her tongue. "I'm going to devour that cunt of yours soon. But foremost, I'm going to keep you on this edge until I am satisfied that once you feel my tongue licking deep inside your wet pussy you'll be screaming and gushing with your release. And you will learn to follow my commands as given or find yourself completely restrained."

He moved his hand over the smooth skin of her ass raise up in offering. Her once pale skin was now starting to bear the remnants of red bruises from the plethora of spankings she had both earned and those for his pleasure. Not nearly enough of them had been for his pleasure yet he had to watch carefully to avoid the purple bruises she had asked not to receive on their first weekend together. So, when he brought his hand down this time, he smacked lower, not hard but enough to leave the stinging red print of his hand on the back of one thigh then the other to apply some natural rouge to her lower flesh.

He reached for one of the leather restraints he had pulled out and slipped one of them around her thigh and buckled it closed, then taking the delinquent hand in his, he clipped her wrist shackle to the leg restraint. That would end that one. Now to see if her other hand would behave.

He scooped up her hair once more and yanked her upright. "Lay your left hand down on your thigh, then softly roll it slightly palm up—"

She positioned her hand exactly as she was told but then came the offensive question.

"What would my Head-Master have me do?"

"I want you to lay your hand on your thigh, palm up."

"Is that all?"

"Yes."

"Nothing else?"

"Wait." The single word spoken as a soft directive.

"I don't understand."

"That is because you are questioning my authority that perhaps I have not been clear of what my commands are." And he went back to the cabinet for one of the clamps he'd set aside earlier.

"No, my apologies. That's not what I meant."

"Isn't it?" he called back to her. "After all, you brought your hand up to direct my eyes, thinking you'd waited long enough, and you wanted me to do something for or to you. And you are about to learn that even in the simplest of commands, I expect them to be followed, unless you want to call your safeword. Is that the case, pet?"

"No, I don't want to use my safeword."

"Very well then. I expect your hand to remain precisely where I told you to put it or it will become restrained as the other is.

"Please forgive me— I—"

"*Shhhh*— now is not a time for apologies. Only learning." And he finished his will, reaching out and plucking one of her nipples between his thumb and forefinger several times until it hardened, then positioned a stainless steel twin screw clamp around it and tightened it down. Tightening each small screw just to the first flinch from his pet.

Now to try out the new sensory toy. First testing the heating element and then the chill plate against his own skin assuring neither would cause any actual burns. Satisfied with the test, he started down her neck, using a combination of heat and its strobing vibration; a sensation created by the internal rollers. A simple mechanical wonder of tumbling weights set off balance to create a toy of endless pleasure.

He watched the sudden hitch in her breath then relaxed. She nearly started down a path of movement, both to give access and again to chase after the wand as he moved it away, but in both she caught herself and stiffened against the movement she'd been forbidden. Her self-will rattled at the chains of his commands, tormenting her and igniting the arousal that came from such a struggle. He moved the toy out across her shoulder and then down the one unclamped breast. He clicked a button, changing the speed so the vibration was more reminiscent of a throbbing pulse and he moved it lower on her body, drawing circles over the jacquard ribbed corset, spiraling down toward the patch of wine colored curls between her legs.

He pushed it directly over her clit and the reward was the sound of his pet's breath hitching in her throat. *Had a woman made a sexier sound as such? Well perhaps they did but few could top the sound of* her *hitched breath.* It was the chocolate confection for a man's ears. The very sensory men enjoyed second best to the wet contact of her body against and around his own. He took great pleasure mapping out and lapping up every nuance of her body's reaction. The new wand's attributes had been a successful selection and he took his time exploring more, watching how she nearly mewed when he flipped its chill plate on and used it to trace between her thighs.

Amelia let out a gasp and her entire body jerked at the touch of icy cold metal against her clit. Completely blind, her one hand strapped to her thigh, the other ordered to remain still, and her left nipple clamped. Now to have the swirling sensation of vibration that changed from heat to cold threw her off. She was struggling to gauge herself for the next sensation.

She felt his thumb brush roughly across her mouth then forced her lips to part, pulling her to open wide and then she felt the blunt end of his cock pushing in.

"Suck it," he hissed.

She closed her mouth around the mushroom cap. She hummed to finally be given a task that was more involved. But her focus wasn't purely on what she was doing; the strange wand was still roaming around her body, some soft sensation that relaxed her, only to alter its course and vibrations, to awake and exhilarate her. She switched her focus back to what her tongue was doing and she swirled it around the shaft as her Master began to pump in and out of her mouth slowly. No sense of rush, just enjoying her mouth at the moment.

He toyed with her, pulling his cock from her mouth and traced her lips with the broad end, pressing against them to be nursed with a suctioning kiss then pushed all the way in until hitting the back of her throat. The girth stretched her mouth wide and she moaned with the full taste of his skin. *Hmm, oh yesss*— the thick hard shaft felt exotically exquisite on her tongue. And she sucked fervently to please him.

The toy he used was wedged then abandoned underneath her at just the right angle of movement that its vibrating pulse made contact and sent shock waves through her clit. His hand fisted into her hair, locked her head firmly in place as he began to move his hips back and forth, picking up in speed. His cock plummeting inside her mouth and back out again. She wriggled her ass down between her heels, lowering down on the wand until she was sitting directly on the forgotten wand. Her Master's hips rocked her back onto it while he pumped her mouth full of his cock. It was everything she desired as she held on.

And then at the drop of a dime, it all stopped. Her Master' cock was pulled from her lips. Her mouth gaped open at the sudden retreat. The hand that fisted into her hair gone and a firm hand held her left wrist. He spoke no words, but in her dark world she realized doubtlessly what she had done wrong. She moved her fingers and conclusively enough, they came in contact, not with her own thigh, but his. In the spell of pleasure, she had reached out, and tried to take ahold of him.

"Now that you are aware of what you have done."

"I'm so sorry. It was an accident, I didn't mea—"

"Shhh— no excuses right now."

The firm words spoken and then her wrist was being moved behind her back. She felt something soft go around her waist. Perhaps the belt from his robe. She felt it tied in place and then her wrist clipped in, so it was now held bent behind her at the small of her back.

"Each offense will find its appendage restrained," he whispered softly in her ear. "Now open your mouth."

She did but it was not his cock that was returning as she licked out to find the mouth piece of a leather gag being inserted and closed over her mouth. She nearly sobbed that she was now being constrained further. She would have begged his forgiveness for having spoken out and questioning him, but that was the purpose of the silencing her, and the leather oral plug prevented her from even trying. The only allowance was a tear that streamed down her cheek.

While she knew she had earned his disapproval, he did not act out in anger, firm and precise, as he had put it— several times, and still she had disregarded him. Now, she was being stripped of her freedoms one by one.

She heard him moving around the room and when he returned, he wasted no time repositioning her. Her dark world capsizing, her cheek landing on the soft suede, then a wedge pillow positioned under her hips, and her knees spread out wide. Blind and mute, with her ass in the air and available, her hands restrained, he made her wait— *again.*

But it wasn't long. This time she wasn't able to defy his commands or perhaps what came next was what he wanted all along when she felt the broad strap slap across her ass. The sudden bite on her skin seared her nerves with its broad sting and then she felt another. The swipes of fat hard leather continued to rain across her ass. Perfectly horizontal across her fleshy bottom, not once coming close to where her hands were locked. And deliberately tame as far as flogging went. Still warming her up when she would have preferred he gave into a frenzy. *How was it, he didn't?*

A wide slap over the left, then right, again, and then a singular upswing whispered past her inner thighs to slap against her mound. Each one minutely kicking up the burst of stars that jolted out from her clit to a new heightened awareness. She let out a pleading moan that the sweet kiss of pain was what she needed. She swayed her hips begging, *please, oh god, please let loose on me.* She wanted it all, wanted to do everything, and be pushed to every succulent limit. Not later, no building, no warming up— *but now.* She lost count in the burning haze of heat and then she felt another stroke come up between her thighs and land over the entrance to her cunt. She yelped against the plug lodged on her tongue and curled her toes. While the final strike in the set had not had the same carried force as the others, the sting was no less felt and it sent a stimulating shockwave out from her epicenter. Then she felt his hand, purring over her skin to enjoy the handy work that no doubt was a display for his eyes.

"Mmmm—" she forced what was meant to be a *please* against the gag, but he didn't begin a new set. She thought for sure she would break down in sobbing and even tried to push a sound of something out to no gain from him.

He lingered behind her, stroking over her skin and the tantalizing fever as it turned a bright red with under tones of dark pink from the previous right before his eyes. It was interesting how he found himself so easily side tracked by just watching her. He'd grown up surrounded with his father's paintings and sculptures. How perfectly she would be placed among them. While she was new to him, she was not new to flogging. It was a topic discussed in depth in their contract and confirmed by Trenton. Yet he watched her body carefully, knowing full well he had not given her instructions for an alternate safeword. But a necessary exception as a matter of peeling away the control she continued to pluck even the smallest of strings to. On the same token, it was reason to play cautiously, enjoying her pleading response for a more fervent landing of the strop while watching for any warning signs. It was a plus he had with her, she was very responsive. Every struggle and yearning clearly displayed over her skin and mewling breaths.

He fingered a tossed strand of her hair, then stepped away. This time giving her no indication to his location in the room. Leaving her a hundred percent removed of her senses— no sight— no sound— no words, and if she moved any part of her body without being told again, he would take the freedom of that movement away as well. He would continue to peel away the layers of her control until she had none left or learned to give it over.

He didn't stay in one spot for any amount of time. He savored circling her, taking in the view from every angle. He went to the bar and poured himself a water and quietly sipped, drawing out the wait. Watching the subtle but reluctant *giving-in* take place. It was finally happening; she didn't want to let go but the struggle to control was slipping.

He stepped closer, kneeling just a few feet away. The creased frustration that skipped across her forehead, her mouth working around the gag then relaxing. Her head turned, still resting a cheek on the ottoman where she was actually waiting for him. It was a tantalizing mimic of sitting on the edge of a great mountain and waiting for the first glimpses of the sunrise coming up. It was just hovering somewhere below the horizon. His pet, waiting in the incandescence of twilight for him.

He glanced down at the ice cube in the glass, then to her, then turned the glass bottom-up, draining the last of the chilled water with little regard to revealing his location then rushed in on her. Without a word, he scooped her up, flipping her from her knees to her back on the ottoman in a sneak attack that had a startled yelp trying to escape from behind the mouth piece.

He grasped both ankles and lifted them up and over until her knees nearly touched her shoulders, then dove down to ravish her cunt with the chill contact of his mouth, letting the cold water spill between them. Deep breaths flared in and out of her nose and she moaned as he pressed his tongue past her moist folds. Licking down their center to part them, sucking up her nectar, then closed his lips over the hooded nestle of nerves. Sucking and near chewing over it with an unleashed hunger. He brushed over the burgundy nest of hair over her mound with his nose then chin. Changing his hold on her enabled him to free up a hand, dropping over her shallow bush and curling his finger into soft hairs, pulling it tight, then plunged his finger deep inside her pudendum. Using the mix of oral play in the bent over attack to work her body up to the very edge of her release.

His eyes locked on the rippling tremors that washed over her body. Her corset hid much of it, but the shaky breathing trapped behind her gag and the tensions that pulled at the muscles around her shoulders and down her arms painted a vividly colored storm of affected sensations that swirled inside her. Sending her plummeting into a whirlpool of exhilarant turmoil. Because just when he had her to the very edge he stopped, brought her legs down, and stepped away for the next item of play.

He wanted to test her level for masochism. He wanted to try so many things, it was hard to settle with just one or two. He was a boy set loose in a candy store with no worry that any of it would give him a belly ache, because when it came to Amelia, no such thing could happen. Addiction perhaps, but he welcomed that. He had already tested her bottom with a thick tawse. The corset hindered a flogger, so he decided to see just how she reacted to a violet wand. Unlike the magic wand, this one didn't vibrate. It gave out no cooling sensation or even any real heat, though some had described a warming sensation.

Violet wands had to be one of those things that must have been made just to appeal to the mad scientist some Doms harbored inside their dark psyche. The handheld plasma advancement of the old Jacob's ladder wand was simply put a static wand and depending on the power source, its handler could control just how shocking the experience could be. For a true sadist and masochist couple, the violet wand was at the top of the list of toys to have, but it could also be used for softer administering even if rarely thought of as anything but for pain play. *They'd been wrong.*

He scooped his pet up in his arms and carried her over to the cabinet, placed her on her feet and bent her over the back of the leather sofa which put her in reach of the wand's power source.

While he wanted to test her with it, he wasn't interested in her level for pain tolerance. Not this time and certainly not while he had her gagged. So he'd planned to keep the voltage setting on low. "I want to explore your body with a violet wand, my pet. Just some light tingling for our first time, but if you get uncomfortable and need to use your safeword, you can snap your fingers three times. Try it now just to be sure." He caressed her back and over her shoulders as he spoke to her and awaited her response.

The fingers of her hand behind her back curled and then she snapped three times.

"Very good and the other hand."

Amelia repeated the snap test with the hand clipped to her thigh.

"Very good, my pet. One snap if you are ready." When she snapped only once, he reached around dropping his hand between her legs and pressed between her thighs, his fingertips seeking out the hooded bundle and massaged over it with the pad of one finger. Already it was swollen and ripe from his touch and he could feel the droplets of silk that made its escape past the locked pressure of a release he'd kept from her. He slid a finger downward to separate her lips to coat his touch in her moisture then back to her clit and toyed with the gold ring she wore. "Damn, you're so hot." He bent over her to breathe the primitive appraisal in her ear.

He stood and licked her dew from his fingers while stepping over to the cabinet for the wand, tested the voltage on the back of his arm "The sensation of violet wand can be intense, so if you find yourself jumping or curling about, you won't be reprimanded for the motion." He gave her his pardon, then brought the glowing pink bulbous wand up and lightly touched it to her skin just in the crease of her ass.

Just a touch for her to experience at first then drew it up to trace around the curve. His own breath deepening with a husky rasp when he heard the alluring moan from behind the leather gag. He knelt behind her and blew on her exposed pussy and reveled in the view as the surface of her skin rose up in chill bumps and it swept them all away with another path of the electrical current circling her ass then down one thigh and up the next.

He pushed his fingers inside her nethers to play in the pool of bliss, still teasing her with the wand. His pet tossed her head, throwing the mop of hair over her back only to trickle back down to the sofa seat and await her next toss.

Amelia's world was tumbling about. She no longer grasped vertical from horizontal. Her Head-Master's finger swept inside the walls of her cunt then pumping into her to build her up. *The wand— how delicious it felt*

even for being so mild a setting, not quite the static shock of a touch. Lines of sensation were drawn across her skin, akin to something between dryer static and a tickle, slowly driving her insane.

She'd never gotten enough of the electrical play in past scenes, it was hard to find a Dom that played with them.

She worked her mouth around the plug and moaned, wishing her pleas would encourage him to turn the current up but then she felt something far better as he dragged it right over her clit. Her knees jumped, nearly going out from underneath her, but the sofa held her as did he. His hand never leaving her, either teasing her cunt to the edge of release or caressing over his flesh.

She sucked in ragged breaths against the confines of her corset and pulled at her restraints waiting and begging for more of anything and everything. Building up to a cliff then teetering so high above the clouds without being given the last tilt to let go and cum.

Her insides boiled with the need but his fingers and the wand always seemed to back away at just that moment when she could be pushed over the edge. *Oh god, please, Master. Please, please let me cum,* she cried in her head, the words themselves nothing more than preverbal mumbles against the mouth piece.

The wand fell away and she felt him standing behind her. *Oh yessss.*

His fingers fanned across her ass now red and fevered from all his attention that his cool touch was a salacious lick over her nerves. And then she felt his thick cock as he played with it, dragging the oozing head of the thick bulb across her skin. Sliding it back and forth between the globes of her ass. *Yesss, fuck me,* she thought and she rose up on her toes to make herself available and pushed back.

The next thing she felt was a hard crack of his hand across her ass too painful to be play. And next she was being lifted and tossed over— she felt his steps and realized he'd tossed her over his own shoulder and was carrying her away. *To where* was something she could not even guess, but when the footsteps stopped, she felt out the movement of his arms busily on a task. Next, she was falling backwards until something caught her and she quickly found herself floating in the air. Her Master repositioned her legs, each being clipped in to hang at just where he wanted them. Her legs suspended wide and immobile by any means over her own will. She heard the rushed tearing of a foil package and then she felt his cock sink inside her cunt. *Ohhhhh*— her head fell back with a sighing moan that would have escaped and filled the room had she been allowed. She felt his grip on the harness that suspended her and the ride began. The force of his arms swinging her to and fro with his hips slamming against her, driving his cock deep inside her with every thrust.

Amelia could do nothing but feel— there was no other definition of where she was. He had taken every ounce of control away and now she was just a dangling body for the fucking and the experience was beyond any exhilarating thing she had ever felt. She was catapulted into a maelstrom of lust and baser sensation. The friction, as his cock filled her core, lit her epicenter like a wild fire.

She smelled the blending of their bodies that perfumed the air around them.

What she heard— she'd never heard before. Such sweetness. His breath growled with every rasping breath. Like pornography for her ears.

He slammed into her. Each thrust driving his claim into her, she was his and he would play and fuck her at his own terms, not hers, and then she relinquished even the attempt to hold her head up.

She let go.

And that's when it all came. The storm rolled in and rushed her like a tumble weed in the wind. Such bliss she'd never felt as she finally surrendered with her head hanging back and her hair sweeping back and forth. The euphoria built up. It consumed her and she began to cry. No, not cry, but she heard her own sobs. Felt them as perfect wonder overwhelmed her, she was not a boss, no longer the Vice-President or a publisher, she was not striving to find anything, she was just here, a woman swinging in the sea of illicit passion, and she sobbed.

"Cum for me, my pet," his rasping voice severed through her crying and reached her ears and she did just that, she came— and then she came apart.

She only vaguely felt the hand cup the back of her neck and lift her. Her world still floating yet she felt powerful arms wrapping around her, lifting, and then carrying her gently away. Still, all she could do was cry.

He cradled her, kissed her forehead and slowly one by one removed the restraints that held her. The gag was carefully pulled from her mouth and he massaged her cheeks and lips; first with his thumb then with his kiss. He rubbed her wrists and arms, drawing the blood flow back into them, then her shoulder as he pulled her hands to her lap, then caressed her cheek while she still cried. And somewhere within all those tears, she told him *Thank you.*

"It was my pleasure, for your surrender is so beautiful, my pet," he told her succulently, still kissing her. The fading connection of his adoring lips pressed to the side of her head and slowly she drifted away to sleep.

After a long nap, dinner was a welcomed feast. And Rashawn took advantage of her languid body throughout the meal by using her as his plate. They started off with hors d'oeuvres of seasoned Taleggio cheese and Mission figs that had been roasted on top of a dark French bread. Each bite melting on the tongue. They followed it with braised cuts of duck with a crispy skin glazed with a sweet-tart cherry sauce.

Rashawn loved every hum from her lips as he fed her small bite-size morsels from his plate with his fingers. Of course, trying to eat a mixed salad of peas and baby carrots from her belly button turned out to be quite the challenge, her giggling didn't help as it tended to send more of the peas running away to make their escape. But the music her laughter made was worth losing food over.

Dessert was a cinnamon pastry cream, but near impossible to enjoy, as he spent more time making a mess of it on her skin then eating it, save for a few scoops of the mess with his tongue to feed to her in a kiss, but more so it was a good excuse to take another shower which led to more playing and she came so beautifully in his arms.

Now with his pet wrapped up in a silk short robe they returned to their picnic spot on the floor in the great room and just relaxed.

ⱷ

"Fur?" Amelia asked, as she spread her fingers out and ran them through the soft wool of the short area rug.

"Wool from an alpaca. Softest of its kind and I assure you the contributors are all alive and well, living out a care free life in the Andes."

Amelia relaxed, resting her head on his lap and let out a sigh. She felt so complete now. And full. She didn't think she had an ounce of strength left in her to do anything or resist if he commanded her otherwise. But she was grateful to simply lay about nestled against him. It was something completely new to her— cuddling, and she felt the smile across her face and the warm glow caused by it. He took her hand and raised it up, placing her palm on his chest. He didn't say a word, and then she felt his heart beating against her hand, strong and steady, and just as content as she was.

"Tell me about your growing up. What sort of school did you go to?" He broke the silence.

Amelia rolled over, keeping her head on his lap, while tucking one hand around his waist and let her fingers play on his back. "I grew up in a transient European family. Part of the time in France. Sometimes in Switzerland, and here in the US. I have three brothers, no sisters."

"And were you daddy's little girl?"

"Oh, that I was and being the youngest. Our mother passed away when I was only seven and my father, fearful I would grow up too heavily influenced by male role models, sent me to a convent school until I was sixteen."

"Ever married?"

"No." She smiled softly, not in the least bit sorry for it. "I was engaged once. Arranged by my father. For two years, I drove both men crazy."

Her Head-Master chuckled, no doubt he could imagine a trillion ways how she might accomplish such.

"How so?" he asked showing his amusement to want to the tales of woe she'd dished out.

"I was fresh out of school, and extremely envious of my brothers. They were already working in the firm for our father. They would go off on these lavish excursions and returning with, bringing back stories of scandalous affairs. The oldest even claimed to have a mistress set up in a penthouse in Barcelona. I was starved of such tales myself. So, I became voracious, both sexually and wanting to excel in our father's firm. I even snuck off to Barcelona without a chaperone and into the bed of three men. Father put a stop to such voyeur travels right away, finding a suitably well-bred young man to tie me down with." She paused amount, licking her lips as she recalled her devilish past. "My fiancée didn't appreciate me moving up the company ladder as I did. He thought

I should stay at home and let him take care of the hefty allowance my father provided me. And quite frankly, I think my sexual prowess frightened him even more. We spent another year dragging it out. Often, we'd sit in a room and never exchange a single word."

"Why bother?"

"Because it took that long for my father to see there was no working this out."

"That was important to you?"

"Yes," she answered matter-of-factly, "I wanted his consent for it to end."

"Anyone else?" he encouraged her to continue sharing about herself, his hands floating over her body, caressing— possessing her all the while. Not just her body but all the things that made her who she was. That's how he made her feel right now. Human and beautiful. His pet.

"There were a few that came into my life, but it's always been the same. My position in the family has made most men feel inferior." She grew saddened a moment, a painful shadow that cast over her face as she looked back into her past. "Even coming home, I would willingly lay that all aside, or try to, at least. The reversal of roles is complicated. Perhaps too much so for any man."

"Perhaps it was your approach."

She turned up at him, she couldn't see him, but she felt him, and she wanted him to know he had her full attention. "What do you mean?"

"It seems you spent a lot of time treating your personal life the same way you did your business life. The challenge for any man was still there, but the relationship's bond should have come first and foremost before worrying about how he would cope with your position in the family business."

"Mmmm, I suppose you're right." She tucked her chin and relaxed on his leg, then glanced back up again. "And what of you?"

"*Pshh*, same as you, I have never been married. But then I had very different role models for parents. I was engaged once. I was young and quite captivated by her, but I kept my lifestyle hidden from her delicate raising. Too long into the relationship, I'm afraid."

"She never knew you were a Master of Bdsm?"

"Well, I wasn't to such experience as that, at the time. But I hadn't been entirely open about myself either."

Amelia giggled unable to imagine this man not taking charge of everything around him even when he was younger. Such a vision was unfathomable as trying to imagine the Dominus being a bunny rabbit as a boy. "However, did you restrain yourself?" she teased him playfully.

Rashawn chuckled; it was rather amusing after all. "Oh, we weren't entirely vanilla. We were part of a spanking society. Very popular at the time. The Victorian naughtiness was very romantic for her. Community gatherings where the ladies dressed up in dainty lace dresses and bottomless nickers. The girls would even stage bickering spats at the picnics so they could all get spankings at the same time. It was a lot of fun."

"So, what happened?"

"Her friends and family— is what happened."

"Oh." Was all she said, knowing full well the judgment of outsiders of any form of the Lifestyle.

"A young girl's mind is very vulnerable to ridicule and her friends at college did not approve. It took them no time at all to convince her that such reprehensible treatment was demeaning and repulsive. We'd been together for four years, yet it wasn't enough to prevent her from being led away by such narrow thoughts."

"Any other memorable relationships?"

"Perhaps one. But it was short lived we were together only a year."

"What happened?"

❧

Rashawn let out a long sigh, as he configured the best way to describe the indifference he'd had with the other woman. "She was a very good submissive, and a masochist, which I took great pleasure in exploring. However, she wanted to be a full time slave. While I have no issues with a twenty-four/seven - D/s, as I struggle to turn myself off when needed. At the same time, her necessity to be tended to around the clock was too much for me. It took away and dulled the allure of the lifestyle for me. She was looking to be completely dependent, and I feared I would find it a burden to fulfill."

"Whatever happened to her?"

"Dominus found her the perfect Master and a forever home."

"And what of you? What is perfect for you?"

Rashawn brought his hand down around her face, using the backs of his fingers to caress down her cheek, dropping under her chin and pressed slightly, tilting her head up so he could enjoy the view of her lips still swollen from endless kissing in their shower. "I crave a strong woman, so that when she submits to me, it means something."

"I have a dear sweet friend, Katianna Dumas, she's also one of my writers. Have you met her before? She belongs to Dominus."

"Yes, many timcs."

"She is his slave in the way you mentioned the other woman you knew was. Does she perplex you?"

"Dominus's Unicorn is an enigma, for certain. I have never met another— not like her. She has such a vitality and curiosity, but her fears get in the way. Trenton Leos gives her a security she lacked within herself. Because of it, she finds a freedom to explore other aspects of herself she'd never been able to before yet being completely given over to him. While I do not think I could be such a Master for a woman such as her, I confess I envy their perfect matching. They are remarkably perfect for each other in their unequal relationship. Her needs compliment his control and his possession sets her free."

His pet let out a soft sigh that brushed his leg like a kiss. "I envy them too."

"Tell me where you work."

"Head-Master, I beg you. I cannot have you visit at my firm."

"Of course not, but I may want to send you a gift or a little something to play with. Maybe even command you to do something— a small inconspicuous reminder of who your Master is until you are returned to me next weekend." He still cupped her chin then carefully lifted her to sit up on her knees.

He moved up behind her. His hands grazing over her shoulders and down her arms feeling the rise and fall of her breaths escalated by just his touch and the arousal stirred from his repositioning her. He reached around, cupping her chin again, and pulled her head all the way back where he could lick over her lips then bit the bottom one before diving in for a deep kiss.

"Do not forget you are contracted as mine for two weekends. That includes every minute between, he nipped her lip in a slow lascivious claim. "Can you imagine yourself at your desk, a small, giftwrapped box before you. The card commanding that you may not open it until lunch time or to wear something at some random time when I send you orders to instruct you what to do with it?"

⚙

The suggestive images were endless. Yet each and every scenario that played out in her mind was delightful.

Rashawn selected a book from one of the many glassed enclosure shelves from the Globe Wernicke Barrister bookcase. It'd been a last-minute detail he'd realized he had to fix, as he prepared for their weekend together, because most of his books were in French. It'd have been a dead giveaway to the all too perceptive woman. However, attempting to find something of the risqué classics on such short notice was no easy feat, but alas he found a copy of *The Way of a Man with a Maid*. An erotic novel penned and published anonymously in the 1930's. While it fell perhaps a decade shy of being a classic, it held some promising Victorian prose toward writing style. Anything of vulgarity in the way of literature was often fun to read, especially aloud.

He made himself comfortable in one of the leather wingback chairs in the great room with his pet propped on a pillow at his feet. He read aloud to her, his fingers absently stroking through the soft tendrils of her hair as he did. Her head rested against his knee where she sat perfectly relaxed. She was beyond compare. The final rebellion in her topping from the bottom had been cracked and peeled away. Her body and mind grasping the raw truth of submission and she'd finally given herself over to it completely now.

It wasn't long, perhaps a chapter or two but the suggestiveness of the book's story along with his pet's transformation was more urging than he could ignore for any measurable length of time. He unzipped his slacks, releasing his cock from its confines, then pulled his pet's head over his lap. "It's time for my pet to show me how talented her tongue is," he instructed then picked up reading where he'd left off.

He gave her loose reins in the task; his fingers raked in her hair merely as a reminder that at any given time he might take over, fisting into the thick locks until her head was rigidly kept in place while he lifted his hips to pump his cock in and out of her mouth. But for now, he allowed her the freedom of her head.

His breath deepened and he let out a light growl. The tantric dance of her tongue that swirled over his turgid flesh was enough to make reading a challenge and he eventually gave it up, letting the book drop carelessly to the floor.

He let out a chain of several more deep groans of pleasure. Both his hands now riding the motion of her head while he buried his fingers in the fountain of burgundy trusses.

The warm wet encasement paired with her tongue was utter deliciousness. He sucked in a hard breath, letting it hiss in through his nostrils then let it out with a gasping sigh. Tension melting away with each breath to be licked away by his pet's sucking.

He had desired Amelia for some time now, but nothing he imagined compared to actually having her in his arms, having her mouth around his cock, and her submission given at his feet. By the time their thirty-six hours was over, he intended to have fully left his mark inside her as well as on her skin. She would be his. Forever, he hoped. However, if that was not possible, he would have everything he could in these last precious few hours. In thirty-six hours, he planned to touch a lifetime of desire.

He pitched back in the leather chair, kicking his legs out at her sides and melted away. He scooped her hair up, lifting it so he could watch her mouth at work. Watching as his cock filled the hollows of her cheeks. Watching the glistening dew her tongue left behind with every savory lick. His pet's wicked tongue making lascivious work over his senses.

Drunk.

That was how he felt with her. She made him drunk with having her. Merde, how he had conspired at lengths to have her attention. In several instances, he nearly compromised his position as the Master to get her to look at him, but lastly, he never allowed the slip to go so far. A relationship without their dynamics—such a thing between them would never work. He was compulsive of his control and her body screamed to find the bliss of being delivered into pure surrender. A desire that continued to slip through her fingers because she just happened to be artfully skilled at topping from the bottom and the very act had been robbing her of the chance for the hungers of her own longing to be slaked.

He'd always gotten such a hard-on watching her in the board meetings at work. How she wrapped those business men around her finger and bent them to her will to serve the company. How many times had he envisioned stepping up behind her after the board had cleared the room so he could bend her over the expansive glass conference table, drawing her skirt up around her waist, and fucking her until they both came, leaving the imprint of her ass on the glass for when the cleaning service came in late at night. He could burn off an entire day's meeting, having listened to MacMinnas or Heldebrange murmur on and on about crunching stocks to squeeze out a higher yield just to watch her.

Drawn back to the present, he was fixated watching her now. A lock of her hair dropped over her face and he brush it aside to keep his unobstructed view of her hollowing cheeks, and the puckered swell of her lips. Before it was over, he was already looking forward to next time he would have her pleasure him over his lap, only without the blindfold. He'd be able to see the brilliant sparks in her green eyes with her tongue chasing after every detail she saw, to taste it as well.

He let out a deep growl, feeling his release drawing close. He pushed her off his cock to let the edge drop back. He wasn't in any rush to be finished off.

He pulled his cock against his stomach, then scooped up his balls and pulled her down to lavish them with some attention. Another growl getting away from him when she dove in not in the least bit shy. She licked circles around each tight globe then sucked them into her mouth one after the other. He let his cock loose, watching it slap her in the face. His pet worked her way up the underside but paused before swallowing him down.

"May I, Sir?"

"*Mmmm*, you most certainly may, my pet." And he surrendered his lust to her divine mouth, certain that she was both a new life and a certain death to him. Both, he would gladly embrace. Because no amount of physical pleasure could compare to what he felt inside himself for his pet. He wished he could tell her so, speak of how she raised the heartbeat of a Renaissance man of this modern world, for there was no greater punishment than to not be able to say what was in him.

His release came— so violent, he gripped the back of her head, and locked her lips around his cock as he shot down her throat. Lost completely to the pleasure, he probably made more sounds in that moment then he had ever before. And he willingly gave them to her as his gift to show his appreciation for the sonance she'd voiced for him. Both in what she gave him physically and what she unknowingly gave to his soul and heart. Because her submission to him touched him more deeply than any touch or that he'd ever allowed in.

Her Head-Master had taken her from his world the same way she went in— cloaked, headphones spilling music into her ears making her deaf to the outside world and blinded to it. She rode curled up against his side while he played with her hand, testing the fitting of their fingers as he stitched them together over and over again. Then he took his time kissing the back of her hand and each finger individually. The ache and dread of parting affecting them both.

When the car came to a stop, she was carefully led out and returned to the care of the Dominus. Her blindfold removed only after her Master's car had pulled away.

"Keep your eyes closed for a moment." She heard Trenton's gentle control talking to her as he removed the sash from her eyes. "Blink a few times. Take your time and open them slowly when you're ready."

Amelia skipped the first two steps and opened her eyes instantly being met with a searing pain as the brilliant noon day sunlight flooded in and she quickly snapped them closed.

"I see you still have yet to learn to follow instructions," he addressed her with a soft chiding.

Words of protest started to bubble up with excuses, but she stopped them. She hurt and he was right, first thing he told her to do she disobeyed, and now her eyes hurt because of it.

She felt his hand over her eyes, shading them, and it eased the pain.

"Let's try this again." His hand became two and cupped over her eyes. "Blink them open." And this time she did as told.

A small amount of light seeped passed his fingers, but not enough to blind her. His hands came away but still shading her face.

"Keep blinking." The slow progression of his hands drifting away, he managed to acclimate her eyes then placed a pair of sunglasses on her face with gentle care.

She sucked in a deep breath and glanced around. They were in the parking lot in front of TL Securities. Just behind Trenton was Diesel Gentry, leaning against Trenton's Conquest Knight and she was certain that somewhere behind the black tinted windows was the face of Katianna Dumas.

"Ready to go home?"

Katianna sat next to Amelia as they rode in the back seat of the monstrous vehicle. Kat's pale, moonlit-snow colored eyes sparkling so brightly Amelia couldn't ignore them any further and she swatted at her young friend.

"Oh, you hush up now." Her face feeling warm it surely turned a beet-red, and still Katianna beamed at her as if waiting for all the juicy details. "Oh, you would be waiting for such a thing, wouldn't you?" Amelia snapped off not needing to hear it vocalized. Amelia couldn't explain why she was so embarrassed, like a school girl caught ogling over her crush.

Katianna merely nodded ecstatically, but still kept silent.

"You know you could have commanded her to not look so eagerly at me too, Dominus." Taking in the assumption he'd commanded Kat to not overwhelm her with questions when they picked her up. But Amelia's fuss was only met with laughter from both alpha males in the front seat. And that only brought on another wave of crimson blushing that spread from head to toe over her body, followed by an unstable smile. She was utterly and blissfully changed.

But as they took the long drive home, something else also began to take place within her that was soon becoming impossible to ignore. She became aware of the growing distance between her and the man who'd not only brought that bliss to the surface but had wrapped it around her, turning her long desires into something tangible for the first time.

Now— now she felt the loss of it as easily as if she had been forced to say farewell to a lover for the last time.

The ache imbued, leaving a riff of pain across her chest as if an earthquake was rattling the crust that protected her heart to tear and crack, exposing the emptiness that had been there for so long. A void she had never taken notice to until now.

Once home, it too, would only compound the loss. A billionaire's palace, that despite its numerous staff members employed to tend to it, would seem just as empty and hollow as her chest felt—

Amelia's thoughts were brought to an immediate halt when she felt the unexpected tear skip down her cheek.

She quickly swiped it away and kept her gaze out the window of the SUV.

Changed.

Yes, that is what she was— like a dream she had known euphoria and pleasure beyond comprehension. She had been *Alison* peering through the looking glass. Now she was awake yet unable to forget the dream and the happiness that had touched her. Such sweet pain, the warmth of his commands, the respite—

Even the sex had been mind-shattering, but the part that was most likely her undoing, was this morning. No scent of morning sex lingered that she could use to convince herself it had been anything but an extraordinary affair of debauchery. Rather he cuddled with her. The firm embrace of his arms coiled around her still spoke a thousand words of possession, while his lips left whispered caresses of loving affection against the back of her neck and shoulders as if he made love to her with his kiss alone.

~~ "Now my pet, sadly I must return you to your world of responsibilities," he whispered softly, with a breath that kissed as much as it tickled against the shell of her ear, "But do not think I have given you up so completely. You are far too precious for me to even consider such absolute absence. I have many desires to experience with you over the week, and there will be rules for you to follow."

He paused a long moment to deliver a shiver inducing line of kisses from behind her ear all the way down and across her shoulder. He took his time like it had never existed. There was no end in sight, no worries of responsibilities except to enjoy her presence to the fullest.

Like savoring a fine glass of wine. It was the first time she had ever felt the true meaning behind the words so often used by the Dominion of Brothers. That until that moment was little more than a playful ambiguity of the word's meaning. A code talk for those who lived the Lifestyle when among mixed company. Yet, while she still laid in her Head-Master's bed, listening and reveling in his affections, she learned it was far more. And she felt herself slip just a little more, though she wasn't so sure there was any farther into the stormy sea of love her little girl heart could fall.

"You are still mine, my pet. I won't have our time shared together marred with you attempting to encounter another. You will find no other Dom can touch your hunger as I do. Am I making myself clear so far?"

"I am yours," she confessed the words before she'd consciously conjured them, though she felt no regrets after. Just warmth— blissful euphoria— the caress of his kiss— the strength of his arms— and the firm desire that pressed against the small of her back with a teasing reminder of all those things delivered. ~~

Another tear escaped and streamed down her cheek, marring her face with the emotional pain of loss she ached with. But couldn't bring herself to swipe it away so quickly this time.

Forever changed.

How could she possibly go back to the empty existence she'd known after such connection with her mysterious man? Not just any man but a Master who understood her needs far better than she did.

She glanced down at her hands, absently mimicking the touches her Head-Master had made while making her suffer the *wait* while he read an explicit tale to her. She could touch her own fingers all day and never be able to provoke the same emotion he had with that simple act alone. And then it struck her, she didn't know what to do with her hands because he wasn't there to tell her what he wanted.

The alarm rang out inside her head like a screaming child. All her life in charge, she had to be stronger than her brothers, better than them, more business savvy than them. She had to prove to any and all watching when she said get the job done, it was done. Such command was expected of her if she was to gain any status with her father. All that boldness, strive, determination had paid off when their father made her the Head Chairman of the family's entire firm over her brothers.

Now she couldn't even perform the simplest of thoughts like what to do with her hand.

~~ "Lay your hand down on your thigh, then softly roll it slightly, palm up—"

"What would you like me to do next?"

"Wait."

"Is that all?"

"Yes." ~~

Amelia closed her eyes and slowly placed her hands down on her legs as she recalled the simple command that she had found so hard to follow before. Yet as she rolled her hands out so they were rested palm up— simple seemed the most comforting thing. To do and do nothing else.

She sucked in a deep breath, feeling the odd relief that came with it, then let it out in a soft sigh that hissed from her nose. A thousand pounds of stress left her in that single breath.

Forever changed.

When the Knight Conquest pulled up her driveway to deliver her to her front door, she felt the panic well up inside her. She wanted to run, scream, and cry. Suddenly she doubted everything. Her *self*. Transition— yet that was what scared her, right now. Going back to what she was. How, if she was changed?

The door opened and there was Trenton's face. Confident, certain, powerful. He knew. His eyes told her so and he held his hand out for her. Amelia hesitated at the step; she glanced back over her shoulder to Katianna who was on the verge of tears herself. "How did you do it?"

Her tears spilled but the most genuine smile crossed their path, "A good friend told me to jump and trust that Dominus would catch me."

Amelia sucked in a deep breath gathering strength from air and she took Trenton's hand and let him lead her inside her home.

She paused inside then wandered into the parlor to deposit her attaché case, then wandered into the great room while Trenton headed straight up the baluster stairs with her suitcase, not bothering to leave the task to her steward.

It seemed wrong, she glanced around as if any minute now her Head-Master would appear and reprimand her for not having her blindfold on. She waited to hear his command that never came and the emptiness she felt screamed inside her—

She found herself running upstairs nearly colliding into Trenton in the hall. She twisted from the arms that would have held her and stumbled into her bedroom.

She froze, unsure what it was she thought she would find, what she wanted to find.

In the evening, when she showered, there would be no one to pat her dry, no clothes set out for her to wear or a note on the table or her pillow with strict instructions on what to do. Her life had been filled with weekends, but none had filled her. None had ever left her feeling so bereft that it was over. Feeling empty and abandoned as she did. She needed him back and she was coming apart inside knowing he wasn't there.

She spun around, her eyes coming around to meet Trenton's. She shook her head— uncertain. "I don't know what this is I feel. I don't understand what's happening."

Trenton stepped in but she countered, taking a step back to keep the distance between them. *Why did she do that? Why did she do or feel anything?* "Dominus?"

"It's okay," he whispered but swept in on her just as she collapsed for the floor.

Strong arms caught and held her tightly, but they were not the same arms as before and she sobbed. "What's wrong with me? Have I gone mad?"

"Shhh, baby girl, it's just a sub-drop."

"What? I don't understand." She shook her head against his chest.

"Of course, you don't. You've never had a deep enough connection or scene, or such a release to have put you in one."

❧

Her bedroom was not the proper place for him to be with her, so he scooped up her legs and lifted her up, keeping her safe and secure in his arms, as he carried her downstairs and into the parlor. Trust wasn't in question, but her emotional whirlwind was. He wanted her to be comfortable, where in the parlor, he knew she would be.

He lowered down on the Victorian sofa and just held her for a moment, then gently eased her down to the floor at his feet where he positioned her to kneel quietly, keeping his hand on the back of her neck. "Close your eyes and take yourself back to him."

He grabbed one of the pillows and dropped it down for her knees, then pulled out his phone to call Deez still waiting outside, they would be staying the night.

Still outside, Katianna and Diesel waited for Trenton to come out, "Deez, what's wrong with Amelia?" Katianna called up to him.

"I suspect she is going into a sub-drop," he answered, looking back over his shoulder at her.

"What's that?"

He waved her to crawl up front with him and once she was in his lap, he brushed her hair from her face with an expression of relaxed adoration. "Her weekend with her new Head-Master turned out as successful as we'd all hoped, and she bonded with him. I suspect they explored some heavy play and now she is feeling some emotional separation anxiety."

"Is it like what I felt when I took off for Florida?"

"No." He shook his head. "More like a precursor. But if not cared for, she could panic and throw her walls back up."

"If Rashawn gave her what she'd always been wanting, why would she do that?"

"Same reason you did. We humans get so adjusted to being unhappy that when given the chance to have the greatest of happiness, we panic and run."

"Like Paris." But she didn't wait for a response he would not give. It was too fresh in his heart. "Is she going to be okay?"

"We'll make sure she is." Just then his phone rang and Kat fished it out from the pocket in his loose fitting jeans and handed it to him.

"What's up?" He listened with a nod, his hand never pausing in the gentle caress on Kat's back. he turned the phone off and handed it back to her to dutifully hold. "Guess we're staying the night." He gave her a playful wink. "Give me some sugar." He puckered his lips to receive his kiss, then scooped her up and hopped out of the SUV before putting her down, then together they went in to stay with their friend.

They found Trenton in the small, more intimate parlor that overlooked the ocean view. The sky turning grey with the approaching late summer storm. Amelia was kneeling quietly at his feet on a pillow and her head rested on his knee.

Katianna joined them, when Trenton's hand waved her to sit next to him. She tucked her legs under her on the small love seat and surrendered herself to his arm's possessive hold.

In another corner, an antique Louis XVI cylinder desk had since been converted into a bar. Diesel opened it up and poured two shots of the platinum tequila she stocked, making sure his amused chuckle was masked well. How a person's personal bar was stocked told you who was welcome in their lives. And he knew on first account there was platinum tequila in every bar of this house. He poked through the small containers but didn't find any limes or hot sauce. *Guess they'd fallen out of visitation habit of late.* He gathered both shots and walked over to Trenton and passed one of them over. "You gonna let her have a glass of wine?"

Trenton fudged his lips and shook his head before tossing back the shot. He stared out the picture window and gritted his teeth with a hiss, then passed the empty shot glass back to him. "No. Easing her pain needs to come from a different source."

Diesel could see Trenton was deep in thought, most likely calculating the best way to care for Amelia without damaging the arrangement between her and Rashawn. It was certainly complicated when she didn't know her new Master was him.

A heavy sigh from Trenton called Diesel's attention back to him and he gave him a questioning look.

"Sit with her, I need to step outside to make a phone call." Trenton got up, waving Katianna to remain with him as he headed out.

Diesel nodded then dropped down in Trenton's spot after he left, reaching over and petting Amelia's hair. "You're not alone, baby girl."

"But the one I want isn't here." She rolled her gaze up to him.

"Then that is good. It means you connected with him well. Now it's time to discover that inside yourself to realize that what you want is greater than what you thought you wanted. When the latter no longer exists, then you'll be ready to welcome him here."

"Would you like for me to refill your glass, Patronus?" Amelia suddenly addressed him by title.

"Are you trying to take over?"

"No, but I would feel better if you gave me something to do." She bowed her head.

He nodded and handed the empty shot glasses to her.

"You know, I still find it hard to believe Dane never took a paddle to your behind when he discovered what you'd done to that desk," he commented to her as she opened up the antique desk to fetch another drink for him.

She shot a fond smile over her shoulder at him, then closed the curled door of wood and brought the drink over. She returned to her knees first then passed the clear liquid up., "Once I explained, he understood."

"No. It should have been restored and kept as a desk," Diesel disagreed.

"No, Sir, it could not have been." Amelia broke out with a playful laugh that sounded good to hear. "My brother left a cigar in it, still lit. By the time it was discovered, the desk had been completely heat scorched to ash. Besides the bar is only an insert made to fit within the original desk but isn't attached."

"That's probably what saved your ass." He chuckled, then sipped at the tequila.

"I wouldn't have minded if it didn't. But it's funny, until that time he discovered the desk, I never knew he was such a connoisseur of antiquity."

"Yeah, you'd never know the dark side of Dane was hiding under all that contemporary and old world mix of fashions."

"I just think it makes him all the more beautifully naughty."

Amelia smiled but it faded quickly.

"What is it?"

"I was just thinking, out of the five of you, I understand Dane the most. I relate to him somehow." She glanced away as if the rest of her words were written somewhere across the room on the volume of books that filled the book units that lined wall to either side of the hearth. "We both have inner desires that are so completely different to the person we display to the rest of the world." She turned to look at him again, a tear trapped in her eyes, "Do people like us ever get to be happy?"

It was doubt that asked. A desperation to be so certain of one's personal desires and still be so uncertain about everything else.

He raised his hand and pointed out the window to the tall man walking across the lawn in the distance, yet his arm around the shoulders of a woman half his height could be distinctly made out. "Look at them. If that isn't love, I don't care. I want what they have because I have never seen any bond more powerful and loyal to each other as theirs." He reached down and took her hand then guided her to come sit in his lap a moment. He cradled her emotional wounds in his thick muscular arms while he watched his brother and his Unicorn heading for the beach. "We all get our doubts from time to time, but those two are living proof when we stop running from the thing we want the most, love happens. What you see in them right now isn't faked. You and I watched it take place. And some of what happened was painful for them. Love is a struggle. It's those rough surfaces that make bonding possible. You just have to stop settling for second best and hold out for the one person imperfectly made for you. And when you find that someone who makes you feel like you're on top of the world and your chest hurts so damn much it feels like it's about to burst, then you'll know you found the right one and don't let anything— and I mean, let *nothing* get in the way of having that right one for yourself.

"How will I know for certain?"

"It will be the one thing that sounds the craziest. Everything you ever experienced didn't work because it's the one you didn't do that was the one meant to work. You'll know because it's going to scare the hell out of you."

Outside, Trenton walked around the guest house that had once been home to his own slave, where he secretly watched over her for four years before pulling her into his life completely. He thought about the oddities of how two very different women needed such similar arrangements to lead them to what they both would be happiest with.

Katianna: a vibrant artist who lived in fear. She had even struggled to accept being happy because she was afraid that in giving herself over to him it would just as quickly be taken away.

Amelia: a powerhouse of feminine strength who feared nothing but the true reality of what she desired most: *Not being in control.*

He walked out on the manicured lawn toward the beach line, knowing the storm brewing off shore called to Katianna. But this time she didn't ask to wander off, she stayed at his side. Trenton pulled her around into his arms and looked down at her as she smiled back, "Do you know how painful it was for me to stay away all those years?" He bent down and kissed her forehead.

"I love you too," she whispered.

"Thank you." He sighed with relief, pulled out his phone, and made the call. A call that for the first few minutes was him bringing Rashawn up to date with Amelia's condition, and the next ten of the man about to make the mistake of throwing their plans into the wind to be with her now.

"Bon sang, Dominus. I cannot sit here and do nothing while she is alone and coming apart."

"She is not alone, I am here with her, and watching over her."

The intense growl that came over the phone told him enough that Rashawn might also be experiencing some drop of his own.

"Rashawn, you listen, and you listen carefully. You have touched her in a way no one has ever done before, but if you show up here and walk in revealing your identity, she will turn and run so fast neither of us will be able to catch her to help her. So for now, you stay where you are, your pet is safe with me for the night and the important thing is to get her to turn to you. So make sure you don't go losing your own senses and be ready to comfort her when she does call."

"I have waited for this for so long."

"Why do you think I went to you? This arrangement was not offered to anyone else, Rashawn. But breaking down that last wall is going to be difficult."

"I don't even know how to chip it away if I can't reveal myself."

"You work with her. You have access to her at the time of her greatest strength. Use that time to blur the lines."

"Blur the lines?"

"Between whom is her Head-Master and who is her co-worker, Rashawn."

There was a long silence on the other end, his presence marked only but the deep breaths. *"If ever there was a doubt that you should bare such an honorary title above others, it does not exist with me. Merci, Dominus, I will be ready for her when she calls."*

Trenton responded that all was good and bid his friend a good night in Rashawn's own language to show his invested support of them, *"Très bien alors. Bonne nuit, mon ami."*

When Trenton returned, he found Diesel had started a game of chess with Amelia. It was a bit more power play than he would have urged her to take back in for the night, but then Diesel still had her kneeling at his feet. And the preverbal threat to spank her when she reached out to make her next move, suggested his brother was playing dirty and there was never any allowance for self-propriety when he did that.

"I should attach Kat's mouth to your cock to level out the playing field."

"I would swear a brotherhood oath, I'd never look at another chessboard for such a gift from you," Diesel chuckled, reaching down to play with Amelia's hair while she looked for a different move that wouldn't displease him.

Trenton went back to the sofa and waved his slave to his lap and stole a kiss from her lips. "Amelia, were you given any instructions from your Head-Master, should you need him or have any issues after you left?"

Amelia's hand paused over her bishop and dropped her eyes to the floor. Her hand followed. "Yes, Dominus, he did."

"I think this would be a proper time to follow them, then."

☙❧

She leaned over and reached into the satchel sitting on the coffee table and pulled the ten inch tablet out. She didn't open it, not yet. It seemed too precious to do so where others could see, but holding it seemed to be enough.

"Open it and talk to him," Trenton disallowed the procrastination.

"I'll be okay, I promise," her lie spoken so softly she wasn't sure he even heard her.

"You seem to think I was asking. Your Head-Master gave you direct instructions to use the tablet to reach him whenever you needed him. Considerable care went into the planning to safeguard against any separation anxiety as well as to be able to address it if the need arose. Now you must follow *His* instructions."

"I don't know, it all seems so silly, I would not want him to be displeased that I couldn't even go one day without him."

Diesel reached around her, capturing her chin and turned her face up to him, a notion neither of the men did often and it touched her. His dark eyes suddenly revealing more colors than she had realized before. All these years she'd known Diesel Gentry and she had never fully looked into his eyes. Smoky grey rings around halos of dark brown woven in with fibers of hazel green looked deep into her.

"Your post-care is as important to him as your surrender, but just as surrender doesn't happen if you don't let go, his care can't be delivered if you don't go to him for it. You have to learn to turn to him," he spoke gently to her.

"It's just—"

"Amelia," Trenton called firmly to stop her thoughts from side tracking.

"But no one has ever been there." She pulled her chin from Diesel's fingers and dropped her gaze to the floor, feeling as empty now as she was when they had brought her home. She heard Trenton get up, felt him when he lowered down behind her.

"You're not even giving him the chance to prove you wrong. You're calling checkmate without allowing him a move."

"I am pretty good at chess." She almost smiled.

"Like a mule." He reached around her and slowly turned open the cover on the tablet, then pushed the power button.

"I'm topping from the bottom again, aren't I?" she asked, watching as the screen came up and there in the upper corner was a small icon of a mask around the scrolling initials: HM.

Trenton took her hand, manipulated her finger then pointed her toward the icon, "Yes— you are," he whispered in a deep resonating tone that sent chills down her spine.

He always had been able to affect her that way. But now she had met a man who affected her in much the same way and so much more. She felt the affirmation of Trenton's kiss press against the back of her head.

"But now you know how to stop and let go."

She nodded.

She did. Her Head-Master had shown her how and she needed to go to him so he could make her head and heart right.

She sucked in a deep soft breath, letting it go and her mind with it, and she touched the icon on the screen.

CHAPTER NINE

<u>MONDAY</u>

Rashawn stepped into the elevator, his thoughts on the days before all up to the second he glanced up finding Amelia inside, her finger poised over the hold button. They stood as if time paused around them. *Did she have any idea how he desired her? Could she feel it?* His hand floated up, resting his fingers over hers and gently pressed them down. The slight variation in her breath told him she had to be feeling something. "*Bonjour, Mademoiselle* Quinneth." He greeted with a savvy tone and deepened in his native French accent.

Her lips moved, it was almost a blushing smile kept under a veil. "Rashawn." His name spoken like a warm tonic of whisky and caramel that brought a much bigger smile to his lips. "Amelia." *My pet.* He stepped in farther just as the door slid closed, standing slightly behind her, then leaned into her, reaching back around to press the 14th floor. He took advantage of the moment, taking in a deep inhale— *mmmm, so good, my pet.* "You smell tantalizing today."

He heard the faint catch in her breath and he retreated politely. He was her Head-Master, but she had no indication it was him. However, the prospects of blurring the lines over the next five days would be an alluring experience. Trenton Leos was a genius.

He stared at the back of her head on the ride up, recalling the softness of her hair, and he let his gaze follow the tendrils flowing down her backside, stopping just above her waist. He recalled how they tickled his thighs as he positioned her to sit over his cock and pressed her head back off her shoulders while he thrust up, deep inside her. He let the mental image in his head transform into a fantasy of more present locations.

She was dressed to kill. The body forming navy-blue hobble skirt hemmed just above the knee had him raising a brow at her frisky empowerment this morning. He could just picture the matching navy heels with the white toe caps she was wearing propped up on his shoulders as he licked her ankles just seconds after putting shackles around them. Her hard, button-sized, nipples wrapped and out of sight inside her white blouse with blue piping still had a mouth-watering effect on him.

He clenched his fists at his side just to hold himself back. For, what he wanted most was to spin her around, and slam her back against the elevator wall. He'd rip that skirt right up its center and capture her legs in his arms, taking the ground on, which she stood, out from under her. Make her completely reliant on him while he ravaged her lips in a fierce kiss. Their kaleidoscope of reflections joining in on the orgy of an unhinged kiss.

Then somewhere between the 12th and 14th floor he would return her to her heels, kiss her forehead tenderly along with a caress of his thumb against her cheek, and then step away just as the doors slid open to deliver them to the day's normalcy. He'd bid her good day with a wicked grin and leaving her with that teasing deposition until she caved later in the day and called him to her office for a *private* conference.

He looked forward to having a few of those.

But alas, the doors did open, his dreamed up escapades of her unventured, and he watched as she stepped off without even a glance back over her shoulder. *If only you would let down that last wall, my pet,* he thought as he too stepped off and headed for his own office in the other direction. But before she got too far down the hall, he pulled out his cell phone, reached behind his back and snapped off a picture. He brought it around to test the captured image and grinned at the only slightly eschewed capture of his pet's perfect *swish* making her way down the corridor in the movement-restrictive skirt. *He had, after all, instructed her last night to wear something prohibitive to the office.* And he had to applaud her for her definition of his command.

Amelia sat back behind her desk after her conference call with one of her brothers still held up in Germany. A few delays there but the business deal was still underway.

She rubbed at her temple and for the first time in however long that she could not recall she did not feel the built up stress that had haunted her. She felt revived in all things, the way a relaxing vacation on a remote island, swinging in a hammock enjoying fruity cocktails and the salty air was meant to cure the compounding stress. Only, no vacation had done such for her. She had escaped to some of the most tranquil and exotic places on the globe and not one had done for her what thirty-six hours with her mystery Master had. She felt so at rest, having found that moment of inner peace that came with letting go that not even her brother was able to push her buttons this morning. A transformation she had chased all her life but never truly arrived to until *Him.*

She logged into her computer, scanned over the remaining itinerary for her day. She had a meeting downstairs with her publishing staff, Business Journal Weekly wanted to do an interview to follow up on the Ümran Global Management's summit that was held in June. Later, she had a board meeting scheduled that was likely going to take up the remainder of her business day. What she would give to be able to fast forward through her day. She'd bribe her driver to push the speed limit to rush her home where the tablet waited for her, so she could wait for His call.

A light knock on her door pulled at her attention. "Yes, come in."

Anna Phillip, her Executive Assistant, poked her head in, her near platinum hair pulled back in a neat bun still stood out in eye catching contrast with the gray skirt and lime blouse. "Miss Quinneth, a package has arrived for you."

"Very well, bring it in, Anna. Where's Robert?"

"Still out on the errand run," she answered curtly.

"Still?"

"You did give him nearly a dozen stops to make." She shrugged back.

Amelia glanced at her watch realizing it'd only been an hour since she sent him out. "It feels like I have been here all day already."

"Perhaps some tea?"

"That sounds good but have one of the others bring it up. I have some files I need you to go through and it won't be any fun. Or a brisk task."

"Yes, Miss Quinneth," she responded, setting the said arrival on Amelia's desk.

Amelia sucked in a deep breath fighting back the warm smile. A plain glossy black bag now sat on her desk. Teal colored tissue spilled from its top and the stem of several red orchids sprouted out over the ruffles.

She noted Anna standing there waiting to hear juicy details. *Not a chance.* And Amelia cocked a brow up at her assistant. "That will be all, Anna."

"Spoil sport." Her assistant of six years playfully frowned at her, but dutifully left.

Amelia waited until she heard the click of her office door close before reaching for the surprise arrival. She pulled the stem of orchids out, bringing it up to her nose even though she knew it would hold no scent. *How had Mother Nature created something as lovely looking as the orchid, but forget to give it the fragrance it was meant to have?* Only it was just then Amelia's nose surprised her. She felt the slight tickle— *it couldn't be.* She inhaled again, but there was no mistaking the naughty mix of male essence and her favorite perfume: Imperial Majesty. She peeked in the bag finding the card:

~~ Such exotic things should smell as beautiful and tantalizing as My pet. ~~

There was no stopping the blush the suggestive message the card and gift sent and she licked at her lips trying to contain the mischievous smile from growing into a permanent feature on her face. Besides— there was more to be found inside her secret black bag. Inside, waiting in turn was a palm size black velvet bag.

She pulled the bag out and poured out its contents and out slipped an elegantly shaped black vibrating egg into the palm of her hand. Her breath quickened with the expectations of his command for her to use it tonight while he watched her on the video camera.

Never taking her eyes off the toy, she reached into the bag one more time and pulled out the final item. Amelia's mouth gaped open and she struggled to take a full breath as she stared at the internet camera. A tag hanging precariously with his orders scribbled on it:

~~ Install it now, My pet. ~~

She felt lightheaded within the swirling warmth that licked over her body, reminding her of the things her new Master could make her feel and how potent that such small items tossed into an inconspicuous bag would bring all those illustrious reactions back to the surface.

She followed his commands, clipping the camera to the top of her monitor and plugged in the usb cable. The computer picked up on the new device and loaded up a driver, and after an approval from her, the same small icon from her tablet appeared on her desktop.

She glanced at her watch, then to her little palm size gift. Too bad she was out of time already. She had to wonder if he had purposely calculated her busy scheduled days to count on them, so his gifts only further teased her with a torturous finesse.

She kissed the cards that held his hand writing, then returned the egg to its velvet seclusion and tucked them away in the top drawer of her desk. But the effects of His gift followed her, lingering in her thoughts throughout the day.

CHAPTER TEN

Amelia forced herself to close Katianna's recent manuscript submission after only a couple of chapters and set it aside on the corner of her desk. She shouldn't have allowed herself to read it, knowing she was under strict commands from her Head-Master not to touch herself. But given her voyeuristic gift from him, when she saw Kat's book had been dropped off that morning, passing up on it was a temptation she had no will to go against.

But now that she'd done so, following orders seemed a battle she wasn't likely going to win. Because Katianna Dumas held the title as her star erotic writer for a reason and this one was her friend's first submission since being collared to the Dominus. The title alone: *Becoming His Slave* did Amelia in and she snatched it up to crack it open before her board meeting later today. Anna knew her all too well, knowing to block all calls when she waved the eight hundred something pages of ring bound paper as she passed.

"You're going to share right?" her assistant whimpered.

Oh, that tid-bit of power-play was what condemned Amelia. Some heavy reading, heavier breathing, and a new toy that needed some breaking in. *Oh, it was good to be me*, she thought proudly to herself and closed the door to her office retreat.

But the next bestseller to hit the naughty hot pages wasn't the only thing she found entertaining; she had one more secret she didn't share with anyone, which brewed a far different salacious ingredient to her private debauchery.

Amelia leaned back in her chair behind her desk, resting over on the arm rest, her eyes flickering to the image on the monitor screen of her computer— and the man she was watching on it.

Rashawn had picked up the habit of remaining in the conference room long after the board had dismissed for the day, or before, as it would seem today. He conducted a majority of his daily tasks in the large opulence it offered. While she had provided him with an excellent office of his own, it didn't have the extraordinary view the board room did, looking out over the Hudson River as it flowed past the green lady. He seemed to have a preference to open spaces. Giving him room to pace as he talked on the phone. Not to mention the view must have appealed to his immaculate taste. Its entire length along the external wall of the meeting hall was uninterrupted tinted glass looking out over South Street.

He'd also seemed to take a liking to sitting in *her* chair. It was amusing, but she liked it better when he kept to his own chair where she could see him unobstructed. Today, was a dark violet colored shirt paired with the silk tie of charcoal gray, creased with metallic shimmering gray. His sleeves rolled up revealing muscular arms tanned from the Mediterranean sun and dusted with dark hairs. She watched with greater anticipation now after the show he'd given her last week, unbeknownst she was certain, but oh how she had enjoyed spying in on him when he pulled his thick cock out and slowly stroked himself to full mast then came all over his exposed chest. She even laughed to herself, watching the devil smear his seed over Stanley Hostimshires' chair before leaving for the day.

So far today, he spent considerable time chewing on the end of his pen and she could just imagine those same teeth closing down over her hard aching nipples. How on earth would she last a whole week before she returned to her Head-Master's feet? The man with no name or face, dropped her off Sunday morning and he'd told her quite specifically not to touch herself in any way until he came for her again. But she couldn't help it, the two day experience had thrown her into a powerful vortex of pleasure she had never experienced before.

He had truly mastered her body into a perfect dulcet of pleasure and pain. Delivering every inch of her body into euphoric bliss like no other had ever brought her to and she ached to relive it again. Even if it was just a moment, here, as she watched an alluring man of exquisite taboo working in her company while she masturbated to the heightened sensation of her blindfolded memory and the salacious words of a talented author.

It was an effort, but she managed to finally get her skirt pulled up, thanks to Lycra infused fabrics. Her heart quickening at her mischievousness as she slid her hand between her thighs. She let out a sigh at the first touch of her fingertips against her wet lips. And when she watched Rashawn spin his chair around to stare out the glass walls while his hand dropped into this lap to stroke at the impressive bulge in his slacks.

Any reservation she had that she should do as her Master ordered were gone and her fingers thrust deep inside the slick folds of her cunt. Her body curled involuntarily as she stroked over nerves still alive from her Head-Master's sadistic lessons and she imagined, for just a moment, her Master had been the handsome young working himself in the conference room.

Oh god, she ached and needed. She was addicted to what her Master could give her and she needed it now. *Tomorrow Yesterday*. She couldn't wait.

And she was digging in the drawer for the present hidden there.

The hunger lashed in her insides until her fingers were not enough, her other hand joined in the wave of self-annihilation she now gave with the vibrating egg from her desk drawer. One hand thrusting inside her while the other circled her clit.

She let her head fall back, succumbing to the self-made visions in her fantasies. Feeling her Master's thick cock sliding deep inside her, one slow slide after another. Building her up in an anguishing wave of pleasure and heat. His firm grip on her hips as he pushed in hard and faster with each sinking penetration.

Her fingers struggled to perform the fantasy. She recalled the warmth of his body as he folded over her, his arms encasing her as she shivered with reckless abandon, and when he told her to cum for him that was when her orgasm hit so hard, she cried out— *Master.*

Amelia clamped her teeth down on her lips as the rippling pulse fired off from her clit. It jolted her body with a shocking wave that threatened to be expressed verbally. She couldn't tell you the last time she had been able to make herself cum at her own hand. Yet here she was feeling the chilled quiver racing down her spine while imaginary visions took over her reality.

~~ The wave ended too soon and only partially sated as she slumped over in her chair letting her breathing return to a calmer rhythm. A light knock on her door roused her and she quickly returned her skirt to its proper place, but her visitor entered before she could do little else.

"Rashawn." She stood to attention, not fully sure why but it was too late; sitting back down would only give her startled position away. To cover her eagerness, she grabbed her attaché and moved around the desk, feeling every bit of her juices on her thighs. "I was just on my way out."

"I had hoped to catch you before you left for the day. I wanted to go over some things."

Caught me in the act you did. "I'm afraid it will have to wait. I'm already running late," she tried to divert him.

Aware that her office smelled of activated cologne and sex. An inappropriate tonic in front of a colleague.

Rashawn quickly stepped in front of her, blocking her escape. "I insist." His eyes impaling her feet to the floor. He slowly reached down, taking one of her hands, and brought it to his lips as he reached for her other. She stared in horror as he slowly lifted her other hand. She tore from his gaze to her traveling hand, aware it still contained the scent and glaze of the cream she had spilled in her orgasm and she fought the urge to pull away.

He paused, his lips brushing the back of her knuckles. She felt the thick knot develop in the pit of her belly. Her eyes glued on him as he sucked in a deep inhale and then she felt his tongue as it laved over her fingertips, hooking one finger, and pulling the single digit into his mouth. His warm wet tongue curling around it and sucked it all the way back leaving nothing unsavored.

He moaned at the discovery and then returned her hands to her sides. His gaze turned piercing. "You have been a very naughty girl, Amelia. I'm wondering if I should just put you over my knee right here and now." His dark voice wrapped around her, holding her tightly in his command.

"Head-Master?" the whispered gasp escaped her lips. ~~

CHAPTER ELEVEN

"Amelia?" Her name was called out shattering the vision in her mind.

Amelia bolted up with a start, blinking hard as she discovered Rashawn standing just inside her office door. Her gaze flickered to the monitor screen sans the man she had been forebodingly fantasizing about and back to where he stood in the flesh.

While his expression reserved some form of naiveté' to what he had just interrupted, his eyes said something completely different. Something all knowing. She sucked in a deep breath to gather her wits and hoped it would cool down the temperature that seemed to surround her.

Keeping her movements smooth and slow, she eased her skirt back down in the safety behind her desk as if doing nothing more than smoothing it out as she regained a more professional posture from the more surrendered one, she was just in.

"Mr. Matisse, my employees generally knock before entering," she snipped.

"My apologies, *Mademoiselle* Quinneth. I did knock. However, I guess I mistook the sound you made as a call to enter. Perhaps you were dreaming." He stepped in farther. "You have been working hard this past week. You must have fallen asleep at your desk."

"I assure you, I did not. Was there something you wanted to see me about, Mr. Matisse?" Amelia closed her eyes for a moment to settle her rattled nerves. She had not meant to be so snippy with him, but she had been caught in an act that was utterly inexcusable. To be sitting here, dreaming of a man so much younger than her and an employee no less. It was about as unprofessional and unforgivable as acts went. *Foolish woman and your guilt. He doesn't know what you were dreaming, only that your hand was halfway up your cunt.* She let out a deep inhale with a streaming pucker. "Please excuse my rudeness, Rashawn. It *has* been a long day." She stood from her desk and walked over to the small bar and washed her hands in the small sink as she felt all the more self-conscious.

"Accepted. I had just stepped in to let you know the final contracts have been drawn up and ready for your approval before being sent out to Ümran Global."

Amelia dried her hands, took a deep breath, and finally turned to face him. "Very good. I'm quite proud of the work you've done to save these companies, Mr. Matisse." Her hand went out to receive the portfolio jacket that contained the reports he was offering.

She flipped through them. It would take some time to read over them all, but a few details jumped off the page at her and she tapped at them with a manicured nail. She glanced up at him. "Are these, time bearing? I have pending plans this weekend—"

"Keep your plans. But I do have other concerns to bring up in the meeting."

"Not today, I hope."

"No, Mademoiselle, but I would like to strongly request to have the platform on Wednesday's meeting."

"It's that pressing?"

"Yes, but a few days will not change any outcome of the contracts."

"Very well, Wednesday's platform is yours. And I'll go through these first thing in the morning." She turned on her toes, taking the reports to her desk, "Also, Business Journals Weekly wants to do a follow up on Ümran Global. I told them you would contact them next week to set up an interview."

"You want me to do the interview?" Rashawn gave her a raised brow with his glance.

"Of course. It is your concept."

"But it is your company, Amelia."

"I take plenty of credit. Please, do the interview, Mr. Matisse." Offering him a proud warm grin. "Now, if you would please get out of my office. I still have another thirty minutes before today's meeting and I want no visitors until then.

Amelia was one of a kind. While her position, and strength to maintain it meant she could scold even the most potent, stubborn-minded men with lasting effects, her face glowed when she was proud of the people she employed, especially when their dedication and knowledge was put to the benefit of all.

It was only a fraction of what he saw in her face now.

"*Avec plaisir.*" He bowed his head, purposely to let his tone drop an octave. Letting the word *pleasure* roll off his tongue like a tease meant to lick her breasts. The visible gasp of air that left her body told him it had worked. But then again, he could smell her honey the moment he'd stepped into the office.

Such fragrant succulence. And *sooo* naughty of her.

CHAPTER TWELVE

<u>TUESDAY</u>

"Mr. Matisse? There is someone here to see you. His accent is pretty thick, but I believe he said he was your father." Riana from the front desk was delivering the message to the boardroom, where he craftily worked void of phones and intercoms that could interrupt him.

Rashawn's face crumpled in surprised bafflement, "My father. Here? Hmm, please tell him I will be right down." He glanced at the gentleman he'd been interviewing to fill the position of assistant sitting across from him. An important need that he had yet to find someone he felt confident of since his arrival. This one was at least going to stay in the running. "Thank you for coming in on such short notice, Donathon. I still have two more applicants I would like to give a chance to impress me, before I make my final decision, but you are certainly among the finals. One last question, if I called you Friday to say you had the position, would you be able to start first thing Monday? I have several international conferences approaching, and need to rush the acclimation I am afraid.”

“Thank you, sir, Monday would not be a problem, if it’s an urgent matter, I could come in over the weekend.”

“No, that’s quite alright. I won’t ever be asking you to sacrifice your weekends. Love your job, but don’t marry it. The pleasure isn’t the same.” Rashawn laughed and stood, signaling even the chatter was over and offered a shake of his hand, “Thank you again for coming in. *Bonsoir.*”

The well-groomed light brunette man took his hand and nodded his thanks and left with Rashawn following behind.

When he got to the reception desk just before the elevator, sure enough there stood Cardiff Matisse.

"Father, what brings you here? Are you not well?” Rashawn quizzed the unexpected visit.

Cardiff spun around as he heard his son’s voice, his face brightening as always. “*Oui* surprise.” Cardiff held his arms out wide to welcome an embrace.

Rashawn hugged his father and exchanged the customary kiss to each cheek. “Surprise most definitely. Why did you not call to say you were coming?” More quizzing but not an ounce of suspicion would he ever throw at his father, but any out-of-ordinary habits from him always had Rashawn concerned after the incident at the Elysian Fields Banquet and Bi-Annual Auction Gathering back in July.

“*Ah,* I have taken on a new commission for a design and I am here in the big city of New York to meet with the man. But I have a new phone and I could not find your number so I came here to find you.”

“Mr. Matisse?” One of the receptionists interrupted.

“Yes.” Her query got a double response from both him and his father.

“What is it?” Rashawn alone followed up.

“Business Journal Weekly is on the line calling back. They’re asking if you could meet them later today for the interview. They’d like to have it out this week.”

Rashawn looked at his watch, thought a moment then nodded his head before returning his attention back to his father and the good news he’d delivered. “I’m glad you are working again.” Rashawn smiled.

“*Psh*—” Cardiff slapped a hand down through the air with a quibbling pucker of his lips, “What was I to do? Fambleush has banned me from the museum.”

“Can you blame him?” Rashawn still wore his grin then waved an arm out to lead his father back to his office, “Come. I have a few things to finish up and then I will take you out for lunch.” Also, to take the conversation away from prying ears. His father was not a shy man, on any subject. Only here, the reception of such eavesdropping may not be the same as from those back home in Paris, France who often would squeal like fangirls to a music concert to overhear such unadulterated words from the *Gramaire* Cardiff Matisse.

“*Hmm* food—” Cardiff glanced around as if worried someone might catch him doing something forbidden, then leaned toward his son, “Hope it doesn’t take long.

I would like to eat without Hitler breathing over my plate."

"Hitler?"

Cardiff shook his head, "You've not spoken to my foolish friend, I see?"

"Only to know you are in good hands at home."

They slowly walked together, his father's presence turning a few heads to get a look at him. He was certainly an eye catcher. Long silver hair that fell well beyond his shoulders like a cascading waterfall with only a faint reminisce of the gold blonde locks he once had whispered through it. His beard trimmed down neat against his face during the summer months, but it was more his attire. He had a liking for salwar kameez and kurtas from Eastern cultures with only a few rare times would the man make an attempt to wear tradition modern European or American clothes. And often it was a mish mosh attempt, pairing up a fine linen dress shirt with thin silk ties, and always a loose flowing skirt that usually touched the floor. Of the few times Rashawn recalled his father wearing pants, they were the aligarhi pajama type. Clothes, his father often said, were too binding. They stifled the soul and choked off the energy used to create art. And it wasn't unusual to find his father painting in his studio completely naked with the windows open to let in the breeze— as well as provide a free view to anyone with binoculars.

Today was a mosh-posh day. A homespun tweed vest of chunky blue and off-white herringbone worn over a light blue button up shirt. His cream jacket was about as crimped and unlovely as spilled out sails. But the final touch was the flowing tan twill, floor length skirt and the sandaled toes that showed with each step. Rashawn chuckled to himself, because there was only so much restrictiveness his father could handle, not even for a new client. Cardiff was his own man and the women loved him.

Rashawn waited until they were in his office and behind closed doors before asking more personal matters, "How are you, Father. Are you well?"

Cardiff took him by the shoulders and nodded happily before hugging him warmly. "I am an old artist. Madness is who I am, but I am well." He tapped his temple with a wrinkled, aged finger. "I still have some good stuff up here before I go up there." He pointed upward. "To join Da Vinci and Angelo."

"I just wish I was made known you were coming for a visit. I would have warned you it is not a good time for me to keep a guest." Rashawn waved a hand to a chair at his desk and closed the door so they could have some privacy.

"*Psh,* who has time for such visit. Neither you, nor I. I've come on business, but I could not be here and not come to see my great son at least once. What sort of father would I be then? I do still have some qualities aside my madness."

Rashawn offered a soft chuckle as he sat down behind his desk, not at all remorseful of the gesture he'd just made before his father. Rather, he knew Cardiff would feel a pride in witnessing the power display. The rendering smile on his father's face just then confirmed it. "Tell me more of this new architect design."

"*Psh,* is not much. But it will be my first sky rise. My new client is looking for a design for his new building project that will suit his eclectic tastes. A penis to tower over all other glass phalluses of the globe."

"But you've returned to architecture. That is good."

"*Oui.* But what choice did I have, I am banished until Fambleush sees fit to say otherwise."

"Can you blame him? He feared you might try to destroy the sculpted Saint Laurent Black Marble sculpture." Rashawn's thoughts going to the magnificent larger than life angel his father had carved. Its large black marble wings reaching overhead toward the ceiling as the fallen angel stretched out over another figure that bore his father's likeness in a pose that suggested the ultimate seduction. It had been the most beautiful thing Rashawn had ever seen made by his father *and* the most disturbing to those who knew his father closest.

"I would not have destroyed it." Cardiff took a defense to the accusation.

"You destroyed the Green Ascota sculpture that resembled that same man."

"But that was in a fit of rejected rage when Paris left. This time it was different. I would not have destroyed the statue. "Okay, perhaps I would have chiseled away the old man under my angel so that I could lay under its raging cock myself, then fucked myself to my utter death."

Rashawn all but dropped his jaw to the floor that his father would openly make such a statement and wondered if letting his father roam around freely was such a good idea or not.

"*Ah—*" Cardiff waved both hands up in the air at him., "Do not worry over me. All Masters have demons and ghosts within them. While they may not define us, they are a large part of what drives us. We are not infallible men. And sadly, I lost myself to a temptation for a time. But I have since made peace with my demons. Why, I even named it Caligula. It seemed rather fitting. Minus the evil tyrant parts."

"And your slaves? How are they taking to such disruptions?"

Cardiff hung his head a moment then nodded his conviction before meeting his questioning gaze. "I have sent them all to a new home and Master. All but Rachel. My loyal and trusted personal assistant."

Rashawn didn't recognize the name. "Father, you never had a slave named Rachel."

"Ah, it is because she is not truly mine. She is Fambleush's Rachel. But she takes great care of me." He waved a finger like an exclamation in the air, "Only the little Hitler demoness reports my every movement to Fam and then he reports to, of all people on the globe, your *maman*. And that vixen tells all my perverted secrets to my doctor. *Putain* femme. When did she become so— uh— how you say? *Autoritaire?*"

"Bossy," Rashawn clucked the translation out, tucked his chin. His mother was anything but that. "Father? Who do you think my mother is?" He was actually more concerned that Cardiff might be becoming sucked into another false illusion.

"Don't question me in such ways. I had an emotional breakdown not a complete detachment of reality. *Your* mother, the royal princess hotelier of Monaco! She came to see me. She waved her little pinky at me and I fell in love with her grace all over again. She has enslaved me now. Put me under her spell. Why, I am being forced to follow a diet and she is behind it all." Cardiff wagged a finger in the air then gave him a wink. "A man should be able to *se laisser aller* in *chocolat* if he wishes," he stammered over his right to indulge in chocolate candies if he wanted to.

"Your French is slipping," Rashawn chuckled.

"*Oui, je suis Français*, 'tis allowed— *psh.*"

Rashawn burst out in a hard laugh. "So where is this Rachel *Hilter* now?"

"I— I sent her on a fool's errand and it must have slipped my mind to tell her I was coming to see you. I won't have my time with you monitored by a cast of hens."

Rashawn could only shake his head at that. But he supposed he couldn't blame him. His father had, until just recently, been considered a renowned Head-Master as well as a sought after artist. While it was perfectly natural and acceptable by society's rules for an artist to go mad. In the Bdsm community however, it was not so welcomed. And there was no keeping it under disclosure as the whole of Trenton Leos' auction guests had witnessed the Master of twelve sexual submissive deviants have a melt down over one he'd not been able to keep. And that incident wasn't so long ago to just dismiss as having been a whim or could be so easily cured.

"Do not worry about me, *mon fils*. My days as a *Gramaire* may be over, but life is still a masterpiece to be explored. Now, you mentioned lunch."

Rashawn smiled, feeling a little better about his concerns for his father. "I did." He tapped a button on his phone.

"*Yes, Mr. Matisse?*" the reception desk answered his call.

"Hold my calls for a bit, I'll be going out for lunch today."

"*Yes, sir.*"

"Shall we then?" Rashawn directed the invite to his father as he got up.

They walked together, Cardiff already making light comments about the beautiful women around the office.

"Monsieur Matisse!" Someone called from behind them and again both men turned to respond.

Rashawn grinned and stopped his father from answering. "He means me,"

"Sorry, sir," Robert, Amelia's personal assistant came running up to catch them, "Miss Quinneth has asked that you stop by her office on your way out to sign some papers."

"Very well," he answered to Robert then turned to his father. "Come, I will give you the grand pleasure of being introduced to my boss."

He should have known his father would turn to the seducer and invite Amelia to join them. So good at the craft, no women could ever refuse him. Surprisingly, not even the Heiress Amelia Quinneth.

And of course, Cardiff had Amelia sitting next to him. Which turned out rather advantageous for himself. His father was still all the French flirt he ever was, such charm and wit poured from him. He exuded perversion in the most proper of etiquette that he'd never known a slap from a lady's hand for his scandalous tongue. However, Amelia blushed often and from here, Rashawn was able to watch every red and pink shade of them.

"So, tell me. Have you not treated yourself with a lovely sub from Dominus's services?"

Rashawn hesitated a moment. He hadn't planned to have such a conversation in front of Amelia just yet, but then again, a small one of the subject might help in blurring the lines some. "No. I have not."

"I am surprised."

"Why should you be? I have had my fill of plenty from such playthings. Now, I am looking for the one that is most fulfilling and I can't possibly do that if the place at my feet is already occupied."

"Ha!" Their small corner of the restaurant filled with the laughter of Cardiff. "You even sound like the Dominus; how you keep such playthings at arm's length and search the globe for precious prizes."

"I have your eclectic taste and my mother's immaculate expectations to blame for it."

❧

Amelia had only been partly following the ebb and flow of conversation between the two, so it took some moments before she realized what they had been talking about. The key words seeping into her inner jumble of thoughts and lit up like Paris's Red Light District. She dropped her fork and looked up at Reshawn.

"Amelia? Are you okay? You look as if you'd seen a ghost."

She quickly regained her composure, tapping her lip with a finger nail. "My apologies, I— I knew you knew Trenton Leos, but I guess I never even gave it any thought that you knew him in other manners."

"Mr. Leos has never been one to be remiss of his Lifestyle. To know him is to know of him and his status."

"This is true." And help it or not, she felt the heat rise up in her face with a full bloom of red. "So you are a Player? I mean you're a Dom?" Amelia sucked in a hard breath trying hard not to out herself or stutter over the subject lines either. She wasn't so certain she was successful of either.

"Dom?" Cardiff spilled abruptly, "Pfft, My son is a Head-Master. He should train if he would just take the time."

❧

That was a touch deeper than Rashawn wanted said between he and Amelia. And a quick glance at his father said as much. Good thing the old man understood, and barely a perceivable nodded compliance was sent back to him while remaining quiet.

"I have— particular tastes. Ones that are not so easily fulfilled. I could have my choice of many submissive ladies. And enough connections to find the ultimate surrender for my bed, but my need's fulfillment comes from a much stronger need from my submissive.

"I—" Amelia fidgeted, her warm red glow spreading across her chest and the evident deep breath rose there as well as he watched with keen interest in her responses, "I, *uhm*— what does that mean exactly?"

"Most submissives want to surrender a moment of time in their day to the care and protection of a Dominant. They find a form of peace and arousal there. Contrary to common misinformation, submission isn't a weakness, but perhaps strength is such a burden to some that their need to surrender it is vital for their wellbeing. I—" he stopped, falling in thought. But there was really no way to explain what he wanted from a woman except what he wanted was called: *Amelia Quinneth.* The smile broke on his face and he glanced up. "I'm not sure how to put it in words. Trenton has a word for it: he calls them *Unicorns.* I suppose that is as good as any. Because after having carried the heavy burden of power throughout the day, her life, her emotions, her heart, her mind— must be turned over to her Master at the end of the day. Complete and total surrender for the rest of her life. When she walks through that door, she knows to shed everything and come straight to me to be rescued from it. It is the greatest need a man could be asked to care for."

"Women with such power over themselves, and others, never surrender in such a way. You'd have better luck chasing a fairy. They just don't exist." Cardiff scoffed at his son's ideals.

Rashawn's eyes shifted to her, pinning her in place, everything seemed to slip away and she fell into the dark pools of his eyes. "She does exist," he spoke the words softly and directly at her.

Amelia didn't say a word. She felt dizzy, and frightened. Because she *was* that kind of woman.

The two men continuing in the debate of her existence as if being heard from underwater. It became hard to breathe. To come face to face with a man who desired what she had wept and cried from because she wanted to let go of everything, just for a moment, an hour, a day, a second, just please take it away, and hold her, kiss her forehead— croon dirty words to her, and make her cum until she cried for other reasons. Why of all the men she could hear it come from was it spoken from a man so much younger than her? Life was so cruel.

"And how will you find such a woman?" Cardiff asked his son, never even noticing the panic she feared was lit in her eyes.

"I will know her by the beauty I could only dream of and within her fire which ignites an uncontrollable urge of desire I cannot live without."

"And if you do not find such a woman? What becomes of you then?"

"It's not finding one, a Dominant should be afraid of. It's finding her and not being able to touch her because she isn't ready. There is no greater torment for him."

On their way back to the office, Rashawn offered an apology to her. "I'm sorry for my father. About the topic he brought up. He has a way of bringing such things out as if everyone in the world were as open as he is. I hope my confessions didn't frighten you. I assure you, I am a private man, and my Lifestyle is harmless. I won't reflect poorly on the firm."

"Harmless, except for maybe the submissive you seek."

"Ah, yes, but she will like it that way." He laughed to make light of it even if she didn't make a joke of it herself. "Let me make it up to you."

Amelia's inside were still whirling around in a turmoil of uncertainty. "How so?"

"Dinner. Thursday night."

So confident, nor did he actually ask. He told with a soft spoken word. She recognized the commanding tone now. Subtle, but strong. Making her weak in her knees to hear another from his lips. But she couldn't give into it. "Oh, I don't know, Rashawn— I *ah—*"

❦

"*J'adorerais te voir,* is what you need to say. I have a shoe box of IOUs from you and now I am cashing in on them. You owe me," he drew firmer, more convincing, taking away the yield he'd allowed for escaping and fidgeting. No more dodging. The window was open, lines were now set in the light. Now it was time for him to blur and narrow the gap between himself as Rashawn and as her Head-Master. He had little time to work with, so every command and suggestion he made was calculated to lure her into her desires and to let go of her inhibitions. "Thursday night."

Amelia nodded before she even realized it.

"*Très bien.* We'll leave from the office to catch an early dinner then a show at the theatre."

"No. Wait— I— I have to check on something first before I can say for certain. Please."

"Very well, but I will be utterly wounded if you disappoint me."

By the end of the day, Amelia sat behind her desk, staring out into the empty space of her office, her thoughts in a torment, while fantasies ran amuck. Self-designed visions of her Head-Master filled her mind, but so did Rashawn's face. The conversation from lunch replaying in her head over and over and became overlapped with the commands whispered in her ear by her Head-Master. Only now in her mind she *saw* Rashawn's lips move as if the words had been spoken by him. She felt the warmth spread across her body and felt the moisture already building between her thighs, then played out a visual of Rashawn's hand slipping under her skirt to finger fuck her in the elevator just to see if he could make her cum before they reached the floor where their offices were.

"Stop. You can't keep doing this to yourself, Amelia," she snapped out loud to herself. Tearing her daydreaming from her mind and redirected her gaze to the computer screen. She pulled up a file and then Rashawn's face came up on her screen, along with all his credentials. Namely his birthdate.

Thirty-five.

He was eleven years her younger. *Why did he have to be so damn young and such a temptation?*

She even knew what it felt like to have his arms around her. They had been in Paris. They had just closed the summit meeting and managed to save two major companies from being closed down. He'd pulled her in so close she was pressed against his body and she felt, or rather she wanted what she felt to be his arousal for her.

"*Ugh*— you're doing it again. Snap out of this," she stammered and pitched up from her desk and began pacing across the floor. "Why do you do this to yourself?" She stopped and fell back against the glass that looked out over the city of New York. She closed her eyes and sucked in a deep breath and pulled her hands up around her head and envisioned her Head-Master wearing his gladiator mask, holding her wrists in one hand, while the other lifted her leg, silently instructing her to wrap around him. And just when she thought he would drive his cock inside her, he spoke. Only it was Rashawn's voice:

~~ *"Miss Quinneth, can I see you in my office? I have something under my desk that requires your personal touch."* ~~

The sultry words she envisioned sent a wave of warmth that licked over her skin and every nerve ending with a scandalous ferocity she was helpless against.

A gentle knock on the door pulled her back to reality and then her assistant poked his head in. "I'm ready to call it a day. I just wanted to check with you before I go. Do you need anything else?"

Amelia glanced around her office, vast and utterly empty. "No, you can go." *Now you have the whole floor to yourself to drive yourself mad.* "No, wait—"

"Yes, Miss Quinneth?" Robert paused at the door.

"Hang on a second, I'll walk out with you."

CHAPTER THIRTEEN

Home wasn't any different. Amelia stood in the kitchen while her steward and cook gaped at her as she abandoned her gory salad for a thick slice of chocolate cake. And wine.

It didn't really wash down well for her palate but it blurred the conundrum in her mind some. Enough that a second bottle was welcomed. Which she finished off while retreating to her posh bed with a new book in good old fashioned print. But not even the succulent words of Katianna Dumas was enough to keep Amelia distracted. Her mind continued to wander, now seeing herself in place of the scenes drawn out in the erotic romance. Her Head-Master shape-shifted into Rashawn and Rashawn turned into her Head-Master. Until she finally chucked the book across the room and dove her fingers into her hair in utter frustration.

The tablet that sat at her bedside called to her. The one her Head-Master had given to her. She rolled over and snatched it up and turned it on to send him a night's journal entry:

Dear Head-Master,

You've awakened something in me. Freedom or a demon. I do not know which. I lust after things I should not. I play with ideas that cannot be. You crumbled my walls and now I can't find the edges that define me. How I wish you were here, to scoop me up and put me together in a way you know is best for me. Tell me who I am and what it is that pleases me. I'm but a little girl who has gotten outside the walls of the convent and now am lost. I fear I will fall fool to things I know I should not want yet I can't stop the temptation from flirting with me. Helpless to liking the attention my mind and body gives it. Yet without the stays of my corset, I can no longer trust myself to maintain properness.

my submission, Your pet

She read it for grammar, knowing her promise to not edit content. She was to send her journal entries as written on impulse. However, she would see to it, it went properly spelled, and she hit *send message.*

She just sat there a moment then finally placed it up on its stand on the nightstand then laid down staring at it from that position now.

It wasn't but a few moments and the soft tone dial rang out as her Head-Master called her on the skype app. The sound of his calling was enough to lift her spirits already.

"Lay face down on the bed, my pet," he spoke instant commands, right away knowing what she needed and was directing her into position for it.

She rolled over on her stomach, adjusted her pillow then relaxed over it so that she could still look at the image of his dress shirt on the screen. He'd released several buttons to let her have a view of tanned skin and a fair wisp of black hairs peeking out with it. His hands covered in black leather gloves, fitted in smooth perfection rested on his leg, propped up on the other.

"Hello, Beautiful."

Despite her melancholy, the greeting warmed her that he should call her beautiful as if it was her name and already her blue mood was lifting. Such power he had over her. "Hello, Sir," she whispered tearfully, pushing up on her elbows.

"Why is my pet feeling so undone?"

"You've changed me and now I don't know what's happening to me."

"Taking your walls down is like removing your corset, My pet. While your body has been trained to take its shape, removing the confines allows your body to shape to what I want it to be, not what the corset has made it. So once free, I can lick a slow line up your spine to taste your skin. Lie back down and close your eyes," he commanded and she lay down making herself comfortable, then closed her eyes though she didn't want to.

She wanted to see him even if she only saw some small part of him. But this wasn't about what she wanted to do but about what she needed and those commands came from him.

He began to whisper tantric things to her, lulling her into a dream land where she belonged only to him. No longer confused who commanded her body and mind.

"I will hover over you, possessing your space and your body. My warmth will become yours. Not just because of proximity but because I will it to happen. When I drop my hips, my cock will slide between the globes of your ass, they too will abide me, make way for my movements, and one day I will slide inside the forbidden channel and experience your silky nethers. I will slip strands of silk rope around your wrists and flip you over so to the tie them to the headboard. I will lift your legs next and guide your feet to rest on the small of my back, while I continue to hover over you. And slowly as I lower down on top of you, encapsulating your desires under my weight, so complete will you feel when your body takes the shape of being completely surrendered to me.

Feel my kiss pressed to your temple as you drift asleep, My pet, and don't fear the loss of your walls. I will let you know exactly who you are and what you need. And I will take you there."

Amelia drifted asleep, her dreams filled with the man who placed her there, wrapped around his body as he reshaped everything she thought she desired to one that felt right.

WEDNESDAY

Morning came like any other, and her Head-Master was gone. The skype window closed, but she'd not been abandoned. A telegram icon waving on the screen that a message was awaiting her said as much. It was a nice and most needed touch. She reached out, tapping the image to expand and a note made to look like a parchment letter filled the 10 inch screen.

~~ Good morning, My pet. I trust you slept well. I want you to wear something in the color of baby blue or an icy blue. Perhaps a scarf or broach. But it must be visible to the eye.

Head-Master ~~

She ended up selecting an icy blue blouse left open low in the front once she undid one of the buttons.

Downstairs another note was waiting for her accompanied by a white Chrysanthemum.

~~ How beautiful you must look this morning. It is my curse to not be there and see you off. However, I want you to have a productive as well as luxurious day, just don't forget to daydream about me when you get the chance.

Head-Master ~~

Could such fairytales truly come true? She wasn't sure but as she kissed the small, folded card that had delivered the rest of His orders for the day, she couldn't help but hope so.

She was just going over her morning itinerary when her Master dropped in on her chat window. His avatar for the morning was a gloved hand accented with a wide bronzed face watch mounted on a wide leather wrist band. There was no mistaking the *Jorg Hysek* design. The HD3 watches were notorious for viewable inner gears and often carried a price tag that exceeded some exotic cars.

"*Good morning, My pet,*" his words spilled over the Skype line.

"Good morning, Sir." She smiled with every bit of contentment that he should visit her.

"Hmmm, I do enjoy your selection of blue today. Tell me, is it a busy day for you today?"

"I'm afraid so. Board meeting with pressing issues."

"I am envious of the others. How I would enjoy seeing you sitting at the lead of the table. I would deliberately sit your opposite and stare at you, envisioning you stretched out on top of it." His tenor rasp echoed back at her and she envisioned him lounging back on the bed immersed in the covers they shared while he masturbated to her voice. *"Glass?"*

"Hum, what?" Amelia blinked herself back to the present, having gotten swept away into the vision. "I'm sorry what did you ask?"

"Glass, is the table glass?"

"Oh, yes, smoked glass."

"How large?"

She licked her lips doing all she could to maintain her proper composure, "It sits twenty-two men."

"Twenty one," his next response corrected her.

"I beg your pardon?"

"It sits twenty-one men, the twenty-second sitting at the head of the table is very much a woman."

And that was it, she was several shades of feminine pink rouge. But before she got swept away by his charm and forgot, she knew she needed to ask him his permission before she could accept the invitation given by Rashawn. "Head-Master? I- I need— I'm troubled over something."

"*Please feel free to speak with me about anything you wish. I would rather you tell me than feel you cannot be open about everything.*"

"A colleague, one of the men who works for me, has asked me out."

"*This is business?*" He's voice drew closer to the microphone, letting her know he'd leaned in, showing her she had his full attention.

"No, Sir. It's kind of a date."

"*You sound nervous.*"

"I— I don't know."

"*Is he a handsome man? Does eh trat you respectfully?*"

"I— uh— yes. He is handsome. And es, he is exceptionally well mannered."

"*I want you to accept and go out with him,*" he cut her off with his answer.

"What? I— I don't rightly understand."

"*My pet, you are a beautiful woman and it is time you realized how much men desire you and your body. To have moments of time when you are treated and adored as a lady to be wooed. And often. I want you to accept and let him treat you like a lady should be treated. I will even allow an in-kind kiss at the end of your date. But nothing more.*"

"I don't know what to say?"

"*Are you surprised I would allow such things without my presence?*"

"Yes. I am," she worried.

"My pet, it is my way of showing you I give you my trust. I feel no need to worry that you are not mine. You did, after all, contact me to ask my permission, but you obviously do wish to or you would not have asked. But I alone have brought you to experience your true submissive needs, so I know you will not jeopardize our relationship. Have a good evening with him. Let him dash you off your feet, then deliver you home where you become mine again."

Amelia was right back inside her storm of swirling lost boundaries. She didn't even know how to respond but it mattered not, her Master had more business to go over. Namely, the gift he'd sent Monday.

Amelia sucked in a hard breath just two steps inside the boardroom when the little gift now placed up inside the walls of her darker yearnings turned on of no power of her own.

She narrowed her eyes and dragged a manicured fingernail over her lip as she gazed over the board already gathered. *What the hell was she thinking, agreeing to her Master's commands?* She fought the urge to lick her lips and instead clenched her muscles around the egg that pulsed in a slow strobing vibration, like a flashing traffic light. *Help me please, I must have asked for this, but let me get through this meeting.* And she stepped over, taking her seat at the head of the table.

Pure reaction from the waist down. *Thank goodness for tables.* This must be how some men feel when they get erections at inappropriate times. *But who the hell gets a hard-on during a board meeting?* Her thoughts went just a touch ferocious briefly before she reined herself back in.

"Gentlemen," she let the word draw out cool and on point, calling their attention to her. "We have quite a bit to go over, so let us begin."

 The rustle and murmuring chatter hushed and their attention turned to her.

"Last week's drop in the Dow Jones—" her mind started into the business that she was pristine at, but behind it all a storm carried on intervals of purring and humming. Miraculously just as she hardened up her internal defense so she could begin the meeting it all stopped. Allowing the respite for thoughts to work unhindered for business calculation. But when she turned the floor over to Jackson. It started back up.

This time a rapid pulse— *hummz, hummz, hummz, hummz*— lighting up between her legs.

She adjusted herself in her seat, tried to cross her ankles, and tucked them under her chair. But that proved to be a dangerous move. Six chairs down to her right sat Rashawn. His eyes intent on Jackson's report glancing away only to jot down a few notes. All the while the strikingly attractive *Mont Blanc* black and silver pen held like a tool of craftsmanship and deeper purpose.

Click click— hummz— hummz— click click—

And the vibration stopped.

Wall Street— a droning conversation, now finished. The matter at hand turning over to Hendricks, while her hand slowly slipped under the table. She drew her knees in just a touch to position her body near side saddle in her executive leather chair. Something clicked in the room and the pulsing between her thighs was back.

Hummz, hummz— pause— *hummz, hummz*— pause.

She rolled her head around— Hendricks' lifeless monotone deliveries could put a forest fire to sleep, but it was not killing the mechanism inside her theca, nor did Hendricks provide anything to keep her thoughts distracted from it either.

She ran her fingers through her hair and drew in a tight breath. The movement in the posture from her, said pure frustration. To the men in the room, it signaled: *get on with it, you are boring me.*

She eased up in her seat, arching her back to just sit straight, what she was really doing was pressing down. Another click and the pulse turned back to the rapid strobing: *hummz, hummz*— *hummz, hummz*—

Click- click.

So close. One more round and she was going to cum. Another click and her eyes went to the pen in Mr. Matisse's hand. His thumb slowly caressing over it and then clicked it again and the vibration started up in an all new delicious suffering that nearly had her gasping.

Oh yes— the flood of sensitized nerve endings firing off at such a heightened symphony she could hardly stay focused on the alarm she should be feeling. *Was Rashawn's pen the remote?* No, it wasn't— couldn't be— *ohh*— her hand came up to mask the gasp that threatened to escape, before pressing it back down to hide under the table. Her mind racing for any possible chances that she could get her fingers up her skirt and clip this ride right off the cliff.

Her gaze went back to Rashawn's hand. He wore a new ring; one she'd never seen before. A thick black ring with an equally black onyx stone set in an oval sterling silver setting. The fingers of his right hand, though still holding the pen like a sex toy, drifted over the new ring worn on his opposite hand with some fondness. She became mesmerized by the movements of his hands. His hand came up to be propped up on an elbow and his thumb twirled the ebony jewel around his finger. And he clicked his fancy pen again.

Hummum— hummum— hummum— the pulse slowed to a steady drawn out vibration. The coil inside her, tightening to the very edge, her breath kicking up and she struggled to prevent it from being too noticeable as she began to teeter at the very cuspate of release.

Another *click* and it stopped.

Damn you, I was right there.

"Mr. Matisse," she cut into Hendricks' report figures. "Have you anything to say?" Her tone tight and demanding as she nailed him under her hawk stare. She'd had enough of these men toying with her.

Rashawn glanced at her, not a touch of mockery on his lips. He was thoughtful in a quick expression then gently met her gaze, not a quiver of weakness but not intent to challenge her either. "Not at this time, *Mademoiselle* Quinneth." He bowed his head in an ever so slight tilt.

"Then *put* the pen *down,* please. And let's allow Hendricks to finish his report." She spoke mildly to presume a calm repose that belied that anything on the contrary was taking place on her insides.

"*Excuse-moi.*" He half chuckled offering his sudden amused awareness that the clicking of his pen had been disruptive, and he set it down, turning his attention back to Hendricks. "*Pardonnez-moi, continuez, je vous en prie.*" He waived his fingers out turning his palm up to gesture to Hendricks the floor was his. His left hand still up, his thumb still caressing the ring on his finger to dance around it.

The eloquent egg vibe she'd received on Monday had sat in her desk for two days, teasing and tormenting her, making her wait. Assuring that she learned this lesson well. *The waiting.* Now her Master taunted her in a new way. Deviant applications awaited the wanton surrender to it. She was on the edge of succumbing.

To hell with all the men about her, as if their sexual freedoms were proclaimed only because they were men, they were Masters of having sexual gratitude even with an audience and not be looked down upon. She was going to scream and moan and cry out *yes* as loud and uninhibited as she could any minute now. *And then she'd write it off as their Christmas bonus,* she felt the arch in her brow move up with her thoughts.

Rashawn turned, his eyes watching her. He had a tendency to do that often. Watching her like she was a seduction in living display. The smoldering embers burning in his gaze as he did. She was clenching her arm rest. He brought his hands together clasping his fingers to knit and suddenly it all stopped.

The very edge she had been carried over to fell away, leaving her with only a heavy silent breath. *Damn Him. She better get a really good spanking for this.*

"Thank you, Mr. Hendricks." She glanced at her watch, noting the time then back to the man still watching her. "Mr. Matisse, as was your request, the rest of our meeting is yours. Please use it wisely."

❦

Rashawn's playing came to an end. It had been about as scandalous as any libertine game went, but then he didn't keep her from anything vital, Jackson and Hendricks were merely going over the weekly reports. Something she would read over later anyways. And Amelia had handled his tryst of deviant trickery so magnificently. The Queen Victoria would have been proud.

But now he had to turn to more business matters. Ones he knew Amelia would not allow such tomfoolery to disrupt her and he certainly didn't want her growing bitter at her Master for violating her business space. She had given over her intimate and personal time, nothing more.

He stood and began passing down copies of a bound report he'd had made for the meeting. Once they each had one and was opening them up to glance through, he moved around the table where he could access the large monitor screen on the wall.

His purpose for being here in New York was motivated by his handling of the Ümran Global contracts. Before he left Morocco to sail here, all was doing well. But new issues were heating up, making Giza and Cairo ground zero, placing their plant there in far more danger than they were just a few months ago. So, time was of the essence to get a contingency plan in motion now or lose everything.

"My apologies, Messieurs, I haven't the time to give for you to read ahead, so please try to follow along as best as you can. If you turn to page two of the proposal, you will find the outline of what I am bringing to you. Which the bottom line of it is we need to move the Carac Ümran Global plant starting now."

"But the original plan included safe guards from Egypt's Chamber of Industries that the plant would be protected."

The questions poured in from one then another and Rashawn answered each with equal importance.

"And they have tried to do so, but we can't place fault on Hameed Alsoudany for unforeseen political and foreign collisions of present day current events. I have spoken with him regularly over the weeks and they are very fearful at this time."

"Does he give any indication of improvements or worsening in the area?" Gerard Ferranti was next to speak up.

"Not in exact terms. At this time, it's safe to assume that any and all conversations we might have with Egypt's government is monitored, so words are selected carefully. But it is with certainty the war between Israel and Gaza are not going to go away anytime soon. So I want to push for a contingency effective immediately."

"We have contracts of production. We can't just shut the plant down and keep our clients on backorder while we spend a year moving," Amelia pointed out.

"Precisely." Rashawn tapped the air with a finger in her direction, "Which if you turn to page twenty-eight, you will see a financial plan for a new plant."

"That's preposterous. A new plant will have exponential costs," Rashawn's good old buddy Stanley Hostimshires barked out, but Rashawn was prepared to counter him.

"True, but if we stay and do nothing, thinking we can ride this out, the cost will come in the form of lost lives on top of the financial loss. Make no mistake, our time in Egypt is now limited. The more time we spend flouncing about, the less time we have to implement a win scenario in this."

Amelia sucked in a noted sigh. She was contemplating.

That what he was proposing was going to be costly was an understatement, but in the long run it was better than a total loss. He just had to make them see that last part.

"Continue," she spoke flatly. It was the open door he needed.

"Morocco is a haven for international trade. Its deep harbors and open ports will make for easy exporting. A new plant will also give us a chance to bring some of the plant's machinery up to date, which will increase production cost effectively." Rashawn grabbed the remote for the monitor screen, clicking it on to show a chart he'd made out, "If you look here, it shows how production has already showed a decline in output. And it's likely to continue on a down grade. If we start building a new factory now, we can have it ready in a year and a half without drawing away from the Cairo location. It's advisable to shift some of the work load to the plant in Istanbul to make up for lost production in the Carac plant. We can hire locally in Morocco, which will boost local support, and once we're ready, transfer as many personnel of those from the Carac plant that can."

"But what the hell do we do with the Carac plant then?"

"The same we would do with any asset, Hugo. We liquidate." Rashawn gave him a triumphant smile, to show the men that Quinneth Global could pull this off.

"You know, we could be looking to use some of the old factory to expand on the new plant. If a safer region is going to incrcasc productions, I think wc should leave ourselves open to it," Carter added, showing where his support vote would land.

"Very well, gentlemen, you have tonight to review the proposal. We'll reconvene tomorrow and take a vote," Amelia cut in, calling the meeting to an end.

"What? Just like that? A proposal like his could take months to review," Stanley was back at the bit and chomping away.

"Except we don't have months," Rashawn intervened, clicking the remote, and brought up CNN's International news. The screen filled with images of bombed buildings while a teletype ran across the bottom in Arabic and English telling of yet another failed cease fire between Israel and the Palestinians. "The clock is already counting down on us."

"We vote tomorrow, gentlemen," Amelia confirmed her call on the matter.

But Stanley wasn't going to agree so easily and he was on his feet tossing the proposal across the table. The folder of papers caught the air and flipped about before coming down on the table with little more than a child's tantrum. "You're just doing this because you're infatuated with him!"

Amelia turned cold to the accusation, and with a cool repose leaned forward, placing her hand lightly on the smoky glass conference table. "And if you would bring to this board even half the proposals Mr. Matisse brings to improve our firm's business managements, I would show a similar infatuation with your work ethics as well." She shot to her feet, keeping her cool repose as she scanned each and every one of them, picked up her copy of the proposal, tucking it under her arm. "Good day, gentlemen." She clicked her lips and marched out with an air that resonated, *don't even think to checkmate me.*

Amelia was just seconds from sitting down behind her own desk when the egg started back up. She should have been pissed, but that tiny whisper of words in the back of her mind reminding her she wasn't in control of something was such a tasty treat she wished to do nothing but sit back and give in to His will.

Rashawn stopped in his office first. His gaze intent on the view of her through the camera mounted on her monitor. He pivoted back and forth in his chair, hands on the desk's edge— *Gripping it— Intensely watching.*

She had been magnificent. Just a moment ago. Such exquisite strength and now look at her— completely turned over to him. She had needed it. She could have rebelled and taken her play thing out, but she didn't. Because she was meant to submit to him.

She was getting close, the shudder of each breath and how she rocked her hips to grind the vibrating bullet around inside to tap her G spot. He wanted to be in there, smell her fragrance when she came. He glanced at the papers on his desk. He needed her signature and immediately snatched them up and headed for her office.

He pulled out his phone swiped the screen over then tapped the icon and the image of his pet filled the screen. *Maudis-moi, My pet, but don't cum just yet.* He needed to be in the room with her, to smell her, watch her, and feel her. Trenton's suspicions had been right, he was experiencing drops himself, and her absence from his nights was driving him insane.

Rashawn had just reached her office when the video feed on his phone showed the mess of burgundy hair spill out over her desktop. He quickly thumbed out a text of his orders. He wanted to witness her hover at the edge a moment longer, torturing himself, wishing he could be there to hold her when he told her she could finally cum. He hit send, then knocked on her door.

There was a slight curse on the other side of the door then she called him in. He sucked in a breath and rolled the tension from his shoulders and entered.

"Forgive my intrusion, you wanted me to go over the expense sheet. I also have some papers that need your signature."

She nodded staggeredly and waved him in.

Putain, My pet, but what a sight you are to my senses.

She looked so tussled. She was fighting it. *Sooo close.* Her breasts heaving with deep ragged breaths. Her facial features stitched tight, trying not to give herself away, but there was no hiding it. The room was swimming with the heightened scent of her body and perfume.

She sucked in a deep breath, her back straightening, her expression turning rigid and she picked up a pen, "The report will have to wait." She held her hand out with a quirk of her fingers commanding him to hand over the papers. He took his time, he needed this, needed a reminder of how beautiful she was when her body was but moments from being turned over to his touch. How delicious she was.

He stopped, standing directly in front of her desk, and handed her the contracts for her to sign. He leaned in, placing a hand on her desk to watch her from his knew perspective, the telltale signs of her thighs clenching showed in the quiver of her stomach and the way her shoulders strained to stay Egyptian straight. He took a deep inhale letting her scent flood his senses with a flare of his nose.

"You smell so good," he whispered.

Amelia's hand froze in mid signature, her face turning up toward him, part horror, part blushing, but the rage that her intimacy was being denied reigned rule this time and the strong willed woman surfaced.

"Get out." She thrust the papers back at him. "Now!"

He tried not to grin, *oh how he tried but* bon sang *he doubted very much that he was successful,* so he did the naughtiest of things and licked it from his lips. Then took the partially signed documents and left.

He closed the door and leaned back on it, pulling his phone back out to watch her, while his left hand played with the remote control ring on his finger and pressed the onyx cabochon three times, sending a signal to the bullet inside his pet to the highest level of vibration. Then sent her his final command:

~~ TXT: Cum for me, My pet. ~~

He would have watched. Had every intention of doing so, but the moan coming from the other side of the door was far more tantalizing and he closed his eyes, leaned his ear in and listened to her release as though she was a symphony of honey on the wind.

CHAPTER FIFTEEN

THURSDAY

Her day, like the three before it, started with little notes of adoration and commands from her Head-Master, touched off with a flower waiting for her at her home or at the office when she got in. Monday's had been an orchid. Tuesday's flower was two nearly black, red Calla lilies. Yesterday's was a large Chrysanthemum in a bed of Baby's Breath. Today's was no exception to the heart touching gifts that warmed her as well as making her the envy of all the other ladies in the office. A heavy bottomed, box shaped glass dish, filled with smooth pebbles then topped off with crystal clear water with a brilliant pink colored Lotus floating in its center, sat at the reception counter waiting for her when she came in. His note read:

~~ You didn't think I would allow you to go on your date without first seeing you spoiled by me, did you, My pet?" ~ HM ~~

She kissed the card, leaving the imprint of her lipstick over the scribed initials HM. Could it ever be possible to fall in love with a man she had never actually met? If the answer could be yes, then it was possible that was what she felt curling up like a purring kitten in the pit of her stomach. And she could imagine herself kneeling at his feet at the end of each day waiting for his touch—*and spankings.*

The day had been hectic. Two calls to Morocco's Chairman of Trade, another long conference call with her brother in Germany, an even longer one with her father in Paris, France. A business proposal discussed with Maxum St. Laurents, which she was sure he couldn't turn down. One that would put his firm overseeing a large sum of aggressive investments, where the bottom line was to hopefully be the primary funding to relocate the Ümran Global plant from Egypt to Morocco.

She considered herself lucky when Maxum said he would get back with her tomorrow with some suggestions. The man did nothing on impulse. And while his peers often scoffed at him for letting prospects get away, he was always the one with large pockets still full of money when seventy-five percent of those compulsive investments fell through. She had to admire the man for that. He stood his ground within a river of trends and his strength to ignore the *must act nows* had made him, as well his clients, extremely wealthy. It just simply took two hours convincing her father to agree to let a competing financial firm handle this particular purse.

And all this was just her morning. By the second lunch order to have grown cold on Anna's desk, Robert showed up, and sat on hers until she had eaten at least half of her Chicken Marsala salad.

"Now kindly get out." She raised her eyebrow at him for the brat he was. "And let Mr. Matisse know I will see him now to go over the financial reports on his proposal."

Robert merely tsk'ed at her on his way out. And she stabbed a bite of chicken from her dish and waved it at him then stuffed it in her mouth before he closed the door. She couldn't resist the need to roll her eyes at him, even though he'd already left. *Little brat.* He was the best PA she'd ever had.

She was just finishing up her late lunch when she got a call on Skype. His avatar for today was a close up of his chin while he dragged his thumb just under the swell of his bottom lip. Her own instantly finding itself captured in her teeth as she reached over and answered the call.

"Good afternoon, Beautiful," the dominantly masculine voice greeted her with a tone that commanded that she believe every word he said, and the avatar phased away and the video chat opened up to reveal this man so carefully cloaked in mystery, always keeping his face obscured from view. Only his dress shirt and his tan hands showed on the screen. Polished and manicured to male perfection. *"I'm glad I caught you."*

"I am too," she purred back. She tried to see around him, but he had taken care in even that detail as well. While it was clear he was sitting at a desk, the room he was in was dark and a desk lamp blared out at an odd angle cast him in its stark lighting. Whatever was behind him was in total darkness.

"I've been thinking about you all night. The wait for tomorrow to come is too agonizing." Every word nearly a

growl of longing. "*So, I will be treating myself to a moment of your time for my own indulgences.*"

He'd already pulled loose the periwinkle and white striped silk tie he wore, letting it hang from his neck around the powder blue tailored shirt signifying an inconspicuous naughty note suggestive of using it to bind her wrists later with. His hand slowly went to one sleeve and released the silver cuff link, letting it drop to the desk with a *clink*, then repeated the process with the other sleeve. Each and every movement, slow and tantalizing for the pure sense of eye candy.

Amelia's mouth began to water, leaving her utterly speechless. Her Head-Master certainly had a body to draw her eyes: tan, like the men of the Mediterranean Sea. Near black hair dusted over his forearms, revealed as he pushed his sleeves up, and matched that on his chest. What little he allowed of his face were brief glimpses of his chin and the shadow of a dark scruff. Evidence he'd forgotten to shave that morning. "*My pet?*"

Amelia swallowed, realizing she hadn't answered yet, "I'm about to be in a meeting."

"*Would by chance, you are having this meeting in your office?*"

"*Uhm—*" she blinked trying to get her head to think properly, though his fingers were now working to undo several more buttons on his shirt, then pulled the crisp linen from its tucking so that his shirt spilled open with the full amount of his chest and firm abdomen exposed for delight. "Y-yes. Meeting— yes— here." She bit at her lip. "My meeting is in my office shortly," she tried making sense, but her attention was full on the happy-trail leading past the ripple of muscles to the loose belt that hung at his hips. She leaned forward as if the very motion would gain her more viewing pleasure beyond the frame of the monitor.

"Splendid. I have been wanting to see you in action. This will be my chance."

Amelia was completely thrown off by the suggestion, which despite trying to form words with her mouth nothing came out. She scratched at her head, then brought her hands together as if some haggard form of prayer could help her get through this, but when her Head-Master's hands fell to his slacks, the telltale movement was a clear indication of what he was doing, she doubted such strength existed in her.

His breath grew coarse as his arm pushed his hand down beyond the view, then up, and his chin tipped back and out of view. *"Oh yes. Watch me, pet. Watch what you do to me."* he growled.

If wishes came true it was teasing the ever living curse out of her now, for each time his arm came up, she caught only the slight visual candy of the reddened cap of his cock, gripped firmly in his fist when what she wanted was to see the full length of his flesh.

The muscles in his arm tensed and flowed like a carnal display of veins slowly dancing at the beat of hot flames and she wished he would let her find him, so she could lick each line over his arms, then beg to suck him until he gave her His prize.

"Do you ache for your return tomorrow evening?" the question spilled out of the speaker in heated breathy words.

She could hardly respond with anything other than her mouth dropping open.

"I would make you wait on the ottoman for me. Pulling your head back with the soft tug on your hair, then run my fingers over your neck and down toward your breasts. Teasing you with feathery glances of the back of my hand. I love how the fullness of your breasts fill the cup of my palm. Just to hold them makes my teeth ache to bite them and leave my mark on them."

And the knock on her door came, slamming reality in her face, turning the haze she had so willingly wandered into to be swept away with dizzying tantalizing dreams. Responsibility and presence brought fantasizing to a painful, screeching halt. "Mm–my Head-Master—please— I—"

"Shhh— use the Bluetooth ear bud I sent you in your care package. He'll never know," he husked out the intent of his deviant trickery.

Amelia's breath left her lungs and made her dizzy when she heard his raspy breath expelled with a hard sigh. She couldn't break her eyes from the flexing cords of muscle in his arm, and the twist of his wrist at the peak of each that pitted against his breath with more growling sounds. She leaned up in her seat as if doing so might actually steal her a better glance beyond the desk that obscured her view from his cock. *Oh please just let me see it, she begged in silence.*

"Pet, do as I say. I will not be denied of you this evening. My need of my submissive pet is great," he growled further. Letting his head fall back as his arm steadily picked up in pace. His free hand moving up over his

chest in a slow liquid movement, then down the center of the rippling abs to join in with the other.

Amelia nearly let out a whimper to protest such teasing, but without even realizing it she'd pulled the small bluetooth from the box tucked away in the foot drawer of her desk and placed it in her ear. Her Head-Master leaned in, sacrificing one hand to tap a command on his keypad, and the audio from his call was transferred to the direct private link in her ear and instantly her spine began to melt with the husky tenor of his heated breaths. *Oh fucking hell,* she cursed when his voice now whispered roughly directly into her eardrum came in tandem of her rapid heartbeat. She chewed her lips because she wasn't going to survive this without begging for something.

The knock at her door came again. "Just a sec!" she called out, halting him long enough to get her game face on.

"Mmmm, maybe you should fire him." Her Head-Master laughed, teasingly, *"Please proceed, but leave the monitor on. Even at work, I will not be denied the pleasure of you."*

She swiped her hand over her hair, smoothing it away from her face, then brushed down her blouse and skirt, she glanced at her desk, at the forgotten plate of lunch crumbs. Good excuse. "Come in," she called, then feigned a last bite from her yet again cold food. She steeled against the urge to make a face, brushed her hands off then gathered up the containers, stuffed them back into the bag they came in and tossed the remnants into a waste basket while Reshawn took a seat across from her. All the while her Head-Master's groans ebbed and flowed in one ear and she fought the urge to look into her monitor.

She became mechanical, holding her hand out for the very papers she purposely didn't finish signing yesterday.

"*Pardonne-moi,* Robert said you would have been finished with your lunch by now. I was under strict orders to not disturb you."

Amelia looked to him then to the monitor and the man clearly sitting before a camera and actively having his way to steal her attention. She felt some sudden relief flooding through to wash away thoughts from the back of her mind. A tension she hadn't realized until now she was carrying as the idea of Rashawn's pen having been in any ways involved with her Hcad-Master's scandalous fun with the vibrating toy he'd commanded her to wear during her meeting yesterday.

Amelia tried to dial in her focus back to the man standing in her office, losing the battle to look, at least a fraction of the second back to the scene on her screen before meeting Rashawn's eyes. "It's quite alright, I— uhm—" she nearly went brain dead when her eyes went right back to the site on her screen. He'd moved. "I got distracted with a— phone call." She dropped her gaze down and scanned over the papers.

"*That's it, my pet. Listen to me while I look at you. Watching you as you work. Your body is such perfection. I can hardly wait to have my cock deep inside your cunt once again. Maybe I'll tie you up using my one of my ties. Will you be ready and wet when I pick you up tomorrow night, My pet? Because I don't know if I will get us to our home before I ravish you.*"

She couldn't even answer, not with Rashawn in the room. Focusing on her employee was hard enough as he talked over the report. She found herself studying his body more than his words. The Marks & Spencer tailored suit, and the light blue shirt, crisp and neat, set off an extraordinary contrast to his tanned hands. Dotted off with silver cuff links. She glanced at the monitor to the pair still sitting on her Head-Master's desk, so similar. So was the shirt, but it wasn't an unusual color. Only, Rashawn's tie was missing. "Where's your tie, Mr. Matisse?"

She snapped her fingers to her lips but it was too late the accusation was out.

He only smiled, never even skipped a beat. "I had a heated conversation with Hameed Alsoudany just before coming to meet with you."

"Is he handsome, My pet? I wonder, shall I have us both fuck you at the same time? Watching you get used and pleasured by two cocks at once? Hmmm, perhaps not. I may not be able to share you. But I might let him watch while I torture you with toys from my collection. Do you think he will pull his cock out to give you a show while I work your body into a full scene while you are strapped to the top of your desk?"

Amelia licked her lips. She sucked in a deep breath as she felt the small clench of muscles between her thighs release a shiver that ran rampantly up her body. When the spell had run its course— "Sorry, you tend to catch me off guard with uncountable frequency with your disrobing, Rashawn. Please continue."

"Picture me sitting across from you in your office, now. Sitting in the chair watching you go over the papers while

I stroke myself to the very edge of my release. And if you're good I might let you come over and sit in my lap and I will do to you what your presence does to me, My pet. See it. See me sitting before you now."

Amelia tried her best to watch inconspicuously, shifting her gaze back to Rashawn whenever he looked up at her from his notes. But it was getting difficult, her Head-Master's voice growing louder and aggressive as his hunger built up, sharing the explicit details of his fantasies and what he would do with her in each of them. The words on the report in her desk blurring into an incomprehensible puddle of grey ink. She could hardly put together a kosher response for Rashawn and unable to make any response to her Master. The dilemma alone which had her all *growly* in her head in bratty rebellion didn't even include the agony her lady parts were in. Her thighs clenching tight with each growl that breathed in her one ear. Her spine melting with the tenor voice that spoke naughtily to her.

"Were it I sitting in front of your desk, would you come around and straddle over me so I can fuck you until you're screaming? Mmmm, bon sang, but I would love to fold you over that desk of yours. Cuff your wrists to the corners and slam my cock into your honey soaked pussy. Ahhh, yes-ss, I am going to cum for you, My pet. I want you to watch me. Turn and look, My pet, watch me while I cum from thoughts of you."

Amelia tore her gaze from Rashawn and glanced full on into the monitor just as her Head-Master was getting up from his seat. "Mmmm," the hum escape her. Finally, he revealed the glossy engorged glans, turned a dark bruised purple, atop the thick shaft being pumped with his fist. The muscles in his arms and legs visibly strained. And her ear was filled with the sound of his gruff heavy breaths. Not even aware her fingers had floated to her lips brushing against them.

"Are you pulling up the reports now?"

Wha- The odd question broke through her hazy thoughts, setting off alarms just in time as a blur of movement came around her desk.

Amelia let out a loud yelp. Her hand snatching the monitor and yanked—

The screen slamming down onto her desk. She sat morbidly frozen at her desk, not even daring to breathe, eyes locked on Rashawn's surprised face while she listened to the vocalized orgasm through the bluetooth, realizing that her reaction drew just as much attention to herself as anything else would.

Rashawn stopped beside her desk, glancing at her, then to the face-down monitor screen, and then back to her. He soon seemed to be fighting back some wicked form of laughter, his dark gaze floating down over her heated cheeks, as though he could see right through her and know every scandalous thought she had. He saw every shiver she felt as her Master came, an erotic melody written for her ears alone.

"Have you been watching porn while I talk business, Amelia?" Rashawn was toying with her.

Amelia rolled her lips in keeping silent, then tapped at her temple refusing to admit to anything of an embarrassing nature.

The laughter Rashawn had been holding back finally rang out like a tease over her sensory. *Oh if only your Head-Master would command that I fucked you too.* The wicked thought danced through her mind before quickly being dismissed. *Oh but he did, he placed me between you both getting fucked by both your cocks.*

Shocked by her randy thoughts, she let out a startled huff and swiped whatever possible telltale expressions from her face to hide behind a hand.

"Very well, Amelia. I see today is not going to be good for this report either, so I will dismiss myself and get ready for the board meeting. I may not be of any good then myself. I am looking forward to our evening together. See you in a few?"

She nodded anatomically, still keeping all that she was, bottled up in a pristine poised pose, keeping her propriety about her. The door clicked closed, and she quickly let the warm flush ripple through her that caused even her head to shake through it. Timidly she reached over and picked up her monitor and returned it to its proper stand. Her Head-Master absent, save for the sinful splatter of his release on the inside of her screen. Nothing moved in the room, the background still lost in dark shadows. Only the empty chair lit up like a criminal who'd been under interrogation. A moment later a shadow stirred against the high back of the leather chair, then a large sheet of paper came into view or rather obscured all other views. A note. And she leaned in to read—

~~You're going to get a spanking for that. ~~

CHAPTER SIXTEEN

Amelia had long since made a habit of keeping a full wardrobe at her office. With a two hour commute home, it was a matter of prudent planning for those spur of the moment evening plans to not have the inconvenience.

While Rashawn seemed to take a liking to secretiveness of his plans for the night, he did give enough suggestion to dress evening semi-formal. However, her Head-Master made no allowance to not be a part of the evening, and before her business of the day was called to a close, a package arrived for her.

The pre-washed soft, cream-colored Chiffon dress fit perfectly, down to the taper of her trained waist. She glanced at her reflection nearly in shock. Katianna would be beating down the door to steal it if she saw this. The scooped hem barely came down Amelia's thighs. While it certainly bore the baby doll delicacy of fashion, the sheer sleeves and a V-neck chiffon overlay brought its look up to decadent class. She would have never picked it off a rack, but seeing herself in it now changed her mind about the design.

When the knock came from her evening escort, she opened the door to meet her date. While Rashawn's chin may have well hit the floor, his eyes were another matter. Two deep brown pools of chocolate wordlessly made love to her, then undressed her, and in that order. He took a step back, shaking his head in disbelief, and he looked like a man who'd fallen in love.

"I—" he shook his head again, "I'm tongued tied. I can think of nothing to say with my tongue because it is busy wishing to do so many other things."

Amelia only blushed, not sure what to say herself to his bold confession.

"*S'il te plaît. Pardonne-moi.*" he stepped in and kissed her cheek one then the other, pausing, then his lips floated up and kissed her temple. "I am a poor excuse for a Frenchman that you take my tongue away from me with a look. I can command only but a singular thought for you." He leaned back gazing down into her eyes, "*De toute beauté,*" he whispered.

And the small blush she wore trailed down her neck and spread everywhere, because she was beginning to like being called *beautiful.*

Dinner was wonderful with a dash of fun thrown in. They'd gone to the well-known La Perigord, only instead of the French menu they were famous for, it was American dish night. A fun twist of doing other cuisine, a rather oxymoron since nearly all American foods were someone else's. Save but maybe the boiled egg and the hotdog.

Rashawn treated them to a New York style pizza reinterpreted by a French cook. The dish might not replace her love for the real thing, her taste buds were in no way upset with the modification. Not to mention Rashawn had her laughing nearly the entire time. They gobbled down slice after slice, dribbling with a mix of cheeses and chased it down with lime laced ales.

The next part of their evening was an even bigger surprise when the car dropped them off in front of a theatre. It wasn't one she was familiar with and the 'Live Girls' flashing in bright neon across the street had her questioning what was beyond the doors of the *Chapeaux of Risqué et Folie Theatre.*

Inside, the fun had just begun, it was all retro and cheesy posh. Red velvet and gold gilt walls lined the lobby and settees of purple Victorian furnishings also trimmed in gold guild, filled the lobby wings for gathering, over hung with gaudy crystal chandeliers. Guests congregated and shared cocktails while they waited for the Maître d' to step out with his long tails and top hat to invite them in for the show. Every step of the way was purposely over done in the style of classical *Moulin Rouge.* And Rashawn adored every giggle that escaped Amelia's lips.

"Oh, you must be joking, Rashawn. What could possibly be playing here that would gather your interests?" Amelia teased him, but he wouldn't relent, leading her on his arm, up the stairs, and into the top mezzanine where they slipped away into a curtained-off balcony booth just in time as the lights dimmed and the large black drapes of the stage drew back with clamorous applause.

A storm of crashing lightning and thunder took up residence in her belly. As the young man beside her had wooed her, charmed her, made her laugh and blush only to now be presented with a live performance of the screenplay: *Quills*. And not at all the wholesome family television version.

On the stage below, voluptuous breasts peeked out over maidens' dresses— a convent raised young lady sucked a hedonic young man's phallus while he recited verses from the Marquis de Sade's *Justine* near the stone hearth— A prisoner in a cell beat off his manhood, while the Marquis man himself, in the cell next to him, recited verses for his next tale to an enamored wash maiden who penned it for him.

Amelia felt like the blushing virgin from the play, having been exposed to such scandalous affairs, her eyes wandering playfully over her young escort's body in a manner not proper for her training.

Her body heated up and she was not so removed she didn't feel Rashawn's eyes on her, or his breath that basked over her neck on the occasions that he leaned in to whisper tantalizing details of the play or the story they told. His hand never let go of hers. Moving only to interchange from fingers laced together to just caressing the top of her hand with a thumb. But the tentative contact never vanished.

~~Picture me sitting in front of you. ~~

She heard her Head-Master's tantric tenor voice echo in her mind, but when she did, it was Rashawn's face she saw. Her thoughts escaped the play a moment and she watched his fingers as he repositioned her hand in his, once more. A glimpse of light caught the polished surface of a cuff link, and she reached over with her free hand and fingered over it. He'd switched out his usual multi time-zone Diesel name brand watch he wore at the office for a Greubal Forsey with an eye catching platinum skeleton face and etched design. Something perhaps most women didn't notice, but she did. She liked a man who changed his attire after work, not to mention his selection of a custom Greubal Forsey fed into her fetish for time pieces. But it told her, that there was more to the man than just work, and his personal time carried a different form of luxury and indulgences.

She let her eyes follow the tie up a well-defined chest hidden under the double-breasted suit coat until she arrived just under his chin. Her face turned a few shades crimson right away realizing he was looking directly at her and let her gaze float up farther until she found his warm eyes watching her too.

Why? She asked the same question again. Why couldn't she find a man her age or older who looked at her the same way as he did? And her Head-Master— what of him? She shouldn't be here. Her new Master had given her an experience she had never been able to find so why was she here with Rashawn?

~~ I want you to go out with him. Can you picture the two of us ravishing your body together— picture me in front of you while you sit at your desk— Is he handsome—?

She felt dizzy— and endlessly confused, but she couldn't run away, not yet. She wanted to be here. If only for just tonight, to divulge in the salacious weave of erotic taboo that had made her laugh and feel adored in a way she had not felt in so long.

The racy play came to an end and the crowd stood offering a standing ovation to a full cast presented for an elegant bow. She and Rashawn walked out, quietly taking their time with no rush to navigate the crowd of others milling out, their heads filled with perhaps too much imagery and wandering thoughts.

Rashawn's car and driver were dutifully waiting for them at the curb just behind a few taxis, but Rashawn led her instead the other direction as if his intentions all along had been to take a city stroll.

Amelia was still swooning from the myriad of effects of the night on her when she blindly stepped onto an air vent grill; the grater snagged her heel as she took the next step, slightly twisting her ankle before she caught herself. Rashawn's hands were already there catching her and holding her steady. But upon closer inspection, she found the strap on her shoe had come undone. "Oh wait, I—" before she could say another word, Rashawn had her under his control.

"Set your foot down, Amelia." His hands asserting her with restored balance.

Then the world slipped away behind a veil taking with it the standard chaos that was New York, as she watched

Rashawn slowly kneel before her. No longer the clatter of car horns arguing to cut in, or the murmur of pedestrians flowing from the theatre. Even the cat calls from across the street to come see live girls perform faded behind wads of cotton in her ears. The bodies that accrued such sounds also drifted away like phantoms moving just outside her peripheral vision.

It was strange, like a charismatic apparition that she was seeing this, that it put her at a loss of words to even describe the sensations swirling through her entire body as Rashawn gently put the ankle strap back in its buckle. His hands moved so precisely as if he'd done it a thousand times and placement was as vital a detail to the shoes' design as anything else. His right hand cupped the back of her heel while his left thumb caressed the arch of her foot. "That's better. How's your ankle? Okay?" he spoke then slowly stood; his fingertips gliding up her leg like ten feathers ghosting over the front and back curves. Then assuredly anticipating he'd set her off balance, one hand took hers, while the other claimed a spot at her back and firmly steadied her.

"A Dom can kneel before a woman like that?" she questioned him, for she was definitely feeling off balance.

"What? Take care of my submissive's every need? I would be a poor choice of a Dominant if I didn't stoop to reset my submissive's shoe strap."

Choice. Spoken so smooth and confidently, he said it as if it was her choice to be kissed or not. And she most certainly wanted to be kissed. Especially when her Head-Master had given permission to allow one.

A little more than another block down, they came to a coffee shop, buzzing with patrons from the theatre house and the nearby nightclubs, pouring in to grab a late night coffee and sweets before heading home.

"Next in line!" a woman called out from behind the counter.

Rashawn leaned in and whispered against her ear, "Do you trust me?"

"Explicitly." She smiled up at him, still glowing from blushing during the play.

His attention went to the counter girl. "Four chocolate covered strawberries, one chocolate croissant, and two amaretto teas. Plus, one Coffee, strong with sugar, all packed to go."

He draped his arm around Amelia as they moved down the counter and picked up their package at the other end.

With cardboard caddy in one hand, the other drifting down to takes its place on Amelia's back, Rashawn led her to the car waiting just outside. His driver, Max spotting them, and hopped out, coming around to get the door. Rashawn passed the cup of steaming coffee over to his driver, keeping the rest for him and his lovely company.

He waited until they were out of the city and on the highway heading out for the Hamptons before opening the box of goodies. "So did you enjoy the play?"

Amelia gave him a blushing smile and nodded her head. Blushing was something he had rarely ever seen her do, yet tonight she had been an art gallery filled with them. An even greater treat than the confections he was about to feed to her.

"I did. I had no idea that theatre existed and I must confess that even if I had, I might not have ever trusted it enough to go in." The shameful blush never fading and while he could not have said for certain if the pink warm glow had reached farther down into her breasts, the slight rise in her breath hinted that it had. Nor did the effects of the erotic risqué on the rest of her seem to be fading.

"It's amazing what one can find when you just let yourself wander. In Paris, some of the best treasures are in and around the Red Light District, yet so many won't venture there because of its lower class risqué reputation. One must get out of the car to discover them." He pulled her hand to his lips. "Something I would never wish to hear you had done without someone to be your protective knight."

"I suppose you have a point."

"I find New York very liberating in a way."

"How so?"

"It's much the same as Paris, but less snobby."

Her laugh was delicate, as if she had done too much that evening and now her cheeks hurt from it all. *Blushing, erotica, and laughter, it needed only one last ingredient. Decadence to dance on her taste buds.* "Open."

She blinked at him a moment, and he held up the strawberry to reveal his intentions. A slight O formed in her lips. He held it out toward her lips and she leaned in, her eyes floating closed and she opened her mouth, waiting.

So many reactions took place in his body, he recalled placing his cock in that succulent mouth, recalled how she'd wrapped her lips around him. The vision went straight down, and he found himself losing on the ongoing war to prevent any tenting in their evening together.

His mouth watered to kiss her, and his breath kicked up with the anticipation of all these explicit wonders he'd had with her and would have again come tomorrow night. But for now, he only placed the chocolate covered strawberry on her lips, traced them then pushed it in so she could take a bite.

He was enthralled watching her lips close around it the same way she had done his cock when she was naughty. And her moan that followed. *Merde, she was killing him.*

Sultry eyes turned up at him in pure bliss. *Bon sang,* he nearly lost his composure when the tip of her tongue peeked out to catch a juicy drop and gave him a sultry smile. Then he fed the last bite of it to her to put himself through the torture all over again.

"So, you're a fan of the Marquis de Sade?" she asked after finishing off the juice bit of strawberry.

"Depends on which version you are referring to. The true libertine was a misogynist criminal, yet we cannot deny his writings have left a mark on society. While the facts of his actions are abhorrent, the fictional romanticizing of who he was has certainly lent a gift to sexual cultures."

"I wasn't aware you were such a voyeur, Mr. Matisse?"

Rashawn chuckled, while he did want to blur the lines between him and her new Head-Master, he didn't want to highlight them in bold just yet. He put on a falsetto of embarrassed laughter and even tried on a soft blush for her. "You must forgive me, Amelia, I was only sharing my thoughts on the presentation of the play. He is after all a part of French history. And my father saw to it I was exposed to many things of the affair as I grew to manhood. All the same, my true interest of the play was I loved the more intimate theatrics of the theatre. I hear they will be showing Bram Stoker's Dracula next week. I am looking forward to seeing what they do with that."

"Well, I am not so sure that fiction should be so influential of our sexual prowess."

Rashawn nodded in contemplation of her statement. A winning business tactic of his was to always provide another perspective, not change one's view but to offer another way of looking at the same thing, "When the true influences are more damaging, it's hard to refute a cleaned up version for influence. Take for example there is a society called Goreans. Not really a kink society, mind you, but a role society of Dominance and submission. And their whole existence is based on a series of science fiction books written by John Norman."

"I see your point. While I don't know any Goreans very well, I have met a few in passing. New York is home to a large community of Goreans."

"You have met members before?"

"Well, yes—" she paused a moment as if correcting her openness, "They are friends of Trenton Leos."

"Ahhh," Rashawn exclaimed allowing the pardon, "Dominus Trenton Leos, now there is a man who lives secretly right out in the open. I have always had such admiration for the man."

"How well do you actually know him?" Amelia inclined. "I mean, aside that your driver is one of his men."

"*Psh,* my father is *Gramaire* Cardiff Matisse, a modern-day libertine who convinced a Monaco princess to bear him a son."

Several colors flashed over her face and drew together in a pleasant smile, "It slipped my mind. I suppose until this week, I'd never given it much thought."

"It's never in kind to assume people know the intimacies of another just based on association of others."

"Would you tell me of something you might do with your perfect submissive?"

"Are you curious of the Lifestyle or just looking to be entertained with a naughty bedtime story?" He shot her wicked grin.

Amelia turned nefariously radiant at that precise moment and the elegance of her smile surged new adoration and hunger in him that he had to take a deep breath just to contain his desires of self-indulgence.

Her eyes dropped, almost playfully shy and her hands came together over her lap to fidget as she hid her own naughty truths. "We'll call it a naughty bedtime story." But he knew what she really meant is she wanted to fantasize about him secretly from where it was safe behind her taboo wall. It was the deepest reach he'd ever accomplished with her and he would certainly fulfill her secret flirting with taboo.

He turned more in the seat to face her more directly, draping an arm up on the back rest and he brought his fingers over his lips tracing them together as he mentally penned her fairy tale. "I will be waiting for her when she comes home from work. I'll instruct her to pour a drink for me. I think maybe a dirty cognac for that night. Then have her undress and wait for me on the chaise lounge in the library. I have a set of stainless steel shackles set out on the coffee table for her, a pair for her wrists, another for her ankles, and a matching collar that when it clicks shut around her neck, her skin lights up with a wave a goose bumps." He halted a moment in order to watch and enjoy with a keen interest as Amelia shivered herself. "I'll take my time, smoothing the bumps on her skin down while I sip from my drink. I might suddenly fist my hand into her hair and yank her head back to whisper naughty things in her ear of what's to come, or maybe just nip her ear and release her head, having said nothing at all." He paused, resting the back of his hand against his lips then dropped it, feeling the intensity of the image he conjured up in his mind. "Can you imagine what it's like to be teased with a bit of leather? The combination of yearning and anticipation can be too much for words. How her body ignites and she wants to beg for a spanking when I remove my belt and loosely drape the length of leather over her body. Provoking her darkest desires to come to the surface with it, because she knows what that sweet sting feels like, and she craves it. Yet, I'll make her wait. I'll slap the belt down over the leather upholstery of the chaise, sending a loud cracking sound out to echo in the room. She'll jump and her bottom lip will roll inward to be snared by her teeth. She'll rock back on her knees a bit, pining for a taste of my belt on her skin—" Rashawn paused and glanced out the window then back to her. "Our ride is almost over and I still have three more strawberries to feed you."

A noticeable exhale came from her as his prize. And he was certain that if ever there had been a doubt he would truly love this woman, it faded with that sound she made for him. It was faint, a bump in the rode could have masked it away from his ears, but he'd heard it, and it was all because of how he affected her.

"Very well," she nearly whimpered, licking over her lips to get them to work properly. "But won't you at least let me serve one to you?"

Serve.

It was a magical word that strummed several cords like music within him.

"I suppose I could be in a giving mood." And his response seemed to do much of the same to her as hers had done to him.

Rashawn was certain they both entertained a number of silent fantasies in their minds as they finished off the last three chocolate covered strawberries, shared the chocolate filled croissant, and washed it all down with the amaretto tea.

The slowing car soon broke the spell and the dark glass that partitioned them off from the front seat of their ride for privacy rolled down.

"We're at the gate, sir."

"Very well, *merci*, Max. Let them know we're returning Mademoiselle. Quinneth home, then pull to the front."

"Yes, sir." The glass returned to its up position.

Rashawn glanced at her, noticing a bundle of both anxiety and exhilarating anticipation.

The kiss. Her *Head-Master* had told her he would allow a singular goodnight kiss. How Rashawn had wanted to take full advantage of that kiss, but in the long ride in the car, he knew full well he would not have maintained to this side of the limits. He would lose himself in her lips and want every bit more that he could have.

"You have something on your fingers," he lied, taking her hand in his and drawing it up to his mouth and slowly, tantalizingly closed his lips around her fingertips. He swirled his tongue around them, licking them clean of essence he only imagined was there. Throughout the tantric moment, he kept his searing gaze on her. Watching as her chest expanded with a hitched breath and her tongue slipped out to lick her lips to plead with him.

She was ready.

The car stopped and he climbed out, pulling her with him and was quickly wrapped around her. "I had a wonderful time tonight. Thank you for joining me." And before she could spill out any formal goodbyes that would put space between them, he leaned down and brushed a kiss to her cheek.

Amelia felt the warmth spread from that small contact all through her body. Then she felt his fingers under her chin, lifting it ever so slightly, and his lips came over hers. Not the chaste press of dry lips, he encased hers, ensuring to deliver the moist contact of his mouth along with the hint of suction that lingered, awaiting for the locks to be released. The kiss in its singleness was pure seduction. Like a true Frenchman. It only took the minute separation for her own lips to part in protest. A move he'd calculated as his fingers gently pushed her chin up and to the side more, placing her at the perfect access. The perfect angle for claiming. Which was exactly what he did. An invasion of compulsive lust licked past her lips, danced across her teeth until he found her tongue. From there it could only be described as an act of untamed love making. It wasn't just his succulent soft lips, or the demanding caress of his tongue; the hand that held her chin moved to her neck firmly bracing her so the full force of his kiss could be given over. The strength of his arm kept possessively wrapped around her waist, expressed in the contact of his hand at the small of her back, pressing her body to his so she felt every inch of his unyielding desires for her.

Her head swooned, relishing the connection. A moan broke from her and he devoured it in their kiss. But before she could consider any shame in the act it was over. Rashawn drifted from their kiss. He pressed his lips to her forehead and hugged her to him, "*Putain,* but I must stop or I will whisk you away. Take you captive to my yacht where I will tie you to a coffee table to make love to you. I would lick every inch of your body. Feast and fuck you for days on end and never let you go until Monday.

"Monday?" Amelia gasped. Her head swooned, not grasping the relevance.

Rashawn pressed another kiss to her forehead and chuckled. "I don't dare be late for work. You might fire me." He leaned back and looked at her.

She felt the flush of color in her cheeks but it was more from the stormy sea of emotions in his eyes than his joking.

He dropped his head to whisper in her ear. Just a few last naughties riding on a breath of warm air that triggered a stream down her spine. "But before my Cinderella could turn back into my boss, the pleasures I'd grant your body would be immeasurable." He sucked in a deep breath. The kind all men did when barely holding their self-control. A sound she had never heard made just for her, save from her new Head-Master— *and now.*

"Perhaps next time, I will do just that. Tonight, however, I will play the behaved chevalier gentleman and take my desires for you home," he vowed reluctantly, despite the swelling cock in his slacks, and he sealed his words with one last kiss upon her lips. Lips that belonged to him. A possession he would find hard to give up. *Such candy.* The swelling fullness pressed and captured by his own. Lips he knew well. Lips he had taken in fierce ravishing while their orgasms shattered them both.

Putain!

He tore himself away before he threw everything away to push the limits with her now. Offering her a sufferable smile.

"Such a woman does exist," he whispered against her hair, then delivered one last kiss pressed to the top of her head. Finished with an alpha growl that had her heavy breath purring against him, and he stepped away to leave before he couldn't.

Amelia caught her breath in a hard double yawn as realism brought her floating feet back to Earth. "You know this can't happen. It's not normal," Amelia called out to him in what she feared sounded far more like *come back* than *we can't do this.*

Rashawn turned, the challenge of a hunt glimmering in his eyes indicating he'd already triumphed. "*Très bien.*" He winked at her, "I'm certain, I would not have expected anything normal when in the presence of such an extraordinary woman." He tipped his gaze, "*Bonne nuit*, Amelia." Then dashed away, disappearing into the back of the Executive Lexus and closed the door. Leaving her with her torn wishes that he would come back, or she would find just inside the front door, her Head-Master, waiting to take over her needs now spinning out of control.

Her Master had opened a bottle, and now Rashawn had her insides fizzing like champagne and there was no capping this off.

Why did he have to be so young?

CHAPTER SEVENTEEN

<u>FRIDAY</u>

How could so many things go wrong in just one day? As if the Gods were throwing everything at him, placing him on trial to measure his worthiness to win over the woman of his desires. For there was definitely something wrong as Rashawn came into Club Pain. The energy and attitude inside was stiff and on edge. An unseen red alert flashed in the backs of everyone's mind stifling the evening's anticipated party affairs.

Derek, the club's head bartender was waiting for him at the bar.

"I'm sorry, Head-Master Matisse. There has been an emergency that has kept the Dominus and Head-Master Dane Masters from coming in tonight."

Rashawn was confused, Dominus knew the importance of this and the timely need. He would not have dismissed it unless the emergency was severe, "Did either say what has happened?"

Derek shook his head, "No, Sir. Only that it was a Dominion matter."

"Dominion? I'm afraid I don't understand."

"Dominus Trenton Leos and Head-Master Dane Masters are brothers at arms along with Patronus Diesel Gentry, Head-Master Marcus Scriven and Master Harper Lancings. The five brothers served together in a special ops team called: the Dominion. So if it is a matter for the Dominion then someone was in great danger. I'm sorry I don't have any further news for you. I will let Amelia know the plan for exchange are canceled until further notice."

"No. I will stick to the plans." He wasn't about to let Amelia slip through his fingers. He'd watched her all week, burning with need that teetered out of control like a wild cat in heat. He'd fought his raging desires daily just watching her and then to walk in on her this afternoon just moments after she had obviously disobeyed his orders to not touch herself, her office perfumed with her arousal had nearly sent him over the edge. He wanted nothing more than to ambush her, fold her over her desk and deliver a hard spanking then fuck her until she was both mindless and sated.

If he didn't follow through with the path, he had taken her down, she would most likely rebuild her defenses and never submit again, unable to feel the loss of this weekend as anything but betrayal. He couldn't allow that to happen. He would have Amelia infuse his dominance into her blood like a drug she was helpless to detox from. Locking her to his life until he could heal the wounds that would restore the bridge of time when he would he reveal himself to her.

He pulled the dark merlot colored scarf from his pocket and offered it over to Derek as if it were the secret to every pleasure. "See that it is delivered to her and instruct her that she is to put it on and wait for her Head-Master."

Rashawn barely had them in the car when he was tearing at her clothes, nor did his submissive red-head hold back any of her own desires, her hands following his to aid in the disrobing at least of vital parts and he soon had his cock wrapped and sinking deep inside her. "There are a number of punishments you have racked up over the week, but the services of my cock's pleasure comes first." He thrust the words into her to be sure she understood the pretenses of them. "Guuhh—" his head kicked back, letting out the gruff growl. He had not anticipated the intense tight world that gripped his shaft. He chewed his lip and moved in to ravish hers. "Mmmm— you're wearing your gift."

"You— told— me to," she gasped a response, fingernails digging into his shoulder.

"Mmmm— yes, I did." His hips surged up, pushing his cock up inside her over and over again. "But I forgot about it."

"Where was my Head-Master's mind to forget such gifts he rained upon me?"

"*Tu me manquais.*"

"You— missed me?"

At present, forming words was certainly a challenge for the both of them for he never relented in his movements, sliding his cock in and out of her wet folds. But fun no less. "No— you were missing from me." It was the true meaning of the French words often lost in translation, losing the essence. And she had no idea how close he'd come to losing her today. Standing before her, seeing the pain inflicted by the fear she had been taken advantage of. How he wanted to wrap her in his arms and explain everything and shield her heart from the news. Keeping silent of who he was to her severed his heart, for there was no greater torture. Such premonitions must have haunted his unseeing eyes.

Last night, as the car drove him away, he'd struggled with his inner lust, wanting to order Max to turn around and take him back. A dream dancing on his fingertips and he feared that driving away would somehow cost him the moment to stake his permanence in her life. Even today, getting through the day at the office had been complicated maneuvering around the damage brought on by one person's greed for flashy headlines.

He'd at least made certain flowers arrived from her Head-Master to set the day off to an excellent start. A large vase of red roses sat at the reception desk. Next to it a velvet egg shaped and exuberantly decorated box waited with them. He'd stepped off the elevator just in time—

Amelia had already gotten in, a beaming smile on her face as she leaned in and inhaled the fragrance of the two dozen roses. The Faberge-like box held delicately in her hand, but when she pulled the ribbon and peeked inside, she quickly shut it and that rare blush he'd been audience to several times the night before was vibrantly alive on her cheeks.

But he wasn't the only audience, a good five or six ladies were trying their best to hover around, hoping to see what had arrived. "What's in it?" One of them asked as he passed by, walking directly behind Amelia.

"*Bonjour dames.*" Rashawn greeted them, getting a closer look at his pet as he passed by. "Beau." he whispered, hoping she heard him.

"Oh, who's getting flowers from you, Rashawn?" Another of the girls called out.

He stopped, turning around with the dozen white tulips wrapped in cream tissue paper and a ribbon to match the color of his pet's cheeks. He was about to pass them over to the woman he'd brought them for when one of the other girls in the gathering popped up bearing news that had put the rest of his day to utter ruin.

"Did you see the cover for Business Journal Weekly?" She held it up with a giddy expression. It was the magazine Amelia had wanted him to do the interview with, but the headline was anything but what he was expecting. There across the top left in bold typography:

~~ Rashawn Matisse – Quinneth Global's Sexiest Chairman and Most Available Bachelor.~~

And there in full cover reveal was the picture they had snapped of him super imposed in front of his yacht: *Matisse Falcon.*

The flowers in his hand were forgotten as he reached out for Sandra to hand the magazine over. His blood beginning to boil over as he read it again, then in flipping to the article he found far more put into the article than he had made them privy to. He had never agreed to a personal interview. He'd even refused them a tour on his yacht. A privilege he rarely even gave over to sailing aristocrats. The article even went as far as to hint to any seeking ladies reading, they might catch him at a local bistro where he frequented for lunch while in New York. Another bit of info he had not granted them.

"You don't look very happy," Sandra commented as if surprised that he may be upset about it.

"I wasn't aware that sending you for the interview would turn into a coup to amuse your ego."

Rashawn turned, unable to wipe the heat from his face as he glared at Amelia. "I assure you that I find none of this amusing, especially when I denied them an interview of any personal content. But you can be certain I will demand an explanation." He nearly thrust the tulips into Amelia's arms. He tried to soften the blow, but to have Amelia glaring at him as she did, accusing him silently of playing the bachelor game with her. He felt violated and the woman he loved was about to slip from his fingers in a wisp of ashes. "*Excuse-moi, s'il te plaît, mais j'ai l'impression que je vais être en retard au travail.*" He turned full French for purchase of some privacy in front of the ever present audience of office staff as he suggested he might be late for work this morning.

"Where are you going?" Her disapproval rang out that he might be trying to call the shots in her firm.

"Il semblerait que je doive d'abord passer par les bureaux de la Business Journal Weekly," he explained he was heading to the magazines office to demand an explanation and stormed off.

But instead, he stopped in the gentlemen's room. He paced, losing his cool and sent his fist into the wall more than once. Scaring the shit out of Hugo who just happened to be taking a piss in one of the stalls when Rashawn stormed in.

He stopped at the sink and fell over his propped arms, gripping the marble edge of the counter top. This couldn't be happening. The contempt that had flared in Amelia's eyes as she read the headline and turned a glaring look at him burned in his mind. *"PUTAIN!"*

He needed to calm down. Then salvage his life and the connection he had had with Amelia last night. He'd have a noose around the neck of whoever spoke to the magazine and leaked out his personal details.

He slapped the cold water on, filled his hands and splashed his face. When he stood the red-headed Heiress Amelia Quinneth herself was standing behind him watching him through the reflection of the mirror. A force to be reckoned with. As angry as she was, all he felt at that very moment was his heart breaking because he hoped her anger was a shield against a similar pain he felt himself and not a matter of her company.

"Did you have fun last night?" she accused him.

Rashawn spun around, taking her arms in his grip. "Don't do this to yourself, Amelia. I would never have done such a thing to you. Nothing I had with you last night was anything but complete respect, admiration, and desire. I went to the interview as you asked, I talked only about when I first started working with Quinneth Global in Paris under your father and the overseas plants in the face of surviving the onslaught of war."

"They didn't ask you questions about your lifestyle?"

Rashawn felt the harsh twitch in her arms. She wanted to trust him, but she also felt pinned. He dropped his hands, not wanting her to feel forced to stand before him. "They did." He nodded, "I didn't answer them. I made it clear I wasn't available for a personal interview. I told you before, I like my privacy. This did not change."

"Perhaps you weren't clear on that. They even went as far as to mention your father and his lascivious libertine lifestyle, and I quote: *So look out, ladies, the young Matisse bachelor may not have fallen far from the tree and turn out to be a kinky catch.*"

Crashing wreckage that weighed in tons fell on his shoulders, shoving him into the ground like a pile driver, obliterating everything he had dreamed and hoped for. Everything he'd worked hard to get and gain, the only remaining thing he wanted the most in his life was standing before him, slamming the doors of opportunity shut. The ache was unbearable. "*S'il te plaît.* I swear I didn't do this to you."

The glare seemed to dissipate, waning away with a dying moon taking with it not only the anger but the blush she'd worn for him, and only him, with it.

She crossed her arms over her chest, wearing them like a suit of armor as she sucked in a deep breath and let it flare out with a frustrated sign. And Rashawn steeled himself for the worst blow to come.

"Did you manage to interview those other two applicants for an assistant?"

"Only one of them."

"And?"

He shook his head, not caring for the irrelevant topic.

"Then I suggest you give Mr. Donathon Brinley a call and tell him the job is his. Stanley's excessively whining because his own assistant is far too eager to help you is getting on my nerves." She turned heading for the door with purposeful added clicks of her heels on the tile floor, she paused half way out, turning back to shoot him her classic raised eyebrow piqued *Scarlet O'Hara* look. "Tell him there's a bonus in it for him if he can get here by eleven to start today. It seems you may need someone to cock block any calls as I won't have a dating service made of my firm. Am I clear, Mr. Matisse?"

A sigh of relief, "Explicitly, boss lady." He grinned.

Later that day, his newly hired assistant was getting the crash course with the help of Amelia's personal assistant, Robert. Rashawn was too deep in conferences overseas, including having one of the Quinneth brothers dumped on his desk for him to deal with *"and keep him out of her red hair for the day."* Her words.

The magazine, while already out, gave over the leak which led to the dismissal of both the interviewer and one of Quinneth's staff, who'd accepted a hefty bribe for juicy details. As far as Amelia was concerned, restitution was made. But for Rashawn, he'd lost far more than she realized. And when his lunch showed up at the office via one of the bistros' cooks to head him off, sparing him the encounter with an already arriving crowd of prowling huntresses, he knew the damage was still very much adherent.

He wanted nothing more than to fast forward to the end of the day. He would gladly don the mask of ambiguity and be her unnamed mystery Master for however long it would take to win her back.

Like the waves of a tsunami, everything had been swept away only to be brought back in a crashing wave of violent lust once he had her in his arms and over his lap in the back seat of the car.

A feminine gasp echoed his own until his turned to a savage growl and was instantly thrusting up into the cunt that undulated against him, teasing, and beckoning him to drive every inch of his hard aching flesh into her wet and heated realm.

The week's passing had been pure agony for them both. Perhaps more so for him, watching her every reaction, knowing she needed him, wanted him as much as he wanted and needed her. So tantalizing she had been, her face aglow with her joyous thoughts having found the perfect Master to surrender herself to. It empowered her all the more. Even in the board meetings, she was different. Now, she controlled the men with the charm of her pinky. It was as though they could smell her exalted Empress vibrations— smell how ripe and in heat her body was that they nearly bayed at her feet to do her bidding. But that all belonged to him. And that powerful aphrodisiac was a greed he'd never had the pleasure of. And *oh putain* how the kinky ideas came to mind of how he would remind her nightly how she belonged to him. His Empress at his feet and in his bed.

His cock had often thickened to such readiness for her that he found himself unable to step away from the table, less he revealed his eager erection that not even his longer tailored suitcoats could hide.

Now his turgid flesh sank into the world it belonged in. Deep inside the euphoria of Amelia's cunt. *His.* She belonged to him. For no Master would ever make her feel so ravenously desired and controlled as he did. And he would make sure she could never deny it after this weekend, for he planned to reveal himself before returning her Sunday morning.

His pet let out a pleasant moan laced with arousal as he tipped her head toward him with a firm grip of her burgundy hair that was certain to pull at her scalp. He slanted his lips over hers, forcing them to open, to accept the sweep of his tongue as it forged its way past her lips, conquering the taste of her tongue in his claim.

He licked every accessible inch of her shoulder with a lustful uninhibited stroke and when he bit down on her shoulder, a cry tore from her throat and he pulled her legs up higher so the head of his cock moved past the luscious folds of slick, soft flesh, and bottomed out deep inside her heavenly pudendum.

"Oh yeah," he mumbled against the curve of her jawline before tracing along it with his tongue, then nipped her again. "You feel so good."

He pressed forward, slowly fighting to breathe as he felt the incredibly snug muscles of her walls grip his shaft. *Bon sang*, she was so tight, it was all he could do to live through the pleasure.

"I was not prepared for how tight you are," he grimaced, his expression growing heavier with lust. His eyes were heavy-lidded, his lips swollen, sensually full. "So tight, I fear I will die of the pleasure before I ever cum."

Rashawn ripped away to suck in several lungs full of air. "Move your body over my cock. Let me feel you fuck yourself over my lap." He gritted his teeth, his hips surging beneath her as she began to ride him with slow, control-destroying movements. There was nothing that mattered now but her. The taste of her, the feel of her. One hand clenched her hip, the other plucking firmly at her clitoris as she began to moan heatedly.

Her soft mewlings begged him wordlessly, her lungs fighting for breath. Her tight pussy glazing his cock with her honey that soaked her thighs. "Please, Head-Master—"

"Please what, my pet? What is it you are begging for?" His hips surged upward, driving him deeper still as the movements on her clit increased.

She thrashed, causing him to hold her tighter, to moan at the tightening of her sleek, hot muscles around his cock. "Harder, harder—" she gulped, grinding down to meet his every movement. " I am not a frail creature."

Rashawn wanted nothing more than to grant such a wish so beautifully pleaded for. To let loose of his control and pound her body underneath his. With little grace he had them on the floor of the Executive, positioning her ankles over his shoulders and folded her under his body as he delivered just what she begged for. Driving down like thunder intent on forging an inferno between them.

As he surged inside the tight depths over and over, she tossed and cried out her rapturous burning, lost under the sea of dark red curls, obscuring his greatest view but he couldn't bring himself to slow even enough to sweep the tendrils aside. Her thighs tensed, pushing against his shoulders and then he felt her inner muscles clamp around his shaft, followed by the shudders that ripped through her body and she cried out with her release.

A work of art she was even in the tormented stages of orgasm. But his awe of her had to stop less he lost himself to his own explosion. With no means for after care, he suffered the brakes of his own choosing instead. He paused over her, staying seated deep inside her soaked walls, staring down at the beauty that she was and he imagined the glimmer he would have seen in her eyes had he removed her blindfold. "Do you see what you have done to me? Reduced me to a savage. I have plundered my pet in the back seat of a car," a husky chuckle kissed the concave skin between her neck and shoulder. A gruff sound that was only echoed with the giddy chime of giggling from a well fucked woman.

"Head Master?"

"Yes, My pet."

"Would it not please you to use my mouth for your pleasure? I promise I would not waste a drop of your prize."

Rashawn was torn between mused laughter and growling his reply of dark lust. That he would be so enraptured with her body, being deep inside her cunt that it had slipped his mind entirely even when he had envisioned his cock sliding past her ruby lips many times over during their meetings over the week.

But he could only laugh at his moment of absolute happiness, for in one swipe and her tongue delivered an overpowering pleasure that met his carnal desires head on and he lost his control to hold out even a moment longer.

CHAPTER EIGHTEEN

Rashawn sat out on the deck, staring out into the dark night over the sea, letting the galloping lull of the vessel soothe him if ever such a thing could be anything more than a fleeting concept right now. The massive fifteen sail, dyna-masts looming twenty stories overhead, hummed as they pivoted, tacking into the starboard side to catch the longitude cross breeze, slowly bringing the Matisse Falcon to pitch to her side. She was hard up to fill her sails but once the tack was completed the linens snapped tight and the scupper yawed forward to head back in.

In the far distance, a grey line cracked the horizon, signaling the coming morning. They were already six hours out with the wind at their backs. It would take almost twice that time to tack their way back in. And he feared the worst was yet to come of a cursed Friday that seemed to not end for them.

Just hours ago, after sending orders to his captain to take the Matisse Falcon out, he caught his feisty red head into leather straps then had his pet tied between the bed posts and teased her with the violet wand and a feather duster. He kept the stimulation a constant, taking her to the edge of one exhilaration then dropping to build her up with a new sensation, skipping her lust across a maelstrom of sensation that his pet never noticed the surge of the yacht's movement until she reached smoother deep water.

When he set Amelia loose, he flipped her over his shoulder and carried her to his desk and ate her cunt to his pure delight, until both his face and her thighs were glazed over and she gushed with his prize.

Another relocation to the great room where he could both enjoy some post cuddling and the dark sea just on the other side of the glass walls that lined the back of the room.

He lay stretched out over the sofa with her spent body draped over him. His hands in constant motion over her body, touching the faint red bruises still left from the weekend before on her derriere, an occasional pass over breasts and to pluck at the one nipple still accessible to his touch to maintain its hard thimble-shape. He ran his fingers through her hair, combing out the tangles he'd put there earlier. He traced her lips with the pad of his fingers as if they contained poetry in braille—

His beautiful pet in perfect submission.

It was in their abandonment of post coideal bliss to each other's arms she broke down and called *Red*.

The initial word shattered through every part of him. Suddenly they were standing back in the gentleman's room at the office. *S'il te plaît*, he begged silently in his mind, *don't do this to me.*

He had anticipated that at some point she would. While their scenes had been scripted out based on both their desires, Amelia's cravings far outweighed the experiences she'd had for some time. The overwhelming stimulation was bound to take its toll on her, but he had not calculated in the effects of today to break her.

The tears suddenly fell, escaping from under her blindfold and streamed down her cheeks.

"My pet, what is it?" He had brushed her hair from her face.

"Red." He'd barely heard the whisper of her safeword and then the sobs came.

His thoughts shattered. He pulled her head to drop back down on his shoulder, wrapping her is in his arms and held her tighter. "*Shhh*, it's okay. You're safe."

"No— I'm not. I'm confused. I don't know what's going on any more and I don't know how to deal with all of this. I'm overwhelmed with so many feelings I don't know if I'm supposed to or setting myself up for heartbreak."

He sucked in a deep breath then maneuvered himself so he could sit up, bringing her with him. She tried to squirm out of his lap, and he allowed her some room but only letting her go so far. She may have used her safeword, but she was still his responsibility. Mostly he needed to help her find her comfort zone again. Repair whatever fissures had shattered her.

"Talk to me, pet. Why do you feel lost?" He kept an arm wrapped around her, his thumb caressing her shoulder, while he reached for her hands, bringing them together over her lap. Then leaned sharply to reach for a tissue from a box on the end table and dabbed her face dry only to witness more tears dribble down.

"I don't know who you are, and then there is someone else and— and I don't understand these feelings I have. It could never work out, and yet he makes me laugh and my heart skip beats. And then when I am with you, my body heats up and I find a tranquil bliss I have found nowhere else, but you're not real! You're here, but I have nothing to place your face in my life, and I am so lost. Because this other man— I see his face and I see how he looks at me. He looks at me the way you make me feel. I want it so much, yet the lines have blurred. Yet—" she shook her head in a motion that seemed to never end. "I can't. I just can't."

"Then why do you trouble yourself over it?"

"He'd brought in flowers this morning," her voice grew distant, "The whole thing disrupted when there was an issue that occurred, but the flowers were meant for me." She swiped at her face trying to compose herself. She wouldn't even turn her face up to him. She hid instead, behind the blindfold and a curtain of luscious hair as she went on with her point of view of what had occurred, "After everyone had left for the day, I sat in my office looking at them, that's when I found a card inside."

Reshawn closed his eyes and tucked her head under his chin, wrapping himself around her. He felt lost at sea himself and holding her tighter was the only way to bring her more into himself. "Was there something particular about the card?"

"It was a quote from something. *'My first vision of earth was water veiled. I am of the race of men and women who see all things through this curtain of sea and my eyes are the color of water. I looked with chameleon eyes upon the changing face of the world, looked with anonymous vision upon my uncompleted self'.*"

"I know this saying; it is from the book House of Incest by Anais Nin."

"Yes, and then under it he added, *'And then I found you in my arms and I became whole'.*"

"He sounds a like a man in love."

"Which is why I am afraid."

"You are afraid of being loved?"

"Yes!" she swatted him away. "No, not afraid of being loved but that the only love I will ever be offered comes from a man afar too young that I could never be with."

"*Shhh.*" He pulled her to rest over his lap so he could cradle her. He kissed her forehead and held her, pulling her head to lean into his shoulder where he held her for a long time. "Maybe your eyes are just out of focus."

He reached for the table again, a new tissue along with a remote and he dropped the lighting until it was pitch black in the great room, then slowly pulled the silk sash from her eyes.

"You're going to let me see you?" She grew nearly frightened.

That was a reaction he had anticipated. He was her mystery romance.

While it may have her spun about presently, losing it was a price he didn't figure she truly wanted to be revealed just yet. "No, My pet. Just as our contract stated, using your safeword forfeits your chance to learn who I am. Nor would I share such when you're emotionally bereft and your strength drained."

"Why would that matter?"

"Because no matter how perfect I am for you, right now you are not ready to accept me in your world fully." He pulled her silk robe from the back of the chaise and brought it over to drape her in. Restoring her.

He held her until she fell asleep in his arms and then he transferred her to *his* bed, where he left her there to sleep.

He went out to his study to pour himself a much needed drink, skipped the fixings, filling his glass to the rim and poured it down his gullet with every intention of torturing himself with the burn of the Hennessy. When his glass was emptied, he filled it again then went out on the deck to stoke and stew.

His second glass was long gone and tossed into the Atlantic Ocean when the steward came up with news of an urgent call.

He wasn't sure he could take any more bad news or urgency at this point. He swiped the back of his hand across his lips then took the satellite phone from his crew mate and waited until he was gone before responding. "Matisse here."

"Rashawn, it's Dane Masters."

"Dane—" it was all that came out, he wanted to say more, but where to start?

"Is Amelia with you?"

"Yes."

There was a sudden sigh of relief on the other end. *"Thank god."* The words set off alarms in Rashawn's head breaking through the curses and heartache.

"What's happened?"

If he thought things could not have gotten any worse than they already had, he was frightfully wrong, as he listened while Dane told him of the horror of Miss Katianna Dumas' being abducted right in front of Club Pain Thursday night.

It was a nightmare no man in love wanted to ever suffer, let alone what his little woman had endured. As cursed as the day had been, Rashawn thanked the mighty Gods that Katianna had already been found and rescued.

It finally made sense why everyone at the club had seemed so upset and why the Dominus had not contacted him or even showed last night, but it changed nothing for him and Amelia.

He went back inside and glanced over at the sleeping heiress in his bed. Such exceptional beauty. She had been everything he fantasized she would be. Now he just had to find a way to convince her she was meant to be his. Because he couldn't bear to let her go now.

CHAPTER NINETEEN

Amelia stirred awake, the rising sun breaking through the windows into her eyes. Her blindfold? It was gone. She twisted sharply in the sheets that wrapped her body in soft luxury. Eyes and hands searching for the silk cloth. It must have slipped off as she slept, but that would not be an acceptable excuse for her Master. She searched frantically, but it wasn't in the bed.

Instinctively her hand came up to her cheek. She'd nearly forgotten and for a moment felt a small shame that she would not have been more attentive. Even if she had not been turned over to a Master like this it was no excuse to be so remiss in her behavior. She glanced about the room, until spotting it lying over the edge of the dresser. She realized while she had been remiss, her Master had not. It was waiting for her and she quickly slipped from the bed and went for it. She found a note tucked under the sash and opened it up. Like all its predecessors, it was artistically handwritten on bluish white parchment paper:

My Pet ~

You will find a robe laid out for you and the door to the head is open for you to use. You may shower and when you finish, your breakfast will be ready for you.

~ Head-Master

Amelia twisted around spotting the robe at the foot of the bed, and in the corner a breakfast table had been set up, draped with white linens and a setting for one.

Her fingers coiling around the silk cloth, something seemed out of place, the note lacked his usual commands, vexing her. She glanced around, uncertain of what she was looking for when something caught her attention, and all motor control came to a crawling halt.

Hung over the back of the chair in the settee was a towel containing the falcon crest with the monogrammed initials RM.

Rashawn Matisse.

Her heart stopped or maybe it races so fast she couldn't detect a distinct beat. But her thoughts shattered.

She was onboard the Matisse Falcon. And like the blind being shown the sun, for the first time she felt the roll of the ship's pitch and yaw under her feet. Far more subtle than the storm inside her own emotions.

The wrong one.

Amelia sank to the floor, a flood of emotions and fear crashing within her, taking her out in one fell swoop. "No, no, it can't be him."

Oh god, how did she not know?

Panic flooded her. Her foolish sexual desires had brought her to this. Her Head-Master had been Rashawn all along. She had fallen in love with submitting to a man far too young for her and a member of the board no less. *Oh god no,* the pain ripped her mind and heart in half.

She had to get out of there. She spun around searching for her clothes, finding only what she had worn last night neatly set aside within the large walk-in closet. None of which did she want to hide in. A little more searching and she gave up, covering up instead in one of his shirts that fell down around her thighs.

She paused, glancing at the assortment of belts hanging on one wall. She reached out and touched the soft worked leather. The whisper of it being pulled from his belt loops as she was made to wait, echoed within lucid wakeful memories. A resounding crack of the strap slapping on the leather upholstery just inches from her, echoing in her ear to tease her senses. She leaned in, pulling one of them to brush against her cheek.

"Fuck, Amelia, what have you done?" she scolded herself. Her feet refusing to flee. Her heart ached, begging her not to run, her mind refusing to accept there were any emotions worth being in the wrong situation. She glanced down at her legs, there just wasn't time, she needed to get out before Rashawn returned and tried to stop her. "I can't— I just can't," she cried out and ran out of the closet.

She cracked the bedroom door open but voices down the hall had her searching for an alternative escape. The far wall looking out over the deck had sliding glass doors and she made a run for them and headed out.

"Stop right there," the stern voice never raising above a spoken command called from behind her, bringing her to a stop just as she reached the steps. "Where do you think you are going?"

Amelia stood frozen in place. She swallowed hard unable to answer him. Unable to face the young man she had so foolishly slept with. *How could Trenton have done this to her?*

"Our contract is not over, Amelia. You are not permitted to leave until I have returned you."

"This is a mistake. I should not be here." She refused to look, caught in a purgatory of panic and a need to restore her demeanor.

"But *here* is exactly where you wanted to be. You went to the Dominus for this very experience, and here, with me is where you received everything and more."

Her Head-Master's voice drew closer. Her heart skipping and beating faster as she felt the warmth of his body pull up behind her.

"Isn't it, Amelia?" His tone so deep— alluring— controlling. Already it called her. Yes, she knew the voice as the Master who'd taken her control away from her just as she had always wanted, never letting her get away with topping from the bottom and with that act delivered her to the most intoxicating bliss she'd ever felt. *Here* was definitely where she wanted to be, except if she turned to look her Master in the eyes, she would see a man eleven years her younger who worked under her. The illusion would be shattered, for that's all this was— *illusion.* There was no Master for her.

"I'm not going to turn and face you," she breathed out the small defense.

"That's good, since I didn't give you the order to do so." His lips dropped over her shoulder, blowing his warm breath through the light fabric of the dress shirt then kissed her neck, slowly making his way up the nape of her neck. A hand sweeping her hair aside as he did.

"You mustn't."

"I can do whatever I like to you, his words seduced her defenses away. "You are still *My pet.*"

"But it's wrong."

His hand gripped under a breast crushing and lifting her at once, his lips and tongue washing her neck farther, more feverishly. Then his hand dropped between her legs and palmed her mound and pressed her back against him. "Does this feel wrong?"

Amelia's head was swimming. *No, it did not.* The commands— his touch— his kiss— his body— they all felt perfect. The cock that pressed between the soft flesh of her ass belonged inside her and she belonged to his every desire. Whatever he wanted of her, she was meant to give. But she couldn't. He was too young for her; it would never work.

She couldn't believe that all this time her mysterious Head-Master had been none other but Rashawn

Matisse. She pulled up the images of the limited view he'd allowed on the monitors, and she glanced down at the tanned hands that held her now. The groomed growth of dark hair on his chin, morphed to the view of Rashawn's face as he leaned down to kiss her after delivering her home. "The Skype call, I watched you on my screen while you were in the room— h-how?"

"That was a tricky one. I taped it the night before, then when I left your office, I rushed to mine to put the note against my screen. I thought for sure the lighting change would have given me away. But your thoughts were well distracted."

No wonder Trenton had demanded she be blindfolded. Had she known she was being turned over to Rashawn, she would have refused. She shook her head, because he'd been perfect. Made her feel the deepest things, made her feel adored. *Why did he have to be so young?*

"You can't rely on your eyes when your desires are out of focus, Amelia."

She was finding it hard to stand her ground. "You're too young for me." Amclia pleaded weakly.

"You think I give a shit about the age difference?" His fingers dove into her hair and yanked her head back, his mouth crashing over hers in a bruising kiss. It melted walls and boundaries. Her knees went weak and his arm tightened, catching her long before she fell. Her head spun and he released her from his kiss only when she was breathless. "If age made a difference, made what we have together better than another arrangement, then I gladly accept it as a factor. Nevertheless, I know how old you are, My pet. More overly I knew your position as my employer and yet I pursued you because I know I am so much more for your body and soul than an inconvenient birthdate."

"And what of me, how should I feel about it?"

"*Quoi?* Are you afraid? Afraid to admit you already like it?"

"Afraid it couldn't possibly last."

"*Psh*— not long enough for you, has it? We could go longer if it is what you need. Is that what your older men do? Do they fuck you for hours until the break of dawn as I do, then make love to you after?"

Amelia's breath gasped from her, "Now you're being immature."

"Don't gaslight. Its beneath you."

She stammered, "What I meant is— the relationship couldn't last."

"Did you now?" He made it sound like he didn't believe a word she said. "So older men stay, do they? You've been dating older men for some time now— how's that working out for you?" His lips brushed up the side of her neck, delivering a heavy breath against the shell of her ear then nipped her as he pressed harder into her, the hand rail catching her, keeping her to his cornering lust.

She was silent, her gears choking and grinding to work properly. He stole every argument she had. Dammit, just like he did in the board meetings. Every time someone said *we can't* he had a way of tearing it apart. Rather than countering with a *why not* he forced the others to relent that the present way was what wasn't working. He turned *we can't* into *we can't afford not to.*

If the current situation was working, change could only bring them closer to a better solution.

❧

Rashawn could see her mind at work, just like it always was, except when he had her under his control. It'd taken some work to get her to that moment of quiet surrender, but once he had managed to get the reins out of her hands, it was beautiful, and she was drowning in the pleasure of it.

Now look at her, almost funny to see someone so in love with surrender, so seduced with her position and yet still cling to a taboo as small as an age gap to come between her and what she wanted. He gave her what no man had been able to accomplish with her and here she was fighting him over something so trivial and irrelevant. Time to get his precious pet back under his control.

"Come now, the great Amelia at a loss for words? Give me one more. Offer me another excuse as to why we can't be together. They say three times the charm. But let's keep this going. I've got a rock solid hard-on for you right now, so the sooner we can get this over with, the better. Let me hear your last excuse, My pet. I assure you— I'll shoot that one down too. And then it'll be done with. Then you and I can get back to what we do best, fulfilling our very eclectic lifestyle needs. Starting with you getting to your knees and pleasing your Master."

"You're being impractical," she whimpered.

"Am I? Come now then, give me another excuse." He dared her heatedly. in her ear as if it were a naughty thing. "Perhaps maybe you can accuse me of being nothing more than a fortune hunter. The young bachelor stud willing to lick your thighs to get to your billions. What will all the girls at the front desk say about the heiress and her rent boy-toy."

"Don't be absurd," she sneered, but inside she was teetering. He had her completely off balance and he clearly had no intentions of allowing her to regain her walls of composure.

"It is, isn't it? But accuse me anyways. I will thoroughly enjoy knocking it from your hands."

She could see he was getting aroused off the argument just as he did in the board meetings when he faced the other men off to have his way. Like a predator, he lived for the fight. Only the fight here was will and words, the stamina of knowing he was right and he could deliver every promise he made. "Very well. Are you?" she agreed to play along.

"You're an heiress of great wealth, Amelia, no doubt about it, but then so am I. *Mon père est* Cardiff Matisse. World renown, the modern day *Leonardo de Vinci. Ma mère* is one of the wealthiest hoteliers of Monaco and owner of one of only three marinas in Monaco bay. And though the royal titles will die with her, she is still a monarch princess. Thus, in my own birthright, I am heir to a fortune of my own. I'd say you're safe from such treasure seeking unless we're to discuss the treasure of that wet pussy between your legs. For I will surely plunder it. I will seek it out and lay claim every night, morning, and every moment in between.

"How can you possibly expect me to continue working with you on the board after this, if we were to remain together?"

Rashawn straightened, pulling back, for the first time, allowing space between them. His gaze locking down on her with the strictest conviction as she looked back over her shoulder at him, her hand clutching at the rail as her only safe line.

"You call this to end, Amelia and my resignation will be on your desk first thing Monday morning. Because if you think for one damn minute that I'll walk into that boardroom and look at you knowing that every Saturday night you go into that damn club all corseted, pierced, and powdered up, kneeling before some washed up crow, who won't come close to satisfying you as I do, that I'll pretend it doesn't bother me? Then it will be the first act you have made that is unforgivable. And I won't torture myself with it."

"And if agreed? What then— how can—"

"I will dole out a harsh punishment for your insolence, not to forget the ones you earned over the week before our weekend is over."

"Punishment?"

"Yes, punishment. We have a contract, my pet. Not to mention we are out at sea. Even having turned back, we're half a day's sail from New York. You're still mine until first thing Sunday morning and I will appease myself with your body until then. I think I'll start with twenty lashes of the cane. Then I'm going to fuck that beautiful ass so I can admire my handy work there and I just might hand out a few bare handed spankings while I'm at it, just to keep up the splendid color on your cheeks."

Amelia's chest heaved so hard she was near panting. Rashawn, not for one second had left his position as Dominant Master and had every intention of having his way with her pending immediate agreement. "Our relationship would only serve to be a distraction at the office."

As with all her other feeble arguments, he countered exceptionally well, "You're already distracted. Either pining to the point of pain for what you can't get with everyone else or distracted watching me when I'm working alone in the boardroom. I do believe I speak for us both when I say at least this past week has been excruciatingly tantalizing and fun."

He turned, circling away from her, putting a good amount of space between them now. Freeing her should she choose to run to the stern of the ship. She would still have to come back to face him. There was no escaping him, barring jumping overboard.

He walked over to the far rail on the portside, turned and leaned back against it, his hands holding it at his sides. The wind whisking through his thick brown hair and sent the soft black cotton of his pajama pants flapping in the wind less lovely than the sails above taut with the breeze that propelled them over the swells of the ocean. He stood there looking at her, barefooted and bare-chested as his robe did much of the same as everything else in the wind.

She slowly crept toward him. Though *overboard* was still a feasible solution to not answering his arguments any more. He only waited. How relaxed he was at sea and how in utter turmoil was she. Her insides felt like a maelstrom filled with the wreckage from the collision of what she knew and what she wanted. But then she saw for the first time, the dark shadows under his eyes. He'd clearly not slept all night.

"So what's it going to be, Amelia? You going to come over here so I can start your punishment?" His voice was lower now, but not one ounce of the heat or the fury and passion was lost. "Or do you want to tell me *you are the Heiress* as your final safeword?"

Safeword— final— no! She— she didn't know. Not final— just maybe, another way. Something— Anything—

She was grasping for strings that he didn't give her to grab. It was all or nothing. Never half. Never a feeble shot. He had her off balance with his explicit demands. He knew it reached inside her. Scandalous connections. Full on and confident all the way.

"I— it would not go over well once the company discovers my private life."

"Are you accusing me of being careless with mine? You never knew I was a Head-Master. Even with knowing who my father is. It never occurred to you how I knew Trenton Leos until I told you."

"I- ah—" she paused in thought. She hadn't known. All this time, she never even suspected that he too was deeply involved in D/s. Cardiff Matisse had designed the office complex building Trenton owned— and the security business. It made sense Rashawn would know him. But it didn't meant it went further. She had not known of Cardiff's lifestyle either. Had she known, she might likely have flirted dangerously with Rashawn, hoping he would discover her own secret and private world.

"Don't let your anxiety kill what you can have. Just think of it, Amelia. You'd still be in control at the office. It's your company and I get so hard watching you boss those old geezers around. But rather than have to wait until the weekends to come to be relieved of such control, it's only a few doors down the corridor and every night you'll surrender to me and I will sate your needs just like you need me to. Why I might even have a generous moment and bend you over your desk to spank you then fuck you while everyone else is out to lunch." His eyes narrowed over her, licking her flesh with devilish temptation, "You'd like that, wouldn't you, My pet?"

Th wind caught her hair and tossed it around, then tugged at the dress shirt she still wore. Her eyes fluttered closed, right away taken up with the image he so mischievously painted for her. And before she knew it, he pushed off, closing in on her again. His footing so sure even in the rocking of the ship, his intense focus on her not even distracted by the hum coming from the masts pivoting overhead to redirect the yacht's position. His arm scooped around her waist and he countered the ships pitch to starboard and he held her steady and plastered against his chest as they leaned into the ship's tack.

There was a strength of Security holding her but another force one far more foreboding present. "Just envision it. You could go to the meeting afterward filling my corner office with your cries of ecstasy. All the men of the board hanging on your every word as you conduct the meeting. Unbeknownst to them, your ass a fiery red, delivering a stinging kiss every time you shift in your chair." He stepped in his body shifty as he anticipated a yaw in the bow then locked on as he came down off a deep wave. All she could do was hold on to him. His experience and skill made him a far better hold than a simple rail at the edge of luxury.

He took her jaw in his grip, turning her lips up to be kissed. He hovered next to them, his breath kissing them, spilling down over her jaw and neck. "Give me a word, Amelia. Tell me, *you are the heiress,* and I will return you to your home and depart. I'm certain you could find a good enough reason for me to return to your father's office in France. Or perhaps send me to away from everyone in Morocco."

Her head shivered out a rejection in answer. "Then tell me *green* and I'll show you what it's like to be mastered without the blinds and masks. I will give you the visual you need to put your Master in your life." He plunged into her mouth, delivering a deep succulent kiss, his hold on her, twisting her so his tongue could delve and lick deeper at the insides of her mouth before tearing away to catch his breath, but left her completely breathless.

The wind spiraled around, while the sea pitched and rolled but he moved with it like a dance, taking her with him until nothing else mattered.

No man had ever kissed her as he did. She had fantasized of him so many times. No man more beautiful and refined as he. A head for business and the gall to go after what he wanted. It just never occurred to her that she would be one of those things he was after. To be desired as strongly as he did. To be mastered, like no other could, by him— *how could she possibly say red to this?*

"You'll be such a distraction," she whispered as she turned her lips up to be kissed again and he instantly took them taking the doubts she tried so hard to hang on to with it.

❦

Rashawn bent over her, surrounding her; he wanted to draw her into every cell of his body as her lips opened, her tongue met his and his senses flamed. Sweet, velvet heat. The taste of her went to his head, the feel of her causing his erection to pulse and pound with a hunger barely leashed. He drove into her mouth until her head fell back from the pressure. He let her slip from him only to taste her skin as his teeth raked her shoulder, her body becoming liquid, pliant. *His.* He allowed his hands to move, rather than holding her to him, roaming her back instead, gathering the shirt up until one hand could smooth over her bare buttock, he would soon spank for being naughty.

Putain! He grinned then remembering she made a comment about distractions. "Of course, I will. I would not be much of a Master if I were not. But then an empty chair at the board table will also be distracting and not in the good way." His eyes danced over her face, looking for her surrender. "I've wanted you a very long time, Amelia. And now I know you are the perfect woman, the perfect submissive for me. Surrender to me."

❦

Amelia backed up against the rail of the deck. She already knew her answer but she had to run it through her mind once more. Once she gave it, there would be no going back, no second chances. No weekend holidays of sexual surrendered bliss.

She thought back to the day she first met Rashawn when he strolled into her office and set his portfolio down in front of her. They went for dinner a few days later. Women melted around him, but she remembered his eyes never left her without ever offending. He kept his dark desires well contained like a polite kiss to the cheek, they were there, but never raked over her flesh with a crude approach. Always refined yet smoldering. She longed to be touched by *le connaisseur déviant de la séduction.*

It was expressly enjoyable having tea over their dessert. He ate and commented over it as if he'd been having mind blowing sex with her right there on the table while everyone in the restaurant was silenced in awe watching them.

She recalled their stay in Paris for the summit earlier that year, watching him work diligently to please her needs within the company. Like a toréador in the bull arena, he dodged every attempt from the other board members to spear his plans to save the two Middle Eastern factories, then he snatched the ribbon from the bull's head, and handed it over to her. Even as they went together to speak with the press, she didn't miss the erection he had and she flew home fantasizing it had been there for her. Now she had to wonder if perhaps it had.

"Why do you always work inside the meeting hall instead of in your office?" She knew there would be a reason, surely a simple one but she wanted to hear it from his lips, but what he told her came as a surprise even in the face of things.

♋

Rashawn moved away. He leaned back against the threshold of the sliding glass doors and folded his muscular arms across his chest, locking his gaze on the woman whose body had already told him she was his. "You don't have cameras installed in my office."

He liked the surprise gasp that broke from her lips. He was surprised she hadn't figured that one out. But the back and forth of her coming and staying had him worn out. He couldn't do it any longer. "Give me a word, Amelia. I want your decision now. No more stalling."

❧

She dropped her eyes, all the argument given still could not convince her to let go of her shields, because one more image came to mind. The one of a magazine broadcasting a scandalous headline:

~~ Heiress Amelia Quinneth caught in the sheets with the Kinky Young Bachelor Matisse. ~~

Rashawn stepped into her space again, catching her chin between thumb and forefinger lifting her face toward him.

Amelia diverted her eyes to the floor.

"Eyes on me."

Amelia's glance merely flicked but didn't follow his command. The glaring image in her mind was too brash to overlook.

"When I give you a command, you will follow. It will remain so until I have returned you. Now look at me."

Slowly, green eyes turned upward and showed him what he wanted to see. What he hoped was there though she fought to deny it.

"You belong to me. Your eyes declare it so. Give in." He leaned in and kissed the bridge of her nose and just like that, she was the little innocent school girl with dreamy crushes on a poster boy. Her heart fluttered as a warm blush started low on her chest and worked its way upward until it escaped from her plump lips like a sigh.

I cannot stay. You know this. She couldn't say the words she knew she needed to say but she didn't truly want to. Her resolve was ebbing. He was right, she wanted this. But Rashawn was more than a couple years younger. There was no getting around it. She didn't want to be labeled the cougar of Quinncth Enterprises. She didn't want to hear the girls snicker as she walked by every morning. Too often she'd seen the insecurities such affairs created in women who fawned over their young cabana boys, always fearful he was slipping off to bed with the lush young ladies while their mistresses slept or worked. *No, he isn't doing this to me,* her thoughts screamed in her mind. She wasn't like them. And Rashawn was no cabana pool boy.

"A million men your age giving you attention will never even come close to that of the one man willing to give you all of himself."

Her eyes fluttered closed, her stomach tightening into a painful coil as her thoughts stormed through her, tearing apart the desires she yearned for the most. "I don't want to be one of them."

"One of what?"

"One of those women running around with men half their age on their arm and everyone knowing its—" her words trailed off.

"*Psh*— you see?" He grew frustrated with her, "You can't even finish what you were accusing me of because it doesn't fit. This isn't about some young penniless pony boy pawning to a woman's needs for currency. This isn't about a woman playing with a young man so she can feel young and vital once more or to make a cheating husband jealous. This is about you needing to feel submission to a Master who can handle you. And it just happens in the most irrelevant detail I am eleven years your younger. I am here because I've been falling for you for some time. Let yourself have what you want." He stepped up brushing against her side as he lowered his lips to her ear, "Submit to me and be perfectly fulfilled under my command. This isn't an affair. Don't you see how much I love you?"

She shook her head, lost fighting him, fighting herself, fighting what she had told herself over and over. "I don't know if I can." But then his last words finally sank in and when she looked at the creation her response made was nothing short of cleaving his heart in half.

Amelia slapped her hands to her mouth, wishing she could take the words back, she didn't want to hurt him, never that. She shook her head in complete violent rejection and bolted for the door.

"STOP there!" Rashawn's stern voice belted out just as quickly.

Amelia found herself responding obediently and stopped. Her hand clamping on the door jamb to steady herself in the inertia of her flight and the pitch and yaw of the sailing vessel carrying her back to normalcy.

"Tell me, Amelia, now that you have tasted a real Dominant, when you go back to your old way of things, will it taste the same?"

So engrossed within the hellish pain she had inflicted, she hadn't even noticed Rashawn had managed to brush past her. Not registering his exit from her until he returned with her clothes in hand. Her attention snared; she gaped up at him where she doubted the horror of being rejected was hidden from her expression. Only the slight tension that twitched at his jaw, fighting that he saw or felt anything.

"You will put these on. But you will remain kneeling until we have reached port," he called from within his room, waving her to step inside.

Amelia's hands ghosted up to the shirt that was his, and slowly and most numbly began to unbutton it.

Rashawn took the shirt from her in exchange for her own. And one by one he handed her each piece of her attire slowly returning her power back to her, save one.

"Follow, Mademoiselle Heiress Amelia."

And she did, down the hall until he paused at a door and pushed it open and waved her in.

She stepped into the familiar room where she'd slept in last weekend

He followed her in and pointed to the foot at the bed, "Kneel."

Numbly she did as told.

"You'll stay here, but while here you will think about what you want. What has been offered and what it is you are running to. You will think about what you enjoyed while under my command and about every tantalizing moment in between from your last visit to this one."

"Rashawn? You said earlier you'd already turned the ship around. Why? Did you know I would refuse you?"

"Trenton's Life-slave was abducted Thursday night in front of the night club."

"Wh- no." She moved her head in a broad sweep back and forth, refusing what her ears heard. "Is she—?"

"*Shhh,* she is safe once more. They were able to find her very quickly and get her back. She is safe at home and in her Dominus's arms once more."

She heard his pain through hers, but his was more personal, Dominus had his but Rashawn's arms were empty because she had refused him. But it wasn't going to be normal when she got back, would it? She would be right where she started before she'd met him as her Head-Master. A power house who longed for the sweet respite of a few moments of not being the head woman in charge. Only that moment would not be there, nor with it the comfort she may very well need as she worried over the little author she'd come to adore over the years. *Would any of the other Doms she knew comfort her through her emotional turmoil?*

Her eyes closed, trying not to confess the dispassionate emptiness that would surely do little more than give her a pat on the back or a peck on the forehead and call her a *good girl*. No deep compassion. No adoration that could be felt in a whisper or slight of touch. No warm arms to wrap her heart and body in and call her theirs. *Please*— she heard her heart beg silently from within. A plea her lips refuted. And she kept silent as Rashawn led her deeper into the bedroom where she had slept her first weekend with him.

She reached out touching tall bed posts, the very contact bringing haunting memories. And then she felt his hand on the back of her neck, pressing her down to her knees— *to wait.*

And so she did. Taking a dutiful position with her legs tucked under her ass and her hands fell into her lap. Her fingers curled into the palm of the other her head bowed and there she remained quietly.

He was almost to the door, "Head-Master?" She whispered still staying in form.

"Yes, what is it?"

"What is it you want from me?"

He was pure business, they could have just as easily been in the boardroom instead of a bedroom. "I want a report, with either a solution and a plan, or your resignation."

Amelia broke her pose, her head snapping up, but Rashawn was already walking out. Her breath pushed from her lungs at the proposed ultimatum. The lines had been drawn, the new contract scripted out— it was time to sign on the dotted line and walk. And walking meant walking for good. If she turned it away, she could never come back and the tear she never thought she would shed for a Master formed in her eyes.

Her head-Master had essentially called Red, when she had refused to say Green.

Rashawn sat at his desk. It was of resound elegance and extravagance. Yet the inlaid design of exotic woods seemed empty without the hope of ever seeing Amelia's luscious body stretched out over it ever again. Only the contract agreement between them sat on it and the questionnaire he'd sent her.

He sat slunk back in the leather winged chair, his fingertips teepee'd over his lap, and his thoughts burned holes toward the cream colored carpet under his desk. The full tumbler of Jenssen Arcana Grande Champagne cognac sitting untouched as the ice cracked to remind him it was melting.

Anger and failure burned through him like a chemical fire that couldn't be put out. Every tiny moment he'd had with Amelia echoed in his head, tormenting him that such perfection would be his last.

When she opened her gift at the firm's Christmas party finding the large bottle of Imperial's Majesty cologne, it'd taken both her hands to hold it up. The bottle alone had delighted her, but then those green eyes rolled closed when she opened it and inhaled.

When he led her into a waltz in the middle of the park one afternoon after lunch.

The way her eyes had finished undressing him when he'd walked into a meeting with his shirt still unbuttoned one time.

When her walls finally broke and she wept after cumming for him, and he held her, safe and sound in his arms and kissed her.

There would be no more of them and the rage sent tears to pool in his eyes and a surge of energy to his arms.

Rashawn jumped to his feet. The need to toss something— break something— getting the best of him.

He swept everything from his desk only to see in hindsight his drink go flying across the room. The sight, and knowing he would have to make another, only ignited another surge and he was two seconds from turning his desk over to its side when the door to his study opened.

He snapped a glare around to the intruder but the wind was knocked out of him when he saw it was Amelia. Standing there in little more than her slip, bra, and the lace blindfold over her eyes.

He froze, more so to prevent any reaction from him. "What are you doing here?" the words came out cooler and considerably more bitter than he had wanted, but he could not tape up his pain.

"My apologies." Amelia took careful steps in heading toward the ottoman, "I think my Head-Master made a mistake when he told me to wait."

"*Pshh— Bon sang*, Amelia. I am well aware you are capable of topping from the bottom. You need not put on a display for my sake now." So angry he did not see the minute flinch in her body from his hurtful words.

"You made me wait in the wrong room," she finished as she crawled up on the ottoman and sat kneeling, her hands going to her thighs and rolling palm up.

He took in a deep breath and let it out. Letting both the breath and the sight of her kneeling as she should, calmed his raging interior. "You should know by now my commands are precise. I expect my orders followed to the letter without any translated variation."

"And as you have taught me, I have stood in the way of my submission for so long I have never had the true experience of it— I cannot find or give it to myself because it is not mine to grant. Only my surrender is mine to give and only with you have I ever learned that." She paused to lick her lips and took a deep breath, perhaps pulling in courage, plucking it from thin air—

And then she said the words he'd longed to hear.

"Green."

"This isn't a scene. I want you in my life completely or not at all. I can't bear the torment any longer."

"Neither can I." She kept her head down as she spoke, "I want to be yours. I want to stay with you. I give you my body and mind to be yours. I surrender to your commands so that you may rid me of my walls and my taboos. So you may lead me to explore a whole new definition of my desires. Just please, do not send me away. I cannot go back to what I was. Who I want to be is who I am when I am in your capable hands.”

“And who am I, Amelia?” She’d stepped in wearing the blindfold, taking reality from her sight, and he would not have it. She would have to name him, acknowledge *who* he was. Not hide behind the blindfold of ambiguity. He stepped up, hooking the lace sash with a single finger, and pulled it from her eyes, tossing it aside. “Look at me and tell me who I am.”

“You are Monsieur Rashawn Matisse, my Head-Master. The Dominant and man I love.”

There were no words more exhilarating or as eloquent ever heard spoken before. They deflated his anger and hurt in an instant. She truly had discovered what her submission was. What it felt like inside rather than what she thought it meant. He let out a soft sigh, feeling the stitches pull the open wounds in his chest closed over his heart, knowing Amelia Quinneth, the heiress of his desires, now resided there, and he never intended to let her go.

Rashawn let his eyes close for a moment. *Relieved.* Everything he had ever worked for, everything he had ever gone after, paled to having her. Now he was complete. “Come to me,” he called her, taking several brisk steps away leading her toward his desk. “But do so on hands and knees.”

She didn’t even hesitate. Her legs unfolded until they found the floor and she eased herself down, and began to crawl across the carpet, still littered with a number of papers, including the contract of consent she had signed.

"That's it," he let out the husky whisper like a beacon to aid her limited sight.

She stopped when her cheek brushed against his leg and he sucked in a deep breath with the empowerment he felt with her gift. For there was no other man on Earth who had been given what Amelia now lay at his feet.

Her surrender to be His sub.

She had wanted this for countless years yet she had never given herself over to it either. Not even a king could grasp the treasure he had now.

He stretched his hand down, letting his fingertips drift like feathers over her hair, then farther down to caress her cheek with the back of his hand. The moment so exquisite he was in no hurry to move past it.

Making her wait.

And she did so perfectly. He dropped down in the chair, using the moment for his emotions and mental state to reset. To exhale the pain, she'd thrust him into when she had intended to reject him. Now she was here retracing her steps to be back at his feet. And he welcomed a moment to enjoy it. He traced her plump lips, swollen from tears created by an over welling emotional delivery. His little pet needed nurturing now. And he couldn't be happier to provide and fulfill that need.

He bent over scooping her up in his arms and pulled her into his lap. Planting a kiss upon the cheek he'd just touched. "Your desires are my command, My pet."

"May I have one request then?"

"Tell me what it is."

"Would you take me to see my friend, with new eyes and to know that she is safe?"

"We are already on our way."

"Then everything else I leave to you." She smiled.

And oh, how much he planned to give, he thought.

He pushed the blindfold from her eyes and let it fall to the floor, raking his fingers into her tresses. "For you, anything, however only when I deem it to be given." His lips curled into a wickedly dominant grin just as he leaned in and kissed her.

"How do we start?" She smiled into his lingering kiss.

He crooked his finger under her chin, lifting her eyes to him, then caressed her cheek with the backs of his fingers, "We start with taking some time to go back over the house rules again." His eyes dropping down at the lingerie she was wearing, "You seemed to have forgotten a few of them."

TO BE CONTINUED—

ABOUT THE AUTHOR

We Came— We Saw— and then we made it sexy.

And that's pretty much how the Twins came to write Erotic Romances and Dark Fantasies. Both Talon and Tarian have been writing together since they were kids, challenging and competing with each other, and always each other's biggest supporters.

Writing has always been an affair creating fictions of Dark Apocalyptic Fantasy and Film Scripts in Action/Drama and Sci-Fi. It wasn't until they began an Ancient History Fantasy together that the works turned to the Erotic Genre and they've been hooked ever since. However, the final product comes out as richly detailed as we believe all stories should be created: holographic worlds of love, pain, frustration, and challenges beyond the every day. We believe a good story should take you on an emotional ride, pluck your heart strings, and zing you about until you're dizzy. All for readers to submerse themselves into and escape from their day when they need or desire, and to whet your appetite for more.

So, make sure to reserve plenty of private time, pour a glass of wine, and find a cozy spot, because as Talon always says—

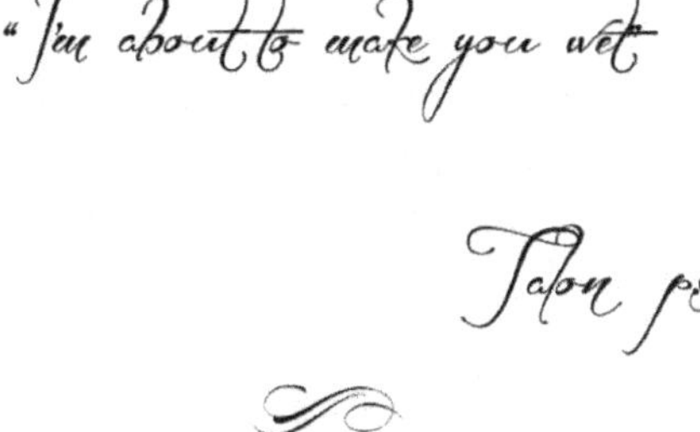

~ RAINBOW AWARDS 2nd PLACE FOR BEST MM EROTIC ROMANCE OF THE YEAR ~

A Place for Cliff

THE DOMINION OF BROTHERS SERIES: BOOK 3

Gay-MM Romance/ Erotic-Romance /
Dominance/surrender / Pain Therapy / Age Gap /
Debonair Meets Cute / Family Drama / Family Bonding /
Voyeurism / Sexy Regatta Races /

Abandoned by his parents and left to tend to his sick sister since he was nineteen, Cliff has done little more than wander through his existence. That is until the Patronus Diesel Gentry sends him to meet Pyotr Laszkovi. A man twice his age except his impeccable looks and debonair sexuality has Cliff falling like a love-sick puppy for the man. Problem is, Cliff is about two threads from coming completely undone as a human being.

Despite this, Pyotr sees in him an irresistible young man who satisfies his needs like no other and is willing to be there to catch Cliff when he unravels and stay at his side during the hardest goodbye of all.

❦

5- Stars, "Never have I seen a relationship between two men as gripping as this one. A Place for Cliff, exemplifies love in a way that is nothing less than awe inspiring (just keep the tissues handy)." ~ Alyn, Guilty Pleasures

*5-Stars "This is not just a book about a romance; it is about love in all forms, about sacrifices for the ones you love, about rage, grief, happiness, sadness, and acceptance. I recommend this to those who love strong but fragile men, hot sex, D**s, slight BDSM, a whole range of emotions to feel, exceptional characters and a happy ending... but I also recommend having handy a box of tissues (for the crying you dirty minded puppies)." ~ MM GoodReads Reviews*

EXCERPT FROM CHAPTER ONE

Cliff looked at the piece of paper in his hand for the twentieth time as he stood outside the VA boarding house, then back at the bronze plaque on the brick wall next to the door. He was at the right place, but damned if he knew why. Why hell, he was still floored that Diesel had taken it upon himself to become Kimmi's Guardian Angel at the treatment center. Not only paying off the outstanding medical bills, but also sponsoring the new biological therapy for her, for that alone, Cliff was forever grateful. But, it didn't make any sense why Diesel wanted him to come here. He wasn't a veteran, he'd never even gotten the chance to consider enlisting, after his parents vanished, leaving him to care for Kimmi on his own.

Hope they're rotting away somewhere— the anguished thought he was always harboring, surfaced in his head.

When he realized what the place was Diesel was sending him to, Cliff had figured it must have been a mistake. So when he saw Diesel at the club again over the weekend, he chased him down to ask why—

~~Did you go?— —It's a boarding house for Veterans back from the Middle East. What was I supposed to do there?— — Did you meet with him? — —No, I never went inside—

Diesel had just looked at him for a long moment then finally spoke again, "Go, meet with him, I think he can help you find exactly what you need."— and with that, the man also known by the title Patronus, walked away before Cliff could question him further.~~

Cliff glanced up the side of the building at the several stories stacked over his head. What the hell was he supposed to be finding here?

Footsteps coming up the sidewalk stirred him from his thoughts and he turned just as a tall, heavily shouldered man with a casual gate walked past with hardly a glance his way him and went in the building. Still, Cliff didn't miss the clear blue eyes shaded by predominant brows of dark brown hair on the man. *Cerulean blue.*

Cliff shook his head. It was unnatural that he should know the name for the particular shade of blue. He owed that much to his little sister. When Kimmi was feeling well enough, she used her innate talent for color to paint. Stained glass mostly, but she'd recently gotten into watercolors and he was forever making stops at the local art supply store to find the exact color she wanted. After several retries, he learned to pay closer attention to the specific shade she was asking for and accepted the fact that there was a bigger difference between Mediterranean blue, turquoise, and blue-green algae then he'd previously cared to know.

"Can I help you with something?"

Once more Cliff found himself pulled out of his wandering thoughts. He blinked, looking up to find the man who'd just walked inside, standing at the door, holding it open. The tall cerulean blue-eyed man had popped his head back out to look at him and it took Cliff's breath away.

Some men you could say were sexy, some were handsome or even pretty. This man was all of the above *and* he was beautiful. Cool blues on a warm European face, topped with thick dark, wavy hair the color of coffee— black, no sugar. A strong jawline fringed with a smoothly trimmed beard that hadn't been trimmed in a few days. The man shifted, resting his forearm on the door jamb, taking a notion that he might be standing there awhile, waiting for the answer. *Oh yeah, he asked something.*

"Is this 1638 Old Country Road?"

The man turned his head slightly, glancing at the bronze plate on the side of the building with the beveled letters that said as much, then back at Cliff with an amused smile on his face. "This is the place."

Cliff scowled as he realized just how stupid he just made himself look. Okay, so that was dumb question number-one. *It's best to space them out a little.* "Can you tell me where I can find a Pyotr Laszkovi?"

The smile that had been dancing in the man's eyes arrived on his face and lined his lips as they stretched out into a dashing grin. "You found me. You must be my next session?"

Cliff thrust his hand out at him. Perhaps too quickly, but since it was already out there, there was nothing he could do but actually shake Pyotr's hand, "I'm Cliff— Cliff Patterson."

Pyotr's eyes dropped to Cliff's hand as if almost surprised by the gesture, then shifted his weight off his arm and brought it down to take Cliff's proffered hand, but he didn't actually shake it— just held it. "You ready to come in?"

"I— *uh*—" Cliff glanced around once more, reminding himself he had no idea why he was here. He felt his hand drop and turned back to the man still looking at him through the propped door.

His smile kinked up to one side like a friendly smirk. "When you are ready then. First hall on your right, second office on the right. I'll leave the door open." And just like that, the blue-eyed Pyotr disappeared inside, leaving Cliff standing out there like some lost dim-wit.

It might have helped if he knew why he was here. Patronus hadn't even give him a hint. What would it hurt to go inside? At the very least, maybe the man inside could explain to him why he was sent here, and if not, then at least another chance to look at those soul dipping eyes.

Cliff followed the simple directions and just as the gentleman said, the door was open. Cliff bent across the doorway, peeking in and there he was— sitting behind a cozy wooden desk, reclined back in his chair. Feet propped on the desk and hands clasped over his lap, sitting there patiently, as if the man had known all along Cliff would eventually come in.

"Well, that didn't take long at all." Pyotr glanced at him with a warm, welcoming expression, nothing more, as if he'd known all along but waited for Cliff to enter on his own terms.

RECIPE BONUS

Taleggio Cheese and Mission Fig Tartine.
[Photograph: J. Kenji Lopez-Alt]

Recipe Thanks goes to Serious Eats and Chef J. Kenji Lopez-Alt

INGREDIENTS:

- 4 slices of hearty bread, such as French pain au levain or sourdough
- 4 tablespoons extra virgin olive oil
- 1 medium clove garlic split in half, and 1 medium clove garlic, minced (about 1 teaspoon)
- Kosher salt and freshly ground black pepper
- 4 to 6 ounces creamy washed-rind cheese such as Taleggio or Morbier
- 12 ripe Mission figs, sliced into 1/4-inch slices
- Coarse sea salt
- 1 tablespoon minced fresh chives

PROCEDURES:

1:

Preheat broiler to high and adjust rack to 6 inches below element. Brush bread slices on all sides with 2 tablespoons olive oil and rub with split garlic clove on all surfaces. Season with salt and pepper. Place on a rimmed baking sheet or broiler pan and broil until golden brown and toasted on first side, about 3 minutes. Flip and broil until second side is toasted, about 2 minutes longer.

2:

Divide cheese evenly between bread slices and spread over top surfaces, trying to cover from edge to edge. Shingle with fig slices. Broil until cheese is melted and figs are beginning to caramelize, about 5 minutes total. Remove from broiler, drizzle with remaining 2 tablespoons olive oil, sprinkle with sea salt and chives, and serve.

DISCOVER THESE OTHER TITLES BY TALON PS & TARIAN PS

DOMINION OF BROTHERS SERIES
Becoming His Slave
Domming the Heiress
A Place for Cliff
Rough Attraction
Taking Over Trofim
Right One 4 Diesel
Touching Vida~Vince

LA SERIE DES FRERES DU DOMINION - {French Edition}
Devenir Son Esclave - Partie 1 & 2
Dominer l'Heritiere
Un Havre pour Cliff
Attirance Brutale

QUANTUM MATES:
Pt 1~ What Torin Wants

DEAR SOLDIER SERIES:
Dear Soldier, With Love
Dear Soldier, With Love II: A Lost Soldier Named Grey

LYCOTHARIAN COLLECTION:
Bond of the Lycaon Concubine

TALON's KEEP COLLECTION:
Feral Dream by Talon ps
Danny's Dom by Nick Hasse

That's My Ethan

Muse Me Only
Inspire Moi Seulement {French Edition}

THE TEDDY BEAR COLLECTION:
Their Plane from Nowhere
Big Spoon & Teddy Bear
Ivan vs Ivan
TIME: Wounds All Heal
Shaggin' the Dead

THE SADOU ORDER – A Dark Taboo Series
Perfect Boy / Perfect Son

TARIAN ALSO WRITES UNDER THE
FOLLOWING PEN NAMES FOR SEPARATE GENRES:

STEPHAN KNOX ~ *Historical Fantasy And Post Apocalyptic Sci Fi*

Anáil Dhragain (Dragon's Breath)

Keeping With Destiny

ROCK HARDING ~ *Adult Coloring Books*

The Adventures of Hugh Jorgan

CONNECT AND FOLLOW THE TWINS:

www.Talon-ps.com

www.ingramcontent.com/pod-product-compliance
Lightning Source LLC
Chambersburg PA
CBHW071357150726
48000CB00001B/65